I0603541

SUMMER'S CONFINE

Rathe Chronicles Book One

ALEXANDRA K. MARTIN

Copyright © Alexandra K. Martin 2020

First Edition 2020 ISBN: **978-0-6450508-8-2**

All rights reserved. No part of this publication may be reproduced, stored or transmitted in any form or by any means, electronic, mechanical, photocopying, recording, scanning, or otherwise without written permission from the publisher. It is illegal to copy this book, post it to a website, or distribute it by any other means without permission. Except in the case of brief quotations for book reviews and articles.

Thank you for not participating in piracy.

This novel is entirely a work of fiction. The names, characters and incidents portrayed in it are the work of the author's imagination. Any resemblance to actual persons, living or dead, events or localities is entirely coincidental.

Cover Art © Dazed Designs 2020

Goddess Reading: Hellhound Publishing

Editor: Emma Luna at Moonlight Author Services

Formatter: Kat Blak

"Success is not final; failure is not fatal:
It is the courage to continue that counts."
-Winston S. Churchill

Please be aware that I'm an Australian writer, therefore this book is written with British spelling in mind.

This is also a Fantasy/PNR Reverse Harem novel, with adult content and is recommended for the mature audience. It may contain some darker elements such as light Dub/Con and Psychological torture, please keep this warning in mind going forward.

Enter at your own risk... Mwahahaha. *Insert evil laugh*

Summer's Confine

Rathe Chronicles Book One

Alexandra K. Martin

This is a beautiful cage, but it's still a cage.

Summer's Confine
Rathe Chronicles Book One

I'd like to dedicate my first published story to my Grandparents Alec, Margaret and Kathy. I love you all endlessly and forever. Without you in my life, I'd be a different person and I'm proud of who I am. Thank you. Also, thank you for getting laid so that I could be here. ;)

Prologue

As my body sinks comfortably into the couch, limbs heavy from my long day, I sigh deeply at another night watching TV alone. The house is quiet except for the low mumblings of the characters on my show because my kids are fast asleep in their beds. I lick my lips and taste the sweet tang of the dried cranberries I'm snacking on. I slowly inhale today's light, familiar scent of incense that still lingers in the air and settles me, but I can't help feeling a low melancholy creep deep in my heart.

No matter how grateful and happy I am with my life, it doesn't dissipate the heaviness in my chest at the betrayal my heart knows. The loneliness that sets in deep into the night. While I'm used to my independence and I know that I'll be okay, I can't help but dream of being loved again.

Deep in thought and distracted, I fail to realise what's happening before it's too late, and my whole world goes black...

Chapter One

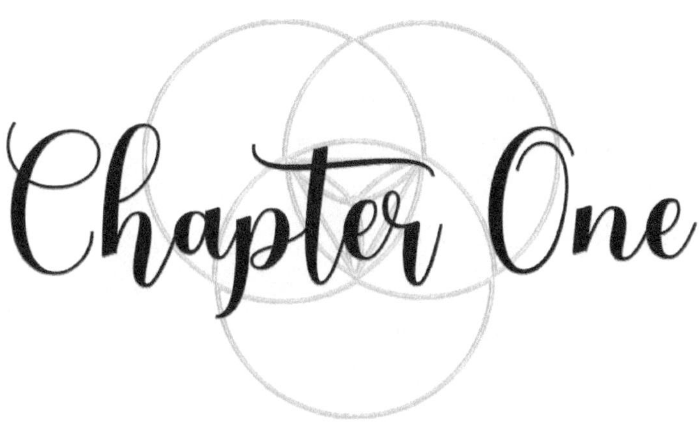

I wake disoriented, confused.

Where am I?

As I carefully sit up, on what appears to be a simple steel-framed bed, I take in the crisp, clean white walls that surround me, effectively boxing me in on all sides, except for the full-sized glass wall centred with a glass door and small circles at head height from one end to the other. The almost immaculate glass would be undetectable if it wasn't for what is surely my only way out of this sterile observatory.

Bed. Toilet. Sink. The quick surveillance of my room leaves me feeling so sterile and cold. My body's as heavy as lead, my mind clouded over and dizzy, and the bright fluorescent lights beaming from the ceiling hurt my sensitive eyes. Oh my God! Am I in jail?

Okay, focus, what did you do last night, Summer?

I was eating cranberries on the couch watching TV, the kids were asleep, and I was alone; as always. I take a moment to look down at myself. Maybe this is a hospital because why else would I be wearing a hospital gown? My kids were sleeping, where are my kids? Please let them be okay.

Slowly I rise, little black spots appear in my vision as I sway slightly. I lean on the wall for support before my mind clears itself. Walking carefully to the glass, I look through, noticing that this place looks more like a prison than a hospital; with its rows of glass rooms and steel walkways. My cell must be a few rows up because the void in the centre of the walkway reaches into an abyss, further down than I can see, giving me no clue as to what awaits me. Feeling suddenly trapped, my heart begins to hammer hard against my ribs as my breaths turn to short, panicked pants, my hands become sweaty, and the taste of bile hits my tongue. I've finally recognised that I'm trapped.

Shaking my head to clear the fog, I give myself a mental slap. I don't have time for a breakdown. I have to find out where I am and what happened to my kids, they're the most important thing right now and I need to know they're okay.

I try the door handle, it jiggles but doesn't give. The harder I pull at it, the more I realise I'm definitely locked in here. What if this is the mental ward and I've finally lost it? Yeah, that kind of makes sense. My sanity was always working on borrowed time, after all, I chuckle to myself.

Calling out, I try to get somebody's attention. After getting no answer, my pleas soon turn louder and more frantic until finally, I get a shaky and hoarse response from a woman to the right of me. Her voice is barely above a whisper, crying that she doesn't know where she is either. It's enough to push me out of my panicked state.

"It's okay, hun, you're not alone." I try to sound calm but I hear her sobs increase through the wall that separates us, to the point of hysterics.

This lady needs to calm down. If we're going to get out of this place then I'm going to need her on my side, and a little more put together.

"Firstly, I need you to breathe and calm down so that we can talk this through together. I'm here with you and I have your back. What's your name, honey? I'm Summer." I make my voice as reassuring as possible.

Her crying eases off until there's a moment of silence, all I can hear is random sniffles, the creaking of a bed, and her breath calming to choppy, quiet sobs before she tells me her name, "Juanita."

I question her about what she was doing before

she woke up here and told her my own story in the hopes of finding a hint as to what's going on.

Juanita replies with a sniff, "I...I was hooking up with a guy from work, it was a bit of a secret thing. I remember going for a shower and that's it. I don't even remember getting home." She gasps, "What if Reno had something to do with this? Why would he do this to me?" Juanita starts to cry harder.

"Oh for God's sake, shut up!"

I peer out of the glass wall, across to where the shout came from; a plus-sized, ash-blonde woman a bit taller than me stands in the cell opposite. Her face and ears speckled with different kinds of piercings, and her thick shoulder-length hair appears wild and unkempt. With her hip jutted out and an almost playful smirk on her face, she stares in the direction of Jaunita's cell, with a quick flick of her eyes to me.

"We're all stuck in this mess, not just you! And I can assure you, we aren't all fucking your co-worker!"

Breathe, don't lose your temper. She's obviously just coping in a really shitty way. Maybe we can all get along and if I play my cards right, I can take control of this situation. It'd be handy to have a different view of this place. There is still the possibility that these women are playing me and are involved in some way. I have to remember to gather as much information as I can, build their trust but remain wary and only give basic information back. People are always more interested in talking about themselves than listening to others anyway.

"Thanks for joining our conversation, Miss bitchy! Was that absolutely fucking necessary?" I ask the new addition. "She's obviously needing support right now, not judgement." My voice comes out clipped and harsh, but I know I need to build bridges, not burn them before they're even up. Taking a deep breath, I calm myself before I carry on. "I'm Summer by the way, this is Juanita. And you are?"

The woman across from me laughs out loud. "I'm going to like you, Summer. The cry baby, not so much. Name's Sabella, but you can call me Bell. Before you ask, I was at a lesbian bar trying to find a lovely new moustache." Bell's boisterous laugh continues filling the room with absolute confidence. "I went to the bathroom and the next thing I know, I'm in this lovely abode listening to '*These are the Days of our Lives*'. So, how do we get out?" She questions with faked indifference but still a touch of humour.

With a heavy sigh, I reply, "I have no idea."

Suddenly, I become aware of the myriad of sounds floating along the hall. I was so focused on us that I hadn't realised we weren't the only ones here anymore. From quiet chattering to sobs of fear and frustration, to shouts of anger and rage, there's pounding on the glass doors and walls, and movement from all around.

Pressing my hands on the cold hard glass, I breathe in deeply, when all at once a realisation hits me, freezing my bare feet to the smooth concrete below them. I look through the glass to the multitude of rooms and terrified people within; we're all women. Pure, unadulterated fear assaults me, shivering its way down my trembling spine, bile threatens me. This can't be good.

I make my way back to the bed, terror still seizing my body making me stumble over my own feet as I go. Finally sitting, I try taking steady breaths to calm myself while I stare down at the shiny white concrete floor and contemplate my unrealistic situation. With vomit rising in my throat once more, from a fury too strong to deny, my stomach churns as I rush to the toilet before violently lurching. Apparently my only content is bile. How long have I been here? The question ricochets around my mind.

Going to the sink I rinse my face with the cool fresh water and gargle my mouth clean, getting rid of the vile biting taste lingering on my tongue. The cold, hard sink under my palms reminds me of my cold, hard reality as I listen to the water swirling down the plug hole. This cannot be happening to me.

Darkness fills my room and those surrounding, enveloping me and everyone here in it. The women around me begin to scream, alarm and confusion reverberating off the walls. My instant reaction is to drop low to the ground, my eyes desperately searching for light, my heart beating wildly in my chest. A slight metallic scent fills the air, as a strange tingling creeps across my skin and body, making me feel weightless and slightly euphoric, then nothing as I pass out.

I give a nice big stretch, my body taught and long, before wiggling back into the mattress. Oh, I'm so thirsty. I open and close my mouth, feeling the dryness of my tongue sweep across my chapped lips. Then it all comes rushing back to me. I open my eyes and yep, I'm still on this fucking bed. But I thought I passed out on the floor. Did someone move me?

I turn my head to the right and see a plate of toast and what looks like a cup of coffee on a tray on the floor. What the hell? Where did that come from?

I slowly get up and head for the tray. Man, I'm hungry. I should probably be warrier about the food here but I don't really care at this point, I'm starving.

My stomach grumbles, as if on queue, like somehow it knows that I'm about to feed it.

As I reach for the tray I spot a man standing on the walkway to my right, he's new, he hasn't noticed me yet so I take a second to suss him out. Damn, he's a pretty big dude. It won't be easy taking him down but I'm pretty sure I still can. He's got to be at least six foot eight, bald with a full dark beard, and covered in tatts. Must be some kind of military, he looks pretty bad ass. He's clad in dark grey clothes that cling to his bulging muscles. His black boots lace up the front and stop halfway up his calf. I also notice the knife strapped to his thick thigh, and the big 'fuck you' gun he's holding across his ripped body. It's pretty hard to miss.

You know what, fuck this. "Oi, Mr Big!" I shout at the bald dick in front of me. As he turns my way, one eyebrow raised, I continue. "How's things? Oh, yeah, and what the fuck, man? Is there a reason why I'm locked in your bloody dolls house?"

The look on his face is priceless. Guess he was expecting me to cry, plead or beg. Ha, jokes on you asshole. I don't do that for any man.

"You can stare at me all day, mouth catching flies, or you can open my fucking door so I can kick your overgrown ass!" I state with a good dose of attitude.

From deep within his chest a burst of rumbling

laughter barrels up and erupts from his mouth, surprising us both with the authenticity of it. Is this motherfucker seriously laughing at me right now? When his laughter dies down he proceeds to speak in an unusually deep voice that oozes with the remnants of his amusement. "Firstly, I highly doubt that you could kick my ass." Wanker. "And secondly, you're not going anywhere so you might as well sit down, shut up, and eat your food. Thanks for the laugh, girly." He turns, stalking off down the hall with surprising swagger and still chuckling at my expense. Dick!

I really want to punch his stupid smug face.

I pick up my tray and sit on the bed. The toast is cold, but I devour it all at a rapid pace regardless. I pick up the mug and inhale deeply. Coffee. My mind throws a mini celebration as I drink all the delicious, though somewhat cold, nectar. I'm surprised to have such a good cup of coffee in a place like this. It has a robust flavour and it doesn't hold an ounce of bitterness. I have to admit I feel a little bit better now than I did before. Food and coffee can fix almost anything, except, coincidentally, the lock on that stupid glass door.

I look across and see Bell leaning against her glass wall looking down the hallway that Mr Big took. "Can you see anything?" I ask hopefully.

"No. Just more desperate women like us. I wonder

who's next to me?" She begins banging on both her sidewalls. "Hello? Are there any girls in there?"

From where I am I can see both the girls on her left and right. The tall, light blonde one to her left rises and goes to the wall before saying, "Yes, I'm Shylo. Sorry, I'm a bit overwhelmed by all this." Her voice catches, "And I'm just not really capable of talking right now." Shylo looks over to me with moist, sky blue eyes and smiles apologetically before sitting back down on the bed and looking at her hands.

"Fine, whatever," answers Bell abruptly, before she turns and leaves Shylo alone, showing that her bark is worse than her bite.

The more petite looking girl on Bell's right hasn't moved from her position at all. She's just lying on the bed, facing away with her long brown hair strewn beside her. Her shoulders move slightly as she quietly weeps.

Bell bangs on the wall again. "Hello? Anybody home?" She raises her voice slightly to be heard.

"Just leave her be," I say. "She doesn't look up to chatting with you, Bell."

"Oh for God's sake. Can you at least tell me your name? None of us should be alone in this," Bell continues.

The girl then turns over, wipes her eyes, and speaks with a renewed pride and heavy dose of arrogance. "Mischa. I am not interested in your attitude. Please be so kind as to leave me alone!" With an exaggerated roll of her eyes, Mischa resumes her original position on the bed.

Bell scoffs and replies, "Oh I see, I'm so sorry, Miss La Di Da. I hope the accommodation is to your liking, madam." Mischa doesn't seem phased with Bell at all.

Man, Bell is going to be a handful to deal with. All the women I've seen here so far seem very different. Mischa is a real natural beauty, even in this place she looks ethereal. I can't help feeling slightly jealous. Unlike her, my look is very basic. I'm only five foot five with honey blonde hair and an everyday kind of face. My best asset is probably either my unique onyx eyes and curvy frame. That seems like nothing next to this beauty. Her tone of voice did, however, come across as haughty. Perhaps it's just her defence mechanism, which is totally understandable.

The difference is just as outstanding in Bell, with her white-blonde shoulder-length hair, bright blue eyes, and plus-sized physique. She's a good looking girl, in her own way, and has a lot of extra character to her face with piercings on her eyebrows, nose, and lips, as well as down the sides of her ears. She's very interesting to look at and it suits her extraverted nature.

The other girl to Bell's left, Shylo, I think it was, looks like a very tall blonde girl but not the typical model type. At least from what I can see of her laying down.

Speaking of neighbours, I had better check on mine. After finding out that Juanita is doing better I knock on the wall to my left. "Are you okay in there? My name's Summer and I thought that I'd check on you."

"Thank you, Summer, I appreciate it." A deep almost melodic voice calls to me, wavering a little as she speaks. "Have you seen or heard any kids here since you arrived? The last memory I have before coming here was reading to my babies and now I don't know where they are or what's happened to them. I feel so sick inside." She chokes on a soft sob before continuing with a more desperate tone. "Do you have any kids, Summer? I have two precious gifts and they're everything to me." Taking in a distant sigh, she almost absently adds, "Oh, I'm Mia."

I have the distinct feeling that Mia is a little too despondent to communicate past this point. She sounds so desolate and empty when she speaks, I don't want to push her any further because I'm not so sure if she can handle it.

I sigh deeply in return, knowing very well the pain that she feels. "Yes." I say, "I have four..."

Chapter Two

"Summer!" Bell cries from across the hall. "Look to your left, there's a different guard coming up."

I leap to the glass and peer down the hall, my face squishing to see through the wall. Yep, that's a different guy alright. This one here is a bit of a looker too. *Okay, Summer, honey instead of vinegar. I've got this.* I pull my shoulders back, fix my hair a bit, plant on a smile, and suppress my inner rage. Bell watches me in confusion before understanding dawns on her face, along with a small, sly, side smile.

"Excuse me, Sir," I say, my voice dripping in honey. He slows down his pace and turns his face in my direction with mild interest. I use the moment to take in his strong set shoulders and unmarked sun-kissed skin. When he realises which room I'm in, he smiles knowingly and strolls over. Oh boy, he is pretty. With his stylish black haircut, proud movements, clean-shaven face, six-foot stature, and his eyes. Wow. His eyes are so blue they're almost translucent, with a black rim making them pop out more. I can't help but notice them shine with a cheeky glint, promising trouble. Hmm, this should be interesting. He saunters towards me with a dignified, yet predatory air. His gaze locked on me, like he knows me, a half-smile planted on his luscious lips.

"Hello, Summer. I'm dying to know what you want to say. Go right ahead." The clear amusement in his voice irks me. *Don't get pissed off.* I visualise him tripping over his feet and smacking his perfect nose on the glass. That'll show him and his stupid, sexy face.

"Oh, I'm sorry, Sir, do I know you?" I ask as innocently as I can muster, feeling better after picturing him with a broken nose. "It's just that you seem to know me."

He steps forward with a little chuckle. A stupid, sexy chuckle might I add.

"Darlin', everyone that works here knows of you. You're the little dynamite that threatened to punch Salvatore in the face." He laughs outright now, his blue eyes shining and crinkling in the corners. "No one talks to him like that, especially not a female. He's well known for his punishing ways, little Miss. I might suggest you keep your fire aimed towards some of the tamer males. 'Mr Big', as you so eloquently put it, isn't tame with any woman, or man for that matter. You sure did cause a whole lot of laughter in the break room today." He chuckles while unconsciously relaxing his body as he leans against the glass, one foot crossed over the other and a hand stroking his strong jawline.

In my line of work, it's important to read people, places, and behaviours. It makes me wonder if this guy's going to be easier than I originally suspected.

"Well, I'm glad to have been some entertainment for everyone, though that wasn't exactly what I was going for," I say with a fake chuckle of my own. "I have to say that you seem like a much more reason-able man." I make sure that my body signals are sending out positive vibes. Chest out, check. Smile sweet, check. Eye contact, check.

Suddenly, he cuts off my mental checklist. "I'm kind of disappointed in you."

Damn it.

"I was ready for a tongue lashing from a feisty temptress, but you're acting demure and receptive. Don't let my looks fool you, darlin', I'm twice the threat of Salvatore," he growls out in a sultry voice, with a side smile.

Shit! He's not bluffing either, intelligence glints behind those clear blue eyes. As he watches me the realisation dawns, that I had in fact been fooled by his stunning looks and feigned nonchalance.

"I haven't told you anything that you wouldn't have found out yourself eventually anyway. Oh and cut the 'Sir' business. Salvatore might get off on that rubbish but I have a name and I'd like it used. I'm Reid, you're going to be here for a while so you might as well learn it straight up," Reid explains bluntly.

I release the breath I'd not realised I've been holding. "Okay, Reid, fair enough, let's cut the shit. What is this place? Why the hell are we here?" I'm not going to bother with the charade, I've got self-respect after all.

"I'll tell you what, Summer." I notice Reid's jaw tightening slightly, eyes narrowing as he looks hard at me. "Boss will be addressing you all later today over the speaker, I highly suggest you listen to whatever he says and take in the rules of this place very carefully. I suggest you explain to the other girls that when one person steps out of line you'll always be rewarded as a group, not individually. That's all I've got for you, darlin'. Good luck!" Reid states with a quick smile before he turns and swiftly stalks away.

I find my heartbeat quicken and a desperate feeling starts to consume me as I watch him walk off, but I control myself and don't call out. It's weird, the further away he walks, the further away my freedom feels. *Get yourself together*.

Distracting myself, I ask Bell if she heard the exchange. "Yeah man, what does he mean by *rewarded?* It didn't sound rewarding." Bell grimaces and fidgets her feet in discomfort.

"I have no idea, but I don't think it's good. Pass it down to your neighbours and I'll do the same. The quicker that message is received, the better," I say acknowledging the dire feeling I'm getting over this whole thing.

Passing down the information to our neighbours, low chatter begins to fill the hall as we all discuss our current predicament. The only exception being Juanita who starts throwing a massive tantrum in her cell, banging and kicking the walls while screaming to be let go. I try several times to calm her down but with little effect. The guards either don't hear her or don't care, and at this point, it's getting beyond ridiculous. I don't want to be an asshole but she has got to stop because the other girls are becoming unsettled with her constant banging and swarm of profanities.

"Calm your fuckin' tits, ya psycho," Bell calls out

to her, breaking through her outburst. Juanita goes quiet, letting Bell finish. "You look like a dildo carrying on like that. Get your fucking self straightened out and stop acting like a bloody baby. So fucking ridiculous!" Bell rolls her eyes, shakes her head and goes back to talking to Shylo.

I sit here, waiting to hear what Juanita does, after a few moments of quiet I hear a snort of frustration and the familiar creak of a bed as she settles back down. I decide to try reaching out to her.

"Juanita, I know you're freaking out right now, but I really need you to try to focus because we want to get out of here just as much as you do. We can't do this without having each other's back. Do you understand?" My voice is soft but firm.

I hear a loud *humph* and then a snapped, "Fine." With a deep sigh from Juanita her tone turns softer. "I'm calm now, this is just all too much for me. I feel like I'm going to have a breakdown or something."

Good, she's thinking a bit clearer and seems to have shaken off her tantrum. "Thanks, Juanita, just try. Go do your thing girl," I say, hoping to dismiss her from more conversation because I need to sit and think this whole thing through.

As I lay on the bed I can't help thinking about how unreal this all is. I can't seem to stop my brain from going through this endless loop of denial, sadness, rage, and hopelessness. I can't keep doing this to myself. It's time to really focus on what's next and move forward through this situation or I'm just going to fall apart.

My eyes feel heavy and I'm emotionally and mentally exhausted, a quick nap to refuel myself won't hurt I'm sure. I close my eyes and drift off to sleep almost immediately.

Beep. Beep. Beep. Beep. The loud, relentless noise snaps me from my sleep.

My eyes pop open in shock, heart pounding. What the fuck? I look around disoriented for a minute before taking stock of my current situation. An alarm. What's that supposed to mean?

Before I can get up to peer through the glass, a man's deep voice fills my room. I look up for the source and discover that there are little speaker holes in the ceiling, I hadn't noticed them before.

"Welcome to Threshold, ladies. I am Boss, your host during your 'vacation' here with us. I hope you have found your private quarters to your satisfaction. Of course, we have many more exciting rooms that you have yet to be able to enjoy, but I assure you they will be open for your use shortly and I am positive they will not disappoint. I am looking forward to having a private audience with each and every one of you in the future." The man calling himself *Boss* speaks, his baritone voice almost cheerful.

"Now onto more pressing business. I am sure that you will have many questions, but for now I suggest that you accept the information I am offering to you presently. Also, my dear ladies, as you are staying in my house, under my roof, I am sure that you will appreciate my desire for you to kindly follow my simple rules," he continues, a nauseous feeling rolls through me. My hand goes to my stomach pushing hard against the anxiety building inside me. This guy must be insane, he's talking like we're willing guests simply staying at his house. This guy clearly has one too many screws loose.

"There are only five main courtesies that I require of my guests. Firstly, I graciously request total conformity to the daily schedule that will be provided to you, as I am sure lovely ladies like yourselves will appreciate how well a household runs when it is suitably organised. My second request is to attend all medical appointments that you will be allocated, as well as taking any medication prescribed to you. It is important that I take excellent care of my special guests' health."

What on Earth? Special guests my ass, how about unsuspecting victims?

"As a third house rule, I would like to express my keen interest in abiding by my security team's wishes. They are here for your best interests and have only the very best intentions for you at heart. For rule number four I would like to stress, for obvious safety reasons, it would be best that you do not attempt to leave Threshold, or the areas provided to you, for any reason without a properly approved escort. Lastly, my dearest ladies, please do acknowledge the designated lights off time with silence and sleep, this will ensure that you are well-rested and happy."

Man, this guy sounds like he believes the crap that he's spouting. Talking like this place is some spa retreat.

"I am positive that your stay will be pleasant and will go off without a hitch. However, if the unfortunate circumstance comes about in which one of my lovely guests is unhappy enough to question or break any of my very reasonable requests there will be a group *reward* received, as I believe in the equal treatment for all. It would not suit my generous nature to reward one over others," Boss explains almost reassuringly. All I can think of is that '*reward*' seems like an interesting choice of words under the circumstances. Tell the security guard to fuck off; here have a candy bar. Stay awake all night; movies for all. Somehow, I don't think that's how it's going to work.

"My prestigious team will be around shortly to gift you a delicious lunch, and your very own new daily schedule to enjoy and commit to memory. This evening will hopefully be your last night of involuntary confinement with everyone's doors opening in the morning to join together over a nice breakfast in the dining room. That is of course, under the condition that all of my guests have fully understood and agreed to my very reasonable expectations. Have a wonderful day ladies and I hope you enjoy a more full view of what we can offer here for you at Threshold on your very special vacation." Boss finishes before disconnecting with a click.

The deafening sound of silence reverberates through the walls and for a moment, even through my mind. I very literally cannot believe this is happening, I've never been more afraid in my life, the reality and seriousness of the situation is crushing me and I feel like I can't breathe. I and many other women have been taken hostage by a madman, a clearly rich and powerful madman. I can't decide whether I should try to run as soon as I can or to make no sudden movement. Oh God. I put my head between my legs and focus on breathing so I don't freak out any more than I already am.

Slowly murmurs begin to rise all around as women start to talk amongst each other. I think about all of the innocent, unprepared women in these glass cells. Some women will be so scared, but some might just be naive enough to feel reassured by Boss's use of certain words and his tone of voice. That is a frightening thought. I need to take care of these women, they need someone that's willing to look out for their best interest and keep them safe; From Boss and from themselves.

Chapter Three

I hear doors opening and closing down the hall, the squeak of what sounds like two trolley tyres, and a light jiggling sound that I assume are our lunch trays. Their slow approach seems to take forever as they start and stop, slowly coming closer to my little piece of hell. I stand with my face against the cold glass trying to catch a glimpse of the trolleys and the people pushing them. I see across from me that Bell is trying to do the same. She's been remarkably quiet since Boss's message was broadcast, I'll keep an eye on her in case she's planning something stupid. I know one thing for sure it would be unwise to take any unnecessary chances at this stage. I need to take full stock of the surroundings here, the guards, and the routines. Any mistakes this early on, especially one

"

fuelled by emotions, could have dire consequences for us all. I have to talk to Bell when I get the chance, to make sure she understands that. Something tells me she's not exactly the patient type, mind you neither am I.

I get the feeling that there aren't as many people in the cells here as I originally thought. By the sound of it, they don't make many stops, but the workers are possibly going slower than necessary. I do think that there are several more floors below me filled with women, as I can hear them talking and crying through the void in the centre of the walkway.

I sometimes see a woman move around in the cell below Bell. She's got short, funky, rainbow tipped hair and big yellow stretchers in her ears, but I can't gauge much else about her from here. Though with hair like that, she has to be interesting, right?

I hear the squeaking get louder and see two men across the hall at Shylo's door. Looks like one guard and one kitchen worker. The first one is armed and in uniform; he looks like a huge Pacific Islander with long hair down his back and tribal tattoos on his neck and arms. The other man is average height and size, but still muscular. He looks to be African American with short cut hair and an apron over his grey clothes, he's also pushing the trolley and handling the food. Both men are very good-looking. What the hell is this place and where do they hire their staff; hunks 'r' us?

Next to me, Mia is getting her tray too, I can hear a quiet exchange between her and a man. Is that a Scottish accent? Oh, the squeaking is coming towards me. *Yay, food.*

I am instantly deflated.

I had to get excited, didn't I? Lo and behold, Mr Big is here to ruin my lunch. As I look at the over-grown man approaching me, I think, *yes I still want to punch you in the face.* I don't know what it is about this guy but he just rubs me the wrong way. The tall, scruffy, red-haired guy with perfect dimples smiling at me as he approaches must be the Scot that I heard. Of course, he's also ridiculously gorgeous, with his face stubble, bulging biceps, and deep green eyes. This is getting annoying now, are they trying to distract us with hot guys so we don't notice where we are? I scoff at the thought.

"Good day to you lass, I've brought you a wee something for lunch, I also added a nice cup of coffee for you. Besides, you gave Salvatore here such a hard time I snuck in a slice of chocolate cake." The Scots light-hearted voice is filled with glee, accompanied by a cheeky wink. All the while Mr Big just stares at me with cold hard eyes meant to intimidate. Those eyes then turn on the Scot when he mentions the cake, that in itself almost makes me laugh out loud. I think I'll use this to my advantage.

"Thank you, I do love chocolate cake," I reply, smiling cooly at Mr Big, egging him on with my eyes. *You don't intimidate me, motherfucker.*

Loud booming laughter fills the air and everyone within my sight turns our way as the Scot lets loose. He looks like a jolly sort, I can't help but wonder why he's here.

"Ah, lass, you're gonna give me a fit. Fuck me, your attitude is brilliant. Salvatore, I believe you met your match, this lass is going to give you a run for your money," the Scot states, every word dripping with humour. "I'm Baine, at your service. I'm here for all your culinary needs, and for you, bonnie lass, probably even more." He finishes with a playful bow and another cheeky wink, and I can't help but let out a small laugh at his antics.

Mr Big steps forward, red-faced and serious. "That's quite enough of that shit, Baine. Remember your place before I put you in it." He turns angrily in my direction, his shoulders back and his head high as he sneers down at me. I hold my ground, there's no way I'm flinching away from his vicious stare. "Your trivial outburst the other day won't happen again, while you're here you *will* call me Master or Sir, nothing less, and you *will* treat me with respect. Keep your eyes down and your mouth shut in my presence, do you hear me, girly?" Mr Big all but snarls.

"Eh, Salvatore, that's a bit rough. Just leave the lass be," Baine says in my defence. However, Baine quickly steps back, putting his eyes down and shutting his mouth the instant that Mr Big slowly turns to focus his menacing glare in Baine's direction.

Mr Big pivots back to me. "I said, do you understand?" I look around at the freaked out women and the worried workers, even the other guard looks like he isn't sure what to do. Well, this is a less than ideal situation I've found myself in, but it *is* me after all, and he's not *Boss*, so what the heck.

"Yes, Mr Big, I understand. You have Mummy issues, right? What, she didn't hug you enough? If you want to be a dick then go right ahead, but I'll put my eyes wherever the hell I want, I'll speak when I want, and I'll never be your little bitch to boss around. There's a Boss here and I'll listen to him because it seems I have no choice, but it's not you, buddy, is it? If you don't like it, you steroid filled asshole, then you can just fuck right off," I spit out with fire in my voice and steel in my spine.

Just then I hear the other guard say, "Holy shit!" Mr Big goes for his keys to unlock my door.

My heart starts thumping wildly in my chest as adrenaline fills me, making me hyper-aware of my surroundings. I have no weapon, everything except my pillow and mattress is attached, and he might just be *too* big for me to take on.

Baine shouts over to the other guard, "Tyrese you've got to do something!" Eyes wide with worry, leaning forward with fists clenched. "Damn it! I'm pressing the alarm." With that he presses a button that I can't see on the wall beside him.

Whooop! Whooop! Whooop!

Red lights begin flashing, the alarm blaring loud, an acoustic to my inner panic. The other security guard that Baine called Tyrese, runs over yelling at Mr Big to stop, but he's too late as my door opens and closes with a bang, locking behind him. Mr Big takes huge strides as he stalks towards me. Oh shit! His eyes. What the—I'm sure they just... his eyes flashed red, bright red. I'm sure of it. Fuck, I've done it now, I just had to go and open my mouth, didn't I?

As Baine and Tyrese fight to get the door unlocked, I retreat quickly, walking backwards until my back collides with the wall, at the same time that his hands slam either side of my head. I look up at his furious face, he lowers his angry scowling eyes down to mine as my heartbeat kicks up another notch. In a deep, low, menacing voice he growls, "Still think you're funny, bitch?"

Knowing I have to think quickly, I decide on

something a little unconventional, I make a split-second decision and reach up with my hands, grabbing the sides of his face. I kiss him, hard, before he can react. His body tenses and freezes under my touch, he stops breathing as I take his mouth with mine, when he gasps in shock at my impulsiveness, I take advantage sliding my tongue in between his lips. He softens his stance and jaw as I glide mine over his tongue and then pull out slightly to nibble at his bottom lip. Salvatore begins to respond with his own tongue, bringing his body flush and hard against mine, his hands move to my waist as he lifts me off the ground with zero effort, pushing me hard against the wall and I begin to slowly, gentle my kiss when I become aware of another kind of hardness. I plant one last lingering peck on his lips, while tenderly stroking his cheek, then I look up at his eyes to see a confused, broken man. Wow. That was effective. Risky, but effective. I can't believe I just did that, who in their right mind would think that's a solution? My dumb ass, apparently. The saddest part is that it wasn't the worst kiss I've ever had.

I smile up at him sweetly knowing I need to remove myself from this situation calmly. "You can put me down now and I don't mean to sound pushy but can you go so I can have my lunch? I'm starving." He steps back with a shocked expression while placing me down. I sweep myself around him and go to the open door to find the three remaining men standing just inside of it. "Is lunch still on the agenda, guys?" I ask looking at Baine, innocently smiling. Baine just stands in front of me staring like I'd grown three heads or something.

Just then Reid and four other formidable-looking men come running down the corridor, with weapons at the ready. They come to an abrupt stop at the front of my glass cell, looking quizzically at the scene before them. Me smiling at Baine innocently, the guys at the door looking at me with different quizzical expressions, and Salvatore in the back of my cell still staring at the wall he'd just pinned me to.

Reid raises his hand at the men behind him in a gesture to stand down once he's determined that there's no imminent threat here. "What's going on? Why was the alarm raised?" He enquires looking from me to the man behind me, still in the exact same position I left him in.

Baine clears his throat before facing Reid, explaining the situation with a look of amusement on his face, while frequently looking from me to Salvatore. Finishing up Baine chuckles deeply, "It turns out that Summer managed to get the situation under control without any need of outside assistance, Sir. She's quite the resourceful lass." Lifting his hand to cover his mouth in an obvious move to stifle further laughter.

Reid looks a bit perplexed at the whole idea and a little more than curious about how the scene played out, pushing some buttons on his watch, the alarm immediately ceases.

Turning toward me for verification he asks, "Is that a true statement of events? Is there anything else that I should be made aware of?"

"Yes, Reid, it's just as Baine said and the only thing I'm worried about is when I'm going to get my lunch, I'm starving but everyone keeps staring at me with their mouths open like they're catching flies. If it's okay with you, can we just get on with it now?" I reply with obvious irritation, the sight of the food trolley makes my mouth water in anticipation.

With clear amusement, Reid nods in agreement and ushers everyone to go back to their duties. Everyone proceeds to leave my doorway except for Baine and the fool still doing a mannequin impression behind me. In this little exchange, I've learnt that Reid has some kind of position of authority here. Good to know.

Baine walks over to the trolley, gets my tray of food and brings it to me, along with some papers and what looks like a bangle watch. "What's that?" I ask him.

"This is your schedule, rules list, and a map of the place. Oh and this is a mandatory watch that everyone has to wear in order for anybody to leave confinement," Baine says before warily adding, "Lass, what was that?" Pointing to Mr Big, who's still in the same position, my inner Goddess rolls her eyes.

I look at Mr Big and chuckle a little to myself. "You might need to call for a different guard to help with your duties, I think I broke that one," I joke, to lighten the mood a bit.

"I actually think you're right. If you're up for it, I could do with some breaking myself." A seductive smile curving his full lips; cheeky bugger.

I decide then that I quite like Baine, he seems like a good guy, there must be a good reason why he's working for such an awful villain. I have decided that's what Boss is, he's a villain and he must be stopped. Now all I need to be is a superhero, but I'll settle with being the anti-hero if I can get us the hell out of here.

"Very funny, you should probably get out of here though, never keep hungry women waiting or they'll eat you alive. It's alright I've got this, I'll call you if I need your help," I say with a wave of my hand to reassure Baine. He nods hesitantly and closes the door behind him, leaving me alone with Salvatore.

I go over to the big oaf and walk around to stand

in front of him so that I can see his face clearly. "Excuse me, Mr Big." My polite tone grabbing his attention as he slowly looks down at me with a dazed expression. "I'm going to need you to vacate my room because I'm hungry and I also need to pee."

"Why did you do that?" He asks in a deep, monotone voice. "I don't understand, it doesn't make sense. You should've fought me or submitted."

I chuckle. "I'll probably eventually hit you but for now, it worked a treat, so why mess with perfection? You need to understand that I don't make sense, get used to that or you'll always be fighting against someone you can't beat. Now, go away!" My voice flat and dismissive, before going to get my tray and then began eating my lunch on the bed, ignoring his presence. I know I'm being a bit cocky with him but at this point I just want him to leave.

I pick up my coffee, inhale the smooth aroma of roasted beans, and drink it down, surprised again by its delicious flavour and enjoying it very much. Who knew Hell was so accommodating to the tastebuds? My insides squeal with delight at the rich and robust taste, as I notice Mr Big sullenly walking away without looking back. Once again I'm alone, kidnapped, and stuck in a white glass room with no way to escape. At least at the moment, I have coffee, food, and chocolate cake, I will relish any victory.

While I'm aware that kissing that big ogre of a man was a very risky move, I knew that I had to de-escalate the situation quickly. I actually thought that my life might've been in real jeopardy. I knew fighting while he was in such a rage was out of the question, especially by how his colleagues had freaked out, I had no chance. I didn't think there was anything that I could've said at that point which wouldn't just fuel him in some way either. I'd nowhere to run or hide, so I just went with my instinct that told me he had never really been touched with any kindness, and hoped that it would be enough to catch him off guard. Thank God it worked, otherwise I would have been screwed.

It may have worked a little too well, even though I used the unexpected to my advantage, I feel kind of bad for the guy. Salvatore was literally so stunned because of a passionate gesture that he couldn't move. What a sad, empty man he must be and what a life he must have had to have ended up that way. I don't plan on being friends with him. He's still an arrogant thug, but I do pity him. If I'm being honest with myself, he smelt like woodfire and leather, it was so good and it made me a little hot under the collar having such a strong, hard body pressed against me. Shaking my head, I get rid of that ludicrous thought.

Sitting on my bed thinking about what happened,

I'm kind of surprised that he didn't just run out of here screaming after being semi-molested by someone who stinks so bad. I lift the front of my hospital gown and take a sniff, wrinkling my nose, old sweat and body odour permeates from it. I really need a shower, that's one thing that this room didn't supply that I miss dearly.

Chapter Four

I finish off my lunch; a chicken sandwich, a fresh cut fruit bowl, and of course my cake, which is delicious. I do some stretching and light exercise to limber up my stiff body, it feels good to get the blood pumping a little bit. I have a full-size hourglass figure, I'm toned and in shape due to my daily fitness regime. I've always enjoyed going out and taking on the world with things like hiking, rock climbing, snow sports, and swimming. I'm lucky to live in such a versatile country, Australia has a bit of everything. My life keeps not just me active but also my kids, we do a lot of family fitness together because those kinds of things are fantastic bonding tools. My kids are my life and I miss them a whole lot, just thinking about them makes my heart hurt.

As much as I would like to say the same about my

ex-husband, I can't because he pretty much did his own thing. We were never really close, we just worked on paper when we were together. I tried for many years to make something out of nothing, but he liked it just the way it was and I eventually gave up trying and concentrated on our kids and my career. Grant, however, found his concentration lingering else-where, which is why we ended things. He travelled interstate a lot for work and apparently to visit his new, entirely different family, too. I found out about it quite some time ago, and he moved to be with them soon after. I assume he's watching the kids while I'm on this involuntary 'vacation'. I hope he's doing right by them, but I know they'll be unhappy there and I need to get home to them.

Seriously, fuck my life. All the good stuff happens to me.

I decide to open up the folder given to me earlier to check out what's inside. I find the five rules that Boss already covered on laminated paper and I wonder to myself if what happened between Mr Big and I would class as breaking rule number three, I guess I'll find out eventually. Fingers crossed that I didn't just fuck up everyone's 'vacation'. Seriously though, vacation? I don't think so.

The next page I pull out is the map of the compound, apparently this is an eight level establishment, but there are only four levels that are open to us. The map says that levels one, six, seven, and eight are restricted areas as they're either private quarters or security concerns. Interesting, I'll check that out when I get a chance.

The other girls and myself are spread out between levels two to five, with our own bathrooms on each level, there are also a few different amenities available to us on each level including a dining hall, medical centre, some entertainment areas, as well as the gym, a garden, and pool on my level, which is five. I can't imagine that I'll be lazing by the pool and catching some rays, but wouldn't it be great if it was outside. If I didn't know any better I'd think that this place was a resort but unfortunately, I do know better. Example A, my stunning room or as I like to call it my cage.

The map looks like a very long and relatively narrow building, with an increase in length at each level starting from level two, working up in length to level five. These are the only levels that we've received the schematics for. It's almost like an upside-down triangle but with the point cut off at the bottom. On the right side of each level are the bathrooms, as well as the meditation space and gym. The accommodation is in the centre to the right of the levels and the other extra rooms stem from the centre to the left of each level, taking up the remainder of the space provided. In between where the left rooms meet the accommodations are two elevators on one side of the hall and a staircase on the opposite. The map is pretty easy to read and I'm sure the building will be simple enough to navigate.

I wonder how many women they have here? I guess I'll find out tomorrow, if this map is showing the rooms correctly then it should be about forty women altogether, ten of us per level; that's no small feat.

I open up the folder and take out the last page, which is the schedule. It's very basic and more free-range than I was expecting. The only weird thing on there is the scheduled medical appointment times, between nine and ten am. It says that each person will have an appointment that will be individually assigned a weekly time, at fifteen minutes per person, it backs up the idea of there being forty women.

6:00am - Doors open

7:00am - Breakfast (1 hour)

9:00-10:00am - 15 minute Medical appointment- day and time will be allocated individually between Mon-Fri

12:00pm - Lunch (1 hour)

4:00pm - Snacks and drinks available (1 hour)

7:00pm - Dinner (1 hour)

10:00pm - Lights out

What I'd really like to know is why on earth we're required to go to medical appointments at all? I better not be some kind of guinea pig. The horrible part is I might be. What if this is the exact reason why we're here? If not then the only other explanation is to sell as sex slaves or something just as creepy. I wonder why we're all women? Maybe I'm just jumping to conclusions, there very well could be a more reasonable explanation and I just haven't thought of it yet, for some reason though, I highly doubt it.

Next item inside the package is the watch. It's a basic, smooth, slim black matte bangle with a small, rectangular, digital 24-hour clock face, there's also a number engraved on it; 240508. It's most likely an ID number of some sort. The watch is unclasped and I can't see any mechanism to close it. I put it on my wrist and try to figure it out when suddenly it closes and clasps itself around my wrist. I pull at it but it's stuck and won't budge, not one bit.

I don't panic because I know something that keeps me calm. I have hands and wrists that are completely double-jointed and can get them out of anything if I need to. I decide to leave the watch on though because there could be someone watching me through a hidden camera and I'd prefer to keep that little nugget of information to myself for now. That way I can use it in the future if I need to, it's good to keep an ace up your sleeve in a situation like this.

Dinner came and went with some random chatter between the ladies, but nothing overly significant happened. The guards and workers that came around were new again and I didn't bother to even acknowledge their presence, I was too busy thinking of home and feeling sorry for myself and my predicament.

I did notice that a beep went off on my watch at every scheduled time from the list given to us, I suppose that's so we can't use the excuse that we forgot.

Five minutes before lights off, the guard in charge with the good hair, Reid, walks down the corridor reciting a loud reminder that unless all women are wearing their watches, that no one would be able to enjoy the freedom that Threshold would like to offer. After all, we're to be treated equally as a group and not individually.

Thanks for the reminder asshat. I guess that means there's at least one woman holding out. I can understand the hesitation but I really hope for all of our sakes that she just puts the damn thing on. Regardless of whether or not she fights it, I'm pretty sure it's not negotiable, might as well just get it over with so we can see what's going on with this place.

Right on time, darkness envelops my cell. I'm awake but it's absolutely pitch black. The only sounds are of women moving around in their cells and my increasing heartbeat. There's something about being in total darkness that can really mess with your mind, especially in a place that you don't feel safe.

Breathing deeply, I try to settle my nerves and let sleep consume me. I'm going to need all of my wits about me if tomorrow turns out to be as bizarre as it sounds.

Chapter Five

I hear my watch beep and the lights go on, opening my eyes I see that my door's still closed, I check my watch; 06:02. Well, it's past door open time, someone mustn't have put on their watch. Deflated, I hop off the bed and go to the toilet before walking over to the glass and peering through. Mischa, Bell, and Shylo are standing at their glass walls as well, looking just as deflated as I feel.

"This is bullshit!" Bell yells in frustration, banging her fist on the glass. "Put your damn watch on!" She screams at the corridor to the unknown perpetrator, her face screwed up in obvious outrage.

Then I get an idea in my head, I wonder if anyone has actually checked the handles? I go over to the door, place my hand on the handle and slowly turn it, hoping to God that it opens.

Click. The latch undoes. Holy shit!

I open the door and walk through, staring wide-eyed at Bell. "Apparently they all did and you're a few beers off a six-pack. Did it seriously never occur to you to try the handle?" I laugh at her with a mixture of relief and awe.

Bell bustles to the door and pulls it open with gusto, rushing into the walkway before turning in circles with arms outstretched, glee written on her face. "I can't believe I'm out of that God-forsaken room."

I totally get where she's coming from, I knew what we were told but I never actually thought that they would let us out. I sigh in relief and feel my shoulders slightly relax for the first time in days as I breathe in deeply, appreciating my moment of freedom.

I look to the right of me and see one cell, a bathroom, and a gym. Juanita and Mischa are in the last cells of the row. When I look left, I see a row of cells on each side. Noticing the numbers above each room, I turn around and find that my number is eight, Juanita has ten, and Mia has six, but Bell's room across the corridor is seven. How did I never notice that before?

I go to the void and look down at the row below and their numbers seem to match the ones above, meaning that I was right, there are ten women in each row, forty women here in total. Holy crap. That is a lot of captives.

I note that at the end of the left corridor there's a double door with two burly guards standing at each side, one of them is the Pacific Islander man that Baine had called Tyrese and the other one I'd seen randomly come and go down the walkway occasionally but never took much notice of him until now. To be honest, he looks like a dickhead because of the deep, unimpressed scowl on his face that he's directing to the women around him. He'd be another good looking dude if it wasn't for the clear disgust written all over him. Even the jagged scar running across one side of his cheek and up to his eyebrow would have been kind of cool. He notices me staring and looks down at me like I'm a bug that he wants to squash under the heel of his boot, point taken Mr, you don't like me. What a douche.

I walk over to Tyrese standing guard, deciding that it's better to ask than assume. "Can we really go through there and see the rooms on the map?" The sound of hope drips from my tongue.

Tyrese looks at me kindly, a sincere smile tugging at the corners of his mouth, eyes squinting in amusement. "Yes, Miss, you can. You'll like the rooms, they're pretty nice and there's plenty to entertain you." As something grabs his attention he looks over my head, I turn to see him glancing at some of the girls at the other end of the hall before continuing. "While you ladies are wandering about, we've been instructed to fix your rooms up with the toiletries and clothes that you might need going forward. If you like any books from the library I was told to tell you that you can take them back to your room if you want to. We really don't want you to be unhappy here, Miss." He seems very sincere when he talks, which is surprising. He's a very big, intimidating looking man, yet he comes across as genuinely kind. What a strange mix of men there is here. The guy standing next to him clearly wouldn't care if I died in a hole. In fact, I think he'd prefer it, he gives me the willies. A shiver runs down my spine at how his angry eyes follow the girls around the room.

"Thanks," I reply, giving him a cordial nod. "I'm going to get a couple of the girls and go for a walk to check it out then."

I turn back around heading towards Bell and the others, before reaching them I detour to the woman I think is Juanita because she's lingering at her doorway, smiling politely as I go. "Are you Juanita?" We introduce ourselves and I tell her about my plan to suss the place out. I invite her along, even though her eyes are narrowed, shoulders tense, and she keeps looking past me or around the room.

Clearly, having had enough of dealing with me, she scoffs. "No, I've got no interest in being here, I'm going back to bed," she snaps back at me before backing into her room and blowing me off.

Okay, she's really not a very friendly person, I'll just give her a day or two to come around. Trying my luck with Mischa instead, I lightly jog over to her retreating form. "Mischa?" My voice raised slightly. "Wait. I'll come with you."

Turning a stern look my way, Mischa looks me up and down very slowly, a twist to her lips and judgement clear as day. "I don't think so, dear. We're not very compatible people. You should stick with your own type." Wow. For the most beautiful woman I've ever seen she's also one of the ugliest, what a shame.

"You're absolutely right, so sorry. I just felt bad for you and thought I'd take you under my wing, I'm sure you'll find someone more suited to your level. Maybe they put you upstairs with us by mistake, after all, you're not too bad to look at. Maybe they assumed you were of higher class because of it. Good luck, honey," I say with fake pity, giving her a pat on her shoulder and then walk over to Shylo, and Bell, who's trying not to piss herself laughing at my little acting job. I couldn't help myself, I don't like it when people think it's okay to look down on another person. I didn't even look back to see how she took it because I couldn't give two shits.

Approaching the girls, I shake my head in disbelief. "Can you believe that girl? I was just trying to be nice to her. Sorry about that guys, I'm usually a lot nicer... and more tactful."

Shylo smiles and says simply, "It's really okay. We're in this crazy place together and we're all doing the best we can, I'm just grateful to not be alone in this. Let's stay together for now if that's okay, I want to look around but I'm too anxious to be on my own."

I have a feeling that Shylo's a pleasant girl to be around and I'm glad she wants to stick with us. "That sounds like an excellent idea. What do you think, Bell? Wanna stick together for now?" I ask, turning to the pierced blonde at my side with a toothy smile.

She looks at me incredulously, one eyebrow shooting straight up. "No shit, Sherlock. Do you think I'm just standing here cuz I like the ambience?" Her sarcasm never seems to cease.

Inquiring if anyone knows who Mia is, Bell points to a brunette girl about my age, maybe a bit younger. She has big, beautiful brown eyes, high cheekbones, short in stature and a pear-shaped body, which suits her well.

Lightly jogging over to where she's standing, I approach with a welcoming smile. "Hi, I'm Summer, your neighbour. A couple of the girls and I were thinking of checking the place out in a safe small group and were wondering if you'd like to join us?"

Rubbing the back of her neck shyly, she returns my smile and agrees to go along with us, then in a quiet voice meant just for me she leans in closer. "Is taking Bell a good idea? She's a bit loud and full-on."

I know where she's coming from but I try to put her mind at ease. "I was just about to talk to the girls as a group about being more quiet and inconspicuous today, and that avoiding conflict is probably best. Plus to be fair, I'm the only one so far to fight with the guards, but I'll be on my best behaviour, I promise." Adding the last bit for humour, "Come on, let's join the others."

We join Bell, and Shylo, taking the three of them aside, I say to them quietly but with purpose, "I think that we should try to take in as much detail as we can about what we see and try to cover as much ground as possible. The best thing to do at this point is to just blend in and go along with whatever they say. In saying that, however, if somebody makes you feel threatened, or scared, or hurts you in any way, call for me and I'll come running. I'm trained in hand-to-hand combat and will do whatever I can to keep you all safe. Does anyone want to add anything?"

Bell scoffs. "Nope, that about covers it, Rambo. Mind you, I've seen your hand-to-hand combat skills, I'd like to know where you learnt that vicious move." Bell then bursts into laughter as the other two look at us confused. Clearly, Bell saw my run-in with Mr Big from her cell.

"Very funny, Bell. That was a one-off and not one of my normal moves, I assure you. How about you guys, anything you want to add?" Mia and Shylo shake their heads, satisfied with my makeshift strategy.

I guess that means that it's time to step through those doors and see where they take us.

Chapter Six

Shylo recommends that we check out our own floor first, which is a great idea and we're all happy to go along with that.

We go to the bathroom first and it's much like the rest of the place; very sparkly white, stark clean glass, and mirrored walls everywhere, reflecting back to us our discomfort in such a cold, sterile place. I'm happy to see enclosed toilet stalls, private shower cubicles, and I open a few doors to find two rooms with baths, the big kind that you can get lost in. I can already see myself lounging in the warm water, covered to my neck and pretending I'm somewhere else. Looking at Shylo I can't help but notice a very recognisable longing in her eyes too as she stares at them.

"I've got to be honest, I'm not disappointed! It's a

bit bleak but we have privacy and baths, so I'm happy with that for now," I say semi-enthusiastically, sniffing at my arm. "I'm in dire need of a shower!"

With an agreeable laugh amongst ourselves we head over to the gym door. The first thing that catches my eye when I open the door is the length of the room and the big sloped stone wall at the opposite end. It's very earthy and beautiful, like the wall of a cave and I breathe in the scent of earth and rock. Maybe we're underground in a big hole and that's why the map is shaped the way it is. *It sure as hell would explain some things.*

We move further into the room and take in the rest of our surroundings, the long walls on either side are the same endless shiny white as the rest. *Naturally.* Along the left wall are cardio machines and on the right a selection of low impact weight machines, including pull up bars and benches, stretch across the open space. At the opposite end, in front of the rock wall, is a larger open space with a soft matted floor and a corner with storage for medicine balls, steps, and other equipment, even a radio. That's exciting, I love music.

Standing around and joking about who will and won't be using the gym we hear a sudden *Buzz*, and our watches vibrate. I look at it, it's breakfast time.

"Let's go eat and check out the dining room next. I'm so hungry and don't want to miss out," Mia chirps in.

"I second that," Bell says, moving back toward the doorway, almost running to leave the gym.

We walk back through the living quarters and I take in each room as we walk past. They're all identical except for the numbers on top. It hasn't escaped my notice that everyone's adapting surprisingly quickly to the rules. I haven't heard of any crazy schemes, or seen any defiant outbursts, though they may be yet to come. Still, I've been expecting the worst, like at any time some girl's going to go off her cracker, shave all her hair off Britney Spears style, and then we're all going to be ushered somewhere for our group 'rewards'. Technically we don't have any razors but that's not the point, the idea keeps me feeling on edge. I don't like the thought of my life not only being in the hands of Boss and his bitches, but also a bunch of unpredictable, scared women.

As I walk through the end doors that lead to the stairwell and elevator area, I'm ridiculously over the recurring theme of stark bleak whiteness. There had obviously been zero thought put into decorating this place, maybe it's part of the plot to drive us all mad.

We follow the flight of stairs down to the third

floor, where the dining room is. Chattering, clanging, and even laughter can be heard through the double doors to my left and silence from the double doors to my right, well I can guess which one has the food. I push the doors open to my left.

The room is long and surprise, surprise, completely white. There are three long tables spanning the room and a kitchen at the end with a buffet and counter in front. At the counter is Baine and the good looking African American guy I remember from yesterday serving the food. Behind them is a very, very large Viking looking man cooking. What the fuck? This is the weirdest kitchen I've ever seen. They really don't have any women working here at all do they? I consider this apparent fact as we walk further into the room.

Bell walks swiftly towards the lineup of women waiting for breakfast and we're not far behind. I can't blame her, it does smell good and my mouth salivates from all the delicious aromas floating my way.

When I finally reach the buffet, my stomach twisting in impatient discontent while Baine stands across from me, with a twinkle in his eye.

"I've got this one, Buck. This is that lass from yesterday. Buck, Summer. Summer, this here is Buck. He's a good type, he'll take care of you when I'm not here." Baine introduces us, and I can't stop the flutter that dips low in my stomach, heading further south than I'd like it to. It's his Scottish brogue, it does incredible things to my body, but the way he looks certainly doesn't help either. I hate that I react to him like this though, it doesn't seem right under the circumstances.

Buck smiles at me warmly, pulling me from my unwanted thoughts of Baine. "Hi, Summer. Nice to meet you properly. You're quite the talk around here."

"Apparently!" I say with mocked frustration. "These are my fellow prisoner friends; Bell, Mia, and Shylo. Girls, these are part of our captors, Baine and Buck. It's okay though because they feed us, so that makes it better." I continue pointedly staring at Baine. I notice both men visibly flinching at my remark, I almost feel bad, but then I don't because I remember it's true.

"Sorry, lass, just trying to be friendly in a bad situation. If I can make the stay here any easier for anyone, I will. It's not an ideal situation, I know, but it can't be helped."

I look at them both, my inner anger slowly rising, but I smile before saying, "And why did you say we are here again?" Knowing I'm not going to get a proper response I say it anyway. I'm feeling slightly irrational and I'm tired of never getting any answers.

They glance at each other uncomfortably before Buck says, "Sorry, Miss, but you're holding up the line. What would you like from the selection?" He looks down and away from my eye contact. I know he's just trying to avoid an altercation but I'm now fully pissed off.

I slam my tray down. All the people around us stop and stare with their breathing halted. Reminding myself not to make a scene or I could be responsible for hurting others, I take a moment to breathe. Before I can stop my mouth, it snaps out, "Nothing!" Giving a direct cold stare at both men. "I want nothing from either of you." And with that, I walk away.

To my great horror, I walk straight into a poor girl returning her plate. We collide, hard, and her plate falls smashing to the ground. My wrist hits the ground with force and my stomach collides with her knee as she falls on her butt, knees bent. Shit, I'm such a dickhead. Not only do I feel incredibly guilty for possibly injuring this young girl, but also I've embarrassed myself while trying to make a cool impacting exit. Fail.

I apologize emphatically to her and ask if she's injured. She looks at me shocked with big, sad eyes convinced it was her fault, which of course it isn't. She's a full-figured girl, maybe in her early twenties or late teens, only short with shoulder-length blonde hair. I hope I didn't hurt her.

Sitting up we stay on the floor next to each other for a minute gathering ourselves. Next thing I know I'm being hoisted in the air with her by the giant kitchen Viking, he seats us in some nearby chairs and drops to his knees in front of us. Woah. This guy has a serious presence. His wide, towering frame is mighty and so is his long, dark blond hair braided down his back, thick beard, and the tattoo covering half of his face. Yet his eyes are so deep and kind you could almost get lost in them.

His deep voice shocks me when he asks several questions in quick succession. "Are you hurt? Do you feel any injuries? Are you well?"

We both just stare at him, unsure what to say.

Baine runs over to us. "Hermes, this is Summer, and I don't know the other lass. Are they okay? Do I fetch the Doctor?" Panic rising in his words.

A girl pushes through the going crowd to check on her friend, whose name is apparently Alice, to see if she's harmed after the fall. Alice looks around and confirms that she's totally fine and jokes that her bum caught her landing, but it goes down like a lead balloon.

"I'm fine too," I blurt out when eyes turn to me. "My tummy's a bit sore and I landed on my wrist weird, but I'll be fine." Trying to sound as reassuring as I can because this colossus man looks so worried.

All of a sudden I'm being carried like a baby down the hall by the Viking, as he calls for Baine to grab Alice, and for Buck to finish serving. Bell goes to jump in front, to intercept the giant man, but he placates her on the way past, telling her that he's just making sure I'm okay. It must be enough for her and the girls because no one follows us down the hall.

What the hell is going on?

"Where are you taking me? Put me down right now, I'm fine. I feel great," I say a little desperately as my body bumps up and down like a ragdoll at his steadfast pace. I kick my feet up and down in protest. "Oh for fucks sake, put me down!"

I look over his shoulder and see Baine carrying Alice down the stairs behind us. It's like we weigh nothing at all, maybe I should enjoy it, it's not often I get carried around by such strong, good looking men. If I was a different kind of woman I could really get used to this, but I'm not. I start to struggle in his arms again, my arms pushing his chest as I try to get one of my legs down. I wiggle and twist until I know it's hard to hold me still.

"Summer, my name is Hermes. I'm the cook here at Threshold, but I'm just as responsible for the well-being and safety of each of you as every other member that works here. It's my duty to take care of you and make sure that you are alright. I know this might seem excessive to you but we're trained to take the utmost precaution with a female's safety. Please don't resist me trying to take care of you, I just would like the Doctor to see that you're well and then you'll be free to roam again. Please understand my need for your safety, little one," Hermes pleads, genuinely concerned as he pulls me closer to his body, a deep frown on his face.

I concede and let him finish carrying me to the medical centre where he places me on a chair inside the waiting room. It's tastefully decorated, with comfortable looking armchairs and fluffy cushions, but the room is still just as white as the others, even if there is at least a more textured feel than just stark repetitiveness.

Baine comes in and places Alice next to me with his eyes facing away from me at all times, head down. Hermes goes to the desk while Baine stands off to the side near us. Hermes speaks quietly, in his baritone voice, with a blond Adonis of a man whom I assume is the receptionist. I'm starting to get a complex now, it's not natural to be surrounded by such good looking people. Thank God there aren't women working here too. Can you imagine what they would look like?

Baine moves to stand with Hermes and the receptionist. Hermes occasionally looks over to Alice and me while talking unbearably quietly, while randomly pointing to us and making some hand gestures. Baine never once looks back at the two of us sitting on the armchairs. I guess his days of being nice to me are over, he's clearly avoiding me.

When the receptionist picks up the phone to make some calls, Hermes leans on the reception desk gazing at us both inquisitively before voicing his thoughts. "Baine and I have to go back to work, please stay here until you've been cleared to leave. I truly hope you're well, I look forward to seeing you at lunch." Pushing off the side of the desk, Hermes walks straight out the door, but not before giving Baine a stern look.

Baine follows him out with his head down, he briefly stops and without turning around asks in a quiet voice, "Are you hungry, Summer? I can bring you food here if you need it, lass." He stands still, looking away, waiting for my reply.

"No!" I reply flatly. I know that it's probably ridiculous and maybe it's because he's being nice but I don't want to be here and sometimes I want to take that out on somebody. It feels like the only power I have left.

He stiffens a moment before walking away.

I kind of hate how stubborn I am sometimes. I'm so hungry, but I had to be a bitch instead of accepting food from someone I'm mad at. He's been nothing but nice to me until now, but I'm having a hard time finding sympathy for someone who's involved with kidnapping and holding women against their will.

Chapter Seven

"Good morning, Alice and Summer, my name's Salem and I'm front of house here." The stunning receptionist pulls up a chair in front of us and sits down before continuing. "Normally we have a scheduled weekly appointment for each of you with your own set doctor. However, we're obviously here for any of your spontaneous needs as well. Both the doctors are just setting up their rooms and will be with you in a second. They're great guys and will take good care of you, your health comes before everything else for them, so you can discuss anything you want and they'll help you out the best they can. If you ever want to make an extra appointment with your doctor you're always welcome to come in and speak to me at any time. Do you ladies have any questions?" Alice fidgets in her seat uncomfortably at the penetrating gaze Salem's directing at her.

I jump right on that one. "Why are we here? Where are we? What do you guys want with us? Where are my kids?" I demand, smiling sweetly, knowing very well that none of my questions will be answered but a girl has to try.

Salem chuckles, the laughter reaching his friendly sapphire eyes as he turns his attention to me. "So, what I hear about you is true?" He quirks a brow.

"What on earth are people saying about me? All I do is ask obvious questions and don't take any shit from you guys. Am I really the only one doing that? It seems hard to believe," I scoff incredulously, arms folding under my breasts.

This time he laughs out loud, leaning back in his chair, while Alice continues to sit quietly, trying to appear unassuming.

"It's the way you do it, this no BS approach to how you talk. We find it very surprising on a woman and on someone who perceives themselves as a pris-oner. I've heard a few stories about the way you've talked to and treated a certain guard, but I didn't believe it until now. What a pickle his brain must be in with the likes of you."

He's definitely talking about Mr Big, I haven't seen him since our last strange altercation. "Where is

Mr Big anyway? Hiding from me?" I ask, amusement lacing my words, and a knowing smile spreading across my lips.

"Probably," he chuckles, "And I can see why, I think you've done a number on poor Baine too, the man can't even look at you. He's going to be feeling guilty over what happened for quite some time. He's a quality male and this whole incident that injured you both is laying heavily on him. If you're hurt in any way, either of you, in his mind it'll be his fault for upsetting you in the first place."

That makes no sense at all and I explain to Salem that it was a small incident and that we're both fine, for Baine to feel responsible is ludicrous. Alice agrees wholly, saying that she feels normal too. I demonstrate that my wrist is back to normal, moving it back and forth, it was just jarred from the impact with no real harm done and there's no need for us to be here.

Alice sighs and looks around the office before staring down at her lap and her wringing fingers. I notice again how Salem's gaze travels over Alice when she's not looking, his eyes holding a question that I don't quite understand, his body leaning toward her unconsciously. She turns her face to him and he quickly looks away, relaxing back into his seat with a congenial smile for us both, like what I'd just witnessed didn't happen. It was a bit of an odd moment but also fleeting and I choose not to linger on it.

I move my hands around to make my point clear. "We're fine, I just have a little tummy ache. It'll feel better after I have a rest."

Salem's eyes darken. "We take tummy aches seriously here, Summer. You could have caught a bug that your body isn't prepared for, we're in a very different place than your body is used to and because of that you'll be exposed to different bacteria. That's why the weekly appointments and medications we prescribe are so vital. We need to ensure your health." His voice takes on a serious note, a small frown hardens his face, which instantly makes my stomach do nervous flip flops. Maybe seeing a doctor is a good idea. Where the hell have they taken me—us?

I look at Alice and she looks just as nervous as I feel, her eyes still on her wringing hands.

A man in a lab coat walks into the room from a door behind Salem, obviously a doctor.

"Which one of you lovely ladies is, Alice?" The Doctor isn't as drop-dead gorgeous as the other men so far, but it could be because of the burn scar that goes from underneath his collar to the bottom of his jaw, with a slither over his cheek. It looks like a particularly nasty wound. I wonder how he got it? Alice raises her hand, apprehension tightening her features as she takes in his scarred appearance. Her sad eyes look at Salem for a split second before gazing at the ground and pushing herself into a standing position, adjusting her gown in embarrassment for her appearance, clearly uncomfortable about her fuller sized figure. "Alice, I'm Doctor Chokey and I'll be your physician while you stay with us." He steps aside with a kind, patient smile in an obvious attempt to make her feel more relaxed. Waiting for her happily, he follows the retreating Alice into the room.

Salem excuses himself, going through the other door, the one I assume my Doctor's in. He comes back out shortly after with a curt, "You may go in now, Summer, the Doctor's waiting."

An apprehensive feeling fills me as I go through the door, but I put on the most nonchalant face I can muster. It's important to me that I always look put together around these assholes, I never want them to feel like they have power over me. In truth though, this doesn't feel great, I know people are taught to trust Doctors, but this whole place gives me the creeps. It'd be weird if it didn't.

Passing Salem at the door, he makes the introductions for us, breaking the ice a little with his big beaming smile showing off his perfect white teeth, and I already feel my shoulders relaxing. I hadn't realised how tense I actually was. "You should know Dr. Orion, this is *the* infamous and incorrigible, Miss Summer." Salem winks at me and walks out of the room.

Instantly, I notice Dr. Orion's appearance, he's older than the men I've seen, probably in his early fifties. With russet-brown skin, bald head, and a large smile adorned with deep smile lines and dimples, he holds an aged charisma that settles my nerves further. I can see from the lines on his face that he's lived life with a smile, deep kindness radiates from him. He must have had a good life, looking comfortable and satisfied, unlike the other men here, they somehow always look on edge.

Dr. Orion stands up from his desk with his friendly smile, coming around it with an extended hand for me to shake in greeting. "It's a pleasure to meet you, Summer. I've been told that you had a bit of a mishap in the dining hall today. How are you feeling? Do you have any aches or pains anywhere?"

I shake his hand and take the seat he's offering me. "It really *is* nothing, Dr. Orion. My wrist was hurting a bit initially, but it feels fine now and my stomach aches a bit but I'm probably just due for my period soon." I give him an honest answer. "To be fair I don't know how long I've been here. If you'd tell me what the date is, I can tell you when I'm due." I hope for any piece of information.

Amusement dances in his eyes, squinting slightly as he tries to keep in another smile. "Nice try, Summer. I applaud your never-ceasing effort to discover the truth, any truth, it seems. I do understand your frustration with the whole situation, but you must understand that it'll all be revealed in due course, but for now, let's just do one day at a time. Where in your stomach does it hurt?" Dr. Orion successfully steers the conversation elsewhere.

I audibly sigh before answering. "Just my lower abdomen. I really do think I'm just getting my period soon, it's not a big deal. I've had ovarian cysts removed in the past though so maybe it's just another one of those trying to cause me some strife. It sucks hard but it'll pass, I'm quite used to it, unfortunately." I shift uncomfortably in my chair. I hate any reminder of the crap that some women have to go through.

Dr. Orion leans over his desk and scribbles something in his notepad before asking, "Is it okay if I do an examination of your lower abdomen to rule out cysts? It's important to Boss that we keep you all in optimal health."

Agreeing, I roll my eyes when he's not looking, it's not going to help me but I'll go along with it.

He then gestures towards the bed which I lay on, gives me a white sheet to cover myself and I lift my hospital gown so that my abdomen is exposed, covering the rest of my lower half. Coming over to me Dr. Orion presses gently around my midsection, putting pressure on different areas and asks every now and then if something hurts.

"If it's alright with you, Summer, I'd like to go ahead with an internal ultrasound to make sure there are no cysts or anything of worry. That way if I do find any cysts I could easily remove them for you to prevent further pain," Dr. Orion says matter of factly.

At this point, I sit up quickly. "I don't think so. Even if I do have cysts, they usually rupture on their own, but if I notice a pain increase I'll come back and we'll go from there. That's as far as I am willing to go at this point, I don't know or trust you. An internal ultrasound is unnecessary, I just fell over in the lunch-room. Are all the women you know so feeble that they jump to the worst conclusions straight away?" I rush out in obvious distaste. Like fuck is he probing anything in me, he might not even be a Doctor for all I know.

Dr. Orion's eyes turn a little cold, his shoulders stiffening. "Our females are not feeble creatures. They're beautiful, mighty women and we're very proud of them. Females are sacred and honoured, besides that, I am just doing my job, Summer. Insults are unbecoming of you," he continues as he pulls my gown back down and stands back for me to sit up, adjusting myself as I do. "We're done here for today but if your pain persists or gets worse in any way please tell the guard assigned to your floor immediately, you may go now." That last remark was a clear dismissal given how sharp he delivered it. He goes back to his desk and starts typing away on his computer like I've already left. *Wow. I'm pissing everyone off today.*

Walking into the reception area I can't help but linger on some of the things he said, *our women, females.* What a strange way to put it. Salem breaks my train of thought as he reminds me of my medical appointment, allocating me a weekly time slot and giving me an unmarked bottle of pills. "Here's your medication to keep you from getting ill while staying with us, take one every night before bed."

"Thanks, Salem, I appreciate your kindness and I'll take the pills, even though it's against my better judgement. What are they exactly?" I look at the tiny red pills inside.

He laughs melodically. "I told you, they're to prevent future sickness from exposure to new environmental factors. You're vaccinated against things where you're from, but this place is different and you need to use preventatives while you're here from our local health variants. It's important that you take it seriously." One eyebrow raised and his smile dropping, his tone of voice deepens, "Do you understand?"

"Yeah, I absolutely understand. Now, where was that again?" I have to keep trying. "Just so that I know what to look out for of course."

Salem laughs out loud again. "Nowhere you've been before, female. Now, off you go, you have many more places to visit and lunch is in an hour."

"Yeah, yeah. You'll tell me sooner or later. Bye Salem," I say with a wave as I leave.

Chapter Eight

Checking out the hallway outside, a locked door greeted me where a descending staircase would have been if the medical centre hadn't been on our lowest available floor.

I go through the opposite double doors to find out the space is identical to my floor except that the voids in the walkways are above and the entire level is just one big floor. I see a couple of girls to my right in room two and I walk over to introduce myself.

A girl around her late thirties, with a grecian nose and olive skin, gets up and shakes my hand. "I'm Vesha, this is my room, and this is my neighbour from four, Arianna."

Vesha seems like a decent lady and she looks like she's adjusting well, too. "It's nice to meet you both." I smile and nod at Arianna in greeting and she smiles back at me sweetly. Arianna has a beautiful dark ochre skin tone with long dark brown hair down to her curvy hips, and eyes almost as dark as mine. Whereas Vesha has short, pixie cut black hair and honey-coloured eyes. They're both quite striking.

Inviting me to sit with them, I stay for a while as we discuss how crazy this whole thing is and talk about where we came from before here. Vesha's from Positano Italy and Arianna came from a little town in El Salvador, that would explain their accents. I find out that our bathrooms are the same, but the only thing they have down here apart from that is the medical centre.

Excusing myself I decide to go and check out the next level and maybe catch a feed before I miss it.

I walk gingerly up the stairs, seeing two guards walking down the same flight, they both stop in front of me, preventing me from passing. I look up at them. One of them is a young guy with blond surfer hair sticking out in all directions and sky blue eyes that bore into me with distaste. He's an angry-looking twat, chewing on a toothpick while glaring at me. The other one is a rounder guy, more middle heavy than I've been used to seeing in the men here at this point, with mousey brown, close-cut hair and hazel eyes. Unfortunately, his unfriendly gaze isn't far off the one his friend's wearing.

"Sorry, excuse me. I'm just going to have a look around the third floor before lunch," I say, feeling like I need to explain my presence in the stairwell because of the heated scowls on the guards' faces.

The young blond one scoffs. "I can't believe you're even allowed out of your cage. You should be made to stay in there like the disgusting little pet that you are." His rough voice sends a shiver of apprehension through me, and my heart pitches a notch. "You're nothing but a dirty little fucking rat, and you smell like one too." He proceeded to wrinkle his nose in disgust, as if to prove his point.

I knew I smelt bad. Inner sigh.

I just stare at him, stunned. Mr Big is a dick, but these guys were the kind of men that got off on hurting innocent people. It's clear as day in their eyes, they're getting a thrill out of taunting a scared young woman in a stairwell. Clearly they're in for an unexpected treat.

I look him straight in the eye. "The only filthy rodent here is you, now get out of my way. If you thought you had found easy prey then you were way off, buddy! Move aside before I move you." I step up nice and close, there's no fucking way these idiots are going to get the better of me.

Blondy actually steps back before catching himself. "What are *you* going to do about it, little girl?" His tone is threatening and his lip turns up into a sneer.

I laugh at him, spreading my legs, centring my body weight, and raising my fists. "Just try me and find out."

A man on the floor above us clears his throat, the deep rumble has us all looking up in unison. There stands Mr Big, towering over the rail of the next stairwell, large hands gripping it tightly and eyebrows raised. I should've known that they were all buddies.

"What the hell do you think you're doing, Simon? You're meant to be guarding them, not threatening to assault them, dickhead," he booms down at blondy.

I stay in my ready position, not quite sure what's going on. The two guards shift around uncomfortably before the chubby one says, "We were just asserting our dominance and showing them their place like you did over that female upstairs. They're beneath us and they should know it."

Mr Big narrows his eyes at them and then glances at me. When he looks from the two idiots to me, I notice his eyes soften slightly. I find that interesting, if I didn't know any better I would think he was concerned for my well being.

"Have they touched you?" His question is short and pointed.

I hesitate for a moment. "No, not yet. But they're

about to touch my fist multiple times if they don't move out of my way." Was it just me or did his lips twitch in the corners?

"Are we supposed to let her talk about us like that? What would you be doing if it was that maniacal woman from level five?" Surfer boy—Simon—whinges. "How did you deal with her?"

Mr Big looks between me and them again before stating, "That *is* the maniacal woman you're talking about. Of all the people you had to piss off, you picked that one. Great job boys, you're officially stupider than you look." He slowly walks down the stairs to us, steps heavy and deliberate, never taking his eyes off the guys in front of me. "The answer to your question is that I didn't 'deal with her', she dealt with me. This delicate female managed to better me in seconds, so I suggest you leave this one alone in the future." His insanely deep, velvety voice sends a new shiver over my skin, standing tall right in front of us, he looks formidable and undeniably delicious. "Understood?" he booms at the boys, his commanding stance making them cower back from him.

"Yes, Sir." They reply in unison, looking like they want to be anywhere but here. They quickly scamper away with Simon giving one last wary look back at me like I've grown extra limbs.

I straighten up and turn to Mr Big, aware that he's already staring at me. "Thank you for your attempt at helping me, but I had that under full control. I could've taken them, no problem." My head held high and shoulders back, fully believing that I could've.

He laughs at me and replies, "I don't know what you're talking about, I was saving *them* from *you*. The last thing my men need to deal with is you going around and molesting them when they least expect it. I need to keep them safe too, you know. You could have ruined their innocence with your unruly behaviour, I needed to get them out of here as fast and safely as possible." With that statement he turns and leaves without a backward glance, while I'm here with my mouth hanging open, shocked and confused. What on earth just happened?

By the time I've composed myself and tried recovering some of my dignity, he's gone. I hate that he had the last word. *Yep, I definitely still want to punch him.*

I enter the third level just as the lunch alarm goes off on my watch and stubbornness be damned, I'm a woman who has got to eat. I stroll into the nearly empty dining hall with no queue. I go straight up, grab a plate and wait for the servers while licking my lips in anticipation. The smell of cooked meat fills the air and makes my mouth water.

Hermes looks up and sees me from the kitchen as I come up to the buffet. Smiling, he walks over to greet me and asks how I'm faring, looking me over carefully with concern on his face. It's so sweet and odd coming from such a large and brutal-looking man. I let him know that I'm doing well and there was nothing to worry about, his face and shoulders relax considerably and the look of relief on his face is almost comical.

"Well, I'm glad to hear it," Hermes booms happily. "What will you have, missy? I might as well get it for you since I'm here."

It hadn't escaped my notice that Baine had gone out the back when he saw me talking to Hermes, he really is avoiding me. For a bunch of big men, they really do act like a bunch of pussies.

Telling Hermes that I'll take whatever he suggests, he happily fills my plate with rice and a beef stew. "You'll like this one, it's hearty and delicious and it will make up for you missing out on breakfast," Hermes states while handing me the plate.

"Thank you, Hermes, I appreciate it," I say, leaving to enjoy what turns out to be a delicious meal.

Chapter Nine

After lunch, I decide to go and check out the sleeping quarters, otherwise known as our glass cells, on level three.

As I begin to walk through the doors I almost knock down another poor unsuspecting victim with my clumsiness. A perky, young blonde that bounces back spryly at the last minute, before we both go tumbling down. "I'm so sorry. Oh my God. That's the second time today I almost mowed someone down. Honestly, I should come with a bell so people can hear me coming," I say horrified with myself.

Her light melodic laughter echoes around us. "It's absolutely fine, I was just as much to blame as you. I'm heading over to lunch and wasn't watching where

I was walking. I'm Janice. Are you from one of these rooms as well?"

"No, sorry, I'm from level five of hell," I joke.

Janice and I chat about what our levels are like and compare amenities. She's a big gym buff so we agree to catch up to spot for each other in the future, but hopefully we won't be here long enough to live that out. We walk back towards the dining room and I stop at the stairwell, before ascending I call back, "See you around, Janice. Oh, and try the stew, it's great."

Level four here I come. If I remember correctly, the level below my own has a library and a TV room – maybe we'll get a local station so I can get a clue on our whereabouts.

Strolling along at a leisurely pace, I turn left, expecting a double door, but instead there's a hallway on one side and a single door on the other. Above the door is the sign, '*Library*'.

Pursing my lips in thought, I decide to go into the library first and check out the hallway after. I open the door, feeling a bit excited to find it's wall-to-wall books alongside a couple of desks and chairs, as well as a few comfy looking couches. It looks just like you'd imagine a normal library to look, not stark and cold like the rest of the facility. The familiar smell of paperbacks gives it a more homely feel despite the cold, smooth concrete floor. Relief and intrigue fill me with the possibility that I can spend lots of time here if I can't find a way home soon. I can't wait to go through the books, perhaps I can find something informative.

Turning back, I follow the hallway to the end where I'm met with a door that reads, 'Games/TV'. *So this is the fun room.* Trying to keep a lock on the buzz that thrums through me, I open the door and peer inside. The room is lengthy and has more colour than any other room; from pops of red cushions, bright, fluffy abstract rugs around the floor, and the colours from the equipment littering the room. There's a pool table, air hockey table, dartboard, chess table, and a card table on the farside. There's also a large, smooth rock wall at the end like the one in the gym. To the right of me, against the shiny glass wall, is a huge television with a big selection of DVD's next to it. How old school is this place? Who has that many DVD's anymore? Facing the TV is a bunch of cinema-style recliner seats and an array of different coloured bean bags to sit on. I have a feeling that this place will always be filled.

Behind me the door suddenly opens and Mischa and Juanita walk in with another girl; tall and gangly, blonde and kind of sickly looking, her skin pale, and eyes gaunt.

"Summer." Mischa sharply nods to me in greeting, gaze hard and shoulders stiff, "If you're looking for Bell and the others they're upstairs in the garden." Her tone is clearly dismissive, I get the feeling she'd like me to leave.

I smile half-heartedly. "Thanks, I'll check it out. Hey, Juanita, who's your friend?" I ask, directing my query to Juanita instead because I'm not in the mood for Mischa.

"I'm standing right here, and I'm Munjulia, a famous designer. I'm surprised you don't know me. Though, mind you, only the best kind of person does," Munjulia replies haughtily, nose in the air, hand lightly resting on her chest, looking me up and down. I call bullshit on this one. Her hair is too stringy and her regrowth is ridiculous, but whatever floats your boat, crazy lady.

"Cool story, bro, I'm gonna head out. See ya," I chirp while walking out of that 'not my problem' scenario.

Remembering that there's more to this level, I check out the other end. As I walk through the hall of cells, Reid stalks down the walkway towards where I am and smiles warmly when he sees me approaching. My stomach flutters unexpectedly.

"Good afternoon, Summer, I take it you're using this time to explore and try to find exits and secret walls for a great escape?" He mocks me with friendly banter.

I snicker a little, tucking some loose hair behind my ear. "You know me so well already, Reid. I was hoping to keep you on your toes for longer but alas, you have found me out. I haven't found any obvious exit as of yet, but it's early days and I'm a stubborn woman. Why are there no windows? Is it perhaps because we're underground?" One eyebrow raised and biting my lip, hoping for some kind of confirmation in reward for my attempts at flirting.

"You really don't give up. I was joking, but clearly my statement was correct. What makes you think we're underground? We could be in space, ever thought of that?" Reid tries to plant doubts in my conviction, but I won't budge on this one.

With my hands on my hips I step closer, my eyes narrowed. "That's all well and good, Reid, except for the simple fact that this place seems to be squished in by rocks. Where else would there be rocks squishing the sides of buildings than underground? Certainly not space! Explain that, smarty pants." Reasoning out my theory. It's logical, he can't deny that fact, space... honestly! That's just insulting my intelligence.

Reid laughs out loud with his head back. Leaning forward he pulls the hair back out that I put behind my ear. "You don't miss much, do you? At least I get a good laugh when I'm talking to you. So where are you off to now, Summer? Should I point you to the secret exit hatch?"

"Yes, that would be lovely, thank you," I sing, a sweet smile dancing on my lips as I bat my eyelashes innocently, aware–and slightly annoyed, that he's dodging my question.

Reid clicks his fingers. "Darn it, seems I've briefly forgotten where it is, maybe next time," he teases with a quick cheeky wink.

I roll my eyes at him shaking my head. "What a shocker. In the meantime, I'm going to see what's at the end of this floor, another rock wall I presume," I say in retort.

"Guess you'll just have to go and find out," Reid whispers, leaning towards me as he passes, continuing on his patrol. Feeling his hot breath so close to my ear and his woodsy scent filling my nose, shivers lick down my spine.

He's an odd guy, something about him seems very old school and otherworldly. Maybe it's the way he walks confidently but with silent grace, and how he speaks eloquently and respectfully, a seemingly true gentleman. Yet, I sense a lot of danger from him, too. Darkness and primal energy lingers there in the depths of his eyes. I don't think Reid is what he seems, there's something more wild in him than he lets on.

Finishing my tour, the only thing I find is a meditation room, so I head back. Reaching level five, there's a locked door that I presume is for the rest of the stairwell going up. Now that's an area I'd be interested in seeing. For now though, I'll go and check out the garden.

I'm curious and excited about what it's going to be like. Is it going to have a path to the outside? I really hope so. The idea of being confined here is stifling, my body needs to see the sunlight and feel a breeze on my face. With my heart clenching tight at the thought of going outside, I hurry my steps to get there sooner.

~

"Oh my God!"

Opening the doors to the garden, my words come out a hushed whisper, my body tingles from head to toe and my heart rate speeds up as the feeling of euphoria spreads through me. I stand there, shocked for a minute, staring at the wondrous sight before me. *Wow.* This is not what I'd envisioned.

This is a utopia, this is a dream. Giving myself a quick pinch just to make sure I'm actually awake.

Thick, luscious grass stretches along the vast ground, the smell of it fresh and familiar. The room is so tall that it comfortably houses different types of beautiful, exotic trees. Birds flutter happily about the room, all different colours and sizes, their blissful chirping ricocheting throughout the garden joyfully. In the centre of the room is a spacious clearing, perfect for picnics and sports, with plant life and beautiful wildflowers growing all around. The very air smells so wonderfully fresh and fragrant, with just a touch of sea air that I can almost taste, it makes me feel nostalgic and calm. At the very end of the garden is the huge rock wall that I'd expected, except for the vast cave pushing through the mass of stone right at the centre, with a series of clear rock pools swirling at the base. Beyond the cave entrance, I can hear the tinkle and rumble of a waterfall coming from within and see the misty spray dissipating in the air. The side walls and ceiling of the garden are the clean, white walls that I'm used to, which somehow doesn't ruin the luxurious feel of this beautiful oasis. I know there has to be a way out nearby because my skin can feel the outside, twitching with expectancy, and I can smell the fresh air. It's the kind of scent that can't be emulated. This place is incredible and I'm full of awe as I slowly glide along the soft grass feeling it slide between my toes.

Between the breathtaking scene, and the euphoric allure of the garden, this place is shockingly real and completely unbelieve.

Women lounge in the garden area, some alone and others in small groups, enjoying each others' company. That's when I spot Mia, Shylo, and Bell sitting together by the water's edge at the entrance to the cave.

Gliding towards them slowly, a calm takes over my mind as I take in all of my surroundings. The sweet scent of jasmine coming from the vines, the grass so soft and bouncy under my feet, the way the birds chirp so happily as if they don't know that we're all trapped in here. This garden almost feels like freedom, if I could just ignore the walls that encompass it.

As I approach the pool closest to the cave entrance, I pay attention to the spray from the waterfall, a ray of sunlight shining through a hole at the top of the alcove where the water flows from. If I were underneath it would I see the sky? Little butterflies flutter softly down through the stream of light and into the cave without care. Their wings glistening beautiful colours in the rays, filling my heart with a joy that only nature can bring. What a glorious sight.

"Summer!" Shylo shouts, pulling me out of my reverie. "Where've you been? We were so worried about you."

I look down at them and see the concerned faces of my new friends, amazed at what a stressful situation can do. Bringing some people together and pulling other people apart.

"I'm okay guys, it's no big deal." Sitting with them, I explain how my day has been, who I've met and what the rooms are like. Stretching my body, I lean back on my hands and look around. "This garden though, wow!"

Bell puts her arm around me and says. "No shit! This is like some kind of Eden or something. Seriously though, where the fuck are we? They have gone to a lot of trouble to keep us all here, and this shit makes me think it's not for just a week. What do you think? Cuz it's freaking me the fuck out." Right to the point as always, Bell's a one of a kind girl, that's for sure.

"I think you're right, Bell. This is way too elaborate to be a short term deal. They have some serious plans for us and don't want us going anywhere, any time soon." I breathe fresh air in deeply, preparing myself to get back to business. "Did any of you notice any hatches or anything that might be useful to check out? I was looking at the door near our stairwell, that might be something. There have to be stairs behind it that keep leading up, we need to keep an eye on the guards around it and see how they get in and out, and if there's any weakness in their setup. Also, I'm wondering if the top of the waterfall goes outside? I think if we can get underneath it, we can have a look and see if it's an option for escape. I'm starting to wonder if we're underground. What are your thoughts?" I stop my tangent and look at the girls gaping at me, eyes wide. "What?" I ask, feeling suddenly self-conscious, brushing non-existent lint off my gown.

Mia chimes in, "What exactly did you say you did as a job before here?"

I chuckle and relax again. "I didn't say. Why, what did you ladies do? It might be handy to know actually, maybe we all have some useful traits we can bring to the table."

Mia scratches her head as her eyes glaze while thinking about her life. "I'm a full-time mum, but before that I was always helping in my dad's retail business. It's kind of a family thing, I never really had to work on my own before. For me, it's always just been family first. Sorry, I'm not very helpful." She bows her head letting out a sigh.

"There's nothing wrong with that, it's very noble and commendable. Never apologise for putting family before anything else. I would have loved to have had the opportunity to do that. What about you, Shylo?" I look at her, waiting patiently for her answer.

"I work full-time again now that my son's in school, I'm a veterinarian. So unless you need help with animals, my skills are limited, but I can also play the piano." Shylo laughs, a beautiful cheerful sound, one that makes you want to laugh along with her.

"It does mean that you have medical experience though, which is more than most people can say. So, if something goes wrong we have you, that's very helpful, Shylo. Don't undersell yourself," I explain reassuringly. "Also, I love the piano, it's a shame there isn't one here. Dare I ask what you do, Bell?" Looking at her, shaking my head and expecting the very worst.

Bell laughs out loud. "What, do you think because I'm loud and obnoxious that I can't have an awesome reputable career?" She manages to get out around her bouts of laughter. "As a matter of fact, love, I'm an architect, a very good one as well. Though I do admit my designs are somewhat unusual and I like to put in a hidden offensive sign or word in every design, because why not. One guy was a real wanker and super homophobic, so I made sure that from a certain angle his design read 'cunt', now that's funny."

The four of us laugh so hard that my stomach hurts. "I have no doubt that you'd do that, you're something else, woman." Calming down, I wipe the laughter tears from my eyes. "With your job, though, you should be able to pick out something that's out of place in the design here, perhaps hidden rooms or something like that. Is that something that you'd be able to notice?" I question Bell, not at all shocked by her previous revelation.

She shrugs nonchalantly. "Yeah, it should be easy enough for me to spot if I'm looking, I'll keep my eyes open and let you know. Are you going to tell us what you do?"

I give a small, tight smile before answering, "I work covertly in counter-terrorism, my job description is on a need-to-know basis. I can tell you, though, that I've worked in many useful areas. My main area of expertise is finding people and information, but I'm highly skilled in clean up, processing, surveillance, disarming, and containing. I'm also well trained in combat, both weaponised and hand-to-hand. I'll have your back and if you need me just say so."

The girls just stare at me in wonderment, a mixture of expressions on their faces, from open mouths to disbelief and maybe even a tinge of fear.

"Are you serious?" Mia asks me nervously, fidgeting on the grass as her eyes shift around.

"No, of course not," I answer laughing. "I'm a forensic psychologist. You guys are hilarious."

They relax and start laughing together. I chuckle softly to myself, *if only they knew...*

Chapter Ten

We spent the afternoon by the rock pool talking about our lives, our ex-partners, and our kids. It was a good time for us to get to know each other a bit better.

We find out that both Shylo and Mia are widows with kids to raise. While Mia knows her kids will be safe with her family, Shylo's son Jett has no one, and her fear for his well-being is potent. Bell, however is a 'love em and leave em' kind of girl. After her ex-girl-friend broke her heart she's been on her own ever since and happy that way. I tell them about my fears for my own kids being stuck with their douche of a Dad. He's never had time for them before and I hope they're okay. Sharing laughter between us and a few stray tears, a special bond forms between us.

After we finish our chat, we have dinner in the dining room and head to our rooms before curfew. No need to rock the boat on the first night, after all. It's been a pretty productive day; I made my rounds, not only exploring the building but also getting information on the others to see if we have anything in common. So far the only thing I've concluded is that we're all women. I even met a few more of the men working here, but I'll keep paying attention because I know that good information is valuable.

When I enter my cell some things are different than when I left. There's a set of white drawers that weren't here before with a clothes basket next to it, and a door and wall around my toilet. Weird, I have no idea how they did that.

Looking through my drawers, I gasp in relief at the clean underwear, *finally*. Opening all the other drawers, there is a similarity about them, they're all cotton and bright white, of course. I find two of each object; bras that attach at the front, triangle bikinis, towels, v neck t-shirts, tracksuit pants, singlets, thin strap maxi dresses, shirt nighties, a dressing gown, and a bath sponge. All things I need and am grateful for, but my fears about us being here for an extended period are growing.

I have forty-two minutes before lights out, I'm

totally squeezing a shower in. I grab a towel, underwear, my sponge, and a nighty, and head for the bathroom, hoping they have soap in there.

Getting into the closest shower stall I close the door, put my stuff on the seat provided and turn on the water. As I strip off my disgusting clothes, I'm overjoyed to see the pump bottles connected to the wall in the shower. They each have a label; soap, shampoo, conditioner, and hair removal cream.

As I hop under the steaming hot water, I moan softly. I can't help but feel a hundred times better as the water runs down my body, trickling away the remnants of the day and making me finally feel cleansed of dirt. I so needed this shower. For a moment, I close my eyes and imagine that I'm anywhere else but here. Totally relaxed, I wash my hair twice, rinse off the day and emerge a new woman. My skin and hair smelling of soft lavender, the towel sensitive against my scalded skin.

After getting changed into my fresh new clothes I go over to the mirrors and see a hairdryer, straightener, and brushes. Quickly, I dry my hair just enough to sleep with it, while I'm brushing it out smooth, I remember that I'm on the clock. Shit, I look at the time. Thank God, I have nine minutes left, I grab my stuff and race down to my room.

As I get to my room, a guard is standing at my door, "Your time is almost up, girl," he sneers at me. "Where have you been? This isn't your castle, you don't get to come and go as you please, princess!" His body leans on my doorway, tense and surly. It's obvious that he's trying to prevent me from getting into my cell.

"Can I please get by? I don't want to miss my curfew, Sir. I didn't mean to run so late." I try talking as sweetly as I can while attempting to squeeze past him. This guy, however, is immovable. He blocks my door even further with his body and smirks down at me.

"What's wrong? Don't you want a reward, little pet?" The way *reward* leaves his mouth makes my skin crawl, like he's excited by it.

I hold my tongue, my heartbeat picks up slightly. I don't like this dumb thug thinking he can refer to me as his pet. "No, I don't. Will you please let me into my room? Why are you doing this to me?" I blurt out, running out of patience.

His cruel laugh eats at my skin. "Doing what, pet? I'm just standing here minding my own business, waiting for you to get your insubordinate, insignificant ass in your room. I'd hurry if I were you, you're running out of time. Tick-tock," he says mocking my inability to pass him and tapping his watch face, his amusement evident.

A warning sound goes off, the alarm calls out loud and clear, "One minute until lights out. One woman is not identified as being in her room. Please make your way within your walls immediately or face group rewards."

"Please, Sir, will you let me in my room?" He stands here laughing at me. All the girls around that can see what's happening to me start shouting over each other; "Let her in!", "Please!", "Don't do this to us!", "Oh god no!".

The alarm starts to count down from twenty and some girls begin to cry. "Please!" I say to him, sweat climbing my palms, fear shivering up my spine as my mouth starts to go dry. "Let me in, they don't deserve this!"

"12, 11, 10..."

Mocking me, he yawns. "You should've thought of that before you had a shower so late, pet. Now you'll all learn."

"6, 5, 4..."

Bam! He gets shoved out of the way by a brutal force, and I get pushed hard inside my cell from behind. I land on my hands and knees with a terrible thud and feel my right knee scream in pain.

The glass door closes with a resounding *Slam!* The

alarm stops and over the speaker, I hear, "Good night, ladies, lights out." Pitch black envelops the cell before I even have time to move or process the pain I'm in.

On my hands and knees in the dark, that bloody landing hurt, *so* bad. I was lucky not to land on my face but I'm very grateful that I was in the room on time at least. That was cutting it pretty close though. I would've felt awful if everyone was 'rewarded' because I wanted a shower.

I slowly turn my body and sit on the cold, hard floor silently in the dark. I hear the dickhead mumbling some profanities to himself before he stomps out of the hallway, somehow seeing where he's going in the dark. Obviously, he's in a bad mood now. I don't hear or see the person who shoved him and me, but I know he's still there.

I feel his eyes burning into me in the dark, it's an impossibility and I know it, this darkness seems to want to swallow me whole. There's no way anyone can see me, but somehow I can sense his gaze upon my skin, it gives me goosebumps all over. I'm probably just overreacting, I'll feel better once I'm safely in bed with my eyes closed. The problem is, from experience, I know when I'm being spied on and I'm never wrong.

I subconsciously fix my nighty and start to stand

but I falter immediately, stifle a scream, and sit back down. My right knee is worse than I thought. I reach down and feel my leg for any obvious injury and it's pretty clear straight away that I've dislocated my kneecap. Shit.

I close my eyes, take a deep breath and pop that sucker back in, I can't help the pained moan that slips out of my mouth because damn, it hurts.

All of a sudden, I hear a deep, and frankly terrifying, growl that sounds like it's just outside the glass right where I'm sitting. The sound travels right through to my spine and stops my heart before making it work overtime, trying to jump out of my chest. What the fuck was that? That sound scared the shit out of me, I'm pretty sure I visibly jumped. Slowly I use my bum and arms together to gently drag myself away to where I think the bed might be, leaving all of my stuff on the floor where I fell. That's tomorrow's problem.

Finally, feeling the bed behind me after what felt like forever, I slowly hoist myself onto it, without putting pressure on my still very sore knee. I get under the blankets and cover myself right up to my chin, like a child would because what the hell *was* that?

Unfortunately, I still have the very distinct feeling that I'm being stalked like prey, but I'm not sure by whom or more correctly—what... My heart runs a million miles an hour, mouth dry as the Sahara desert, palms sweaty, and my breathing, loud and raspy.

This is going to be a long night.

Chapter Eleven

It *was* a long night; between feeling watched, the odd scary growling, and the pain in my leg, it was definitely not the best night of my life. Mind you, I've had worse.

Waking up in the morning, everything is the same as the night before, but the things I'd left on the floor are now in my hamper. Someone had come into my room when I'd finally fallen asleep, which is surprising because I'm an incredibly light sleeper and can't imagine anyone getting by me.

As soon as the doors are opened Bell, Shylo, and Mia are by my side with a million questions fuelled by concern for me. Subduing their worries and assuring them that I'm fine, I ask Bell, "Did you see who got me inside on time?"

"Nah, man, it was so fast. I was too busy worrying about you. The overgrown baby went flying, then so did you, and then the lights went out, it was nuts. I thought that there was another guard on duty though but can't think of who. Maybe one of the other girls noticed? They're more likely to notice men than me. I *can* tell you about the chicks here in great detail though." Bell adds a wink and her own little humour to a humourless situation, and I so appreciate her for it.

I nod in understanding and then try to get up, flinching as I put my legs over the side of the bed.

Bell jumps to help me up. "Shit, you hurt yourself, didn't you?" She looks horrified.

"Nope, someone else did it for once." I laugh a little. "I'll be fine, it's just my knee."

"Fucking smart-ass." She smiles in return though. "You want me to take you to the medical centre? Get the Doc to have a look at it."

I know she's being nice but the last place I want to go is back there. "Honestly, I'll be fine. You go down to breakfast with the ladies and I'll just take it easy for a bit, it's not like I have any pressing plans. I'll catch up with you afterwards. How about we meet at the pool for a swim around 10am? I don't know about you but I'm dying to get in there." I smile at her to get her off my back. I hope it doesn't look as fake as it feels, my knee is throbbing something fierce.

Agreeing, she pats me on the back and she goes to join the others, who are already walking out the door.

Listening carefully, I hear everyone slowly disappear from the walkway and go down to the dining room, finally. I take a peek at my knee, it looks swollen but it'll be alright. I'll just elevate it for now and go from there. Getting the pillow from behind me, I place it carefully under my knee with a wince.

It's so weird being in this situation and having to act like this is totally normal, what a shit show. I miss my kids and I just want to go home, not to mention that I still don't know where I actually am or why I'm here.

"Daydreaming, are you, Miss Summer?" I hear Reid say from the doorway. It makes me jump and I flinch in pain at the sudden movement. He scowls slightly at my response.

I sit up. "Shit. Sorry, I didn't hear you coming. I'm not normally jumpy." I straighten my nighty top to make sure I'm not accidentally revealing myself. "What can I do for you, Reid? I'm not really in the mood to entertain you right now."

"May I enter?" Reid asks, surprising me, standing straight with his hands resting behind his back.

Taken aback, my voice pitches a bit. "Sure, it's never stopped you guys before. Why ask now?"

He steps in hesitantly before saying, "We're not meant to enter your rooms without your permission, unless under urgent circumstances. What happened with Salvatore in the past was an unfortunate anomaly that should not have occurred and he was given a severe speaking to for disregarding Threshold rules. I assure you, that incident will not transpire again."

"What about last night?" Looking at the stoic expression he's giving me, I would bet that he had no idea someone was in my room last night. So, I elaborate for him. "When I involuntarily tumbled into my room last night as the lights went off, I'd left all of my belongings that I was holding strewn all over the floor and just got into bed. This morning when I woke, everything was put away. That would entail someone other than myself being in my room while I slept, and let me tell you that it didn't make me feel great when I figured that out."

He stares at me in silence for a moment. "Are you quite sure, Summer?"

Pursing my lips I give him a cold 'are you serious?' look before answering, "Yes, Reid, I am *quite* sure."

Reid then looks down and around the room as if studying it and searching for something. He then proceeds to walk over to my washing basket, pick up my discarded clothes and then shocking the shit out of me, he smells them. Actually put my stinky garments to his nose and sniffed like a dog. What on earth?!

"What the fuck are you doing?" I spit at Reid, furious that he's smelling my bloody clothes, feeling totally violated. What a perv. "My knee may hurt but I will still kick your ass if you're gonna be acting like a freak in my room."

He looks at me as though he just realised what he did, puts my clothes back quickly and steps away. "I'm so sorry, I was just seeing if there was a type of cologne or something lingering on them that might give away who moved your things. I can see now that it was probably not an appropriate action to take. My apologies, Miss Summer." Reid bows his head slightly to emphasize his apology.

I shift uncomfortably in my seat with my face scrunched up in disgust. "Yeah, okay. Please don't do that again." I want to gag at how bad they would've smelt. "What did you want anyway, Reid? Why are you here?" I want to get to the point so he'll go away.

"Yes, well..." Reid looks uncharacteristically uncomfortable now but continues. "We have heard different accounts of what happened with you at curfew last night and as such my superiors would like to have a word with you and the guards involved to get to the bottom of the incident. It's important that we discover who the reprimanding will belong to. This is not negotiable, do you understand?"

I'm going to be responsible for everyone getting 'rewarded' after all, there's no way they're going to listen to a prisoner over a guard. Might as well get this over with and plead my case as best as I can.

"Can I get dressed before we go? Or am I going in my PJs?"

"I am sorry but we must be on our way, your attire will not matter." Reid gives me a quick smile. "Come along." He walks to the door and turns to wait for me to catch up.

I slowly get up from the bed and start towards Reid, trying not to lean on my right leg and failing miserably. *Ouch.*

Next thing I know, Reid is holding me in his arms. "What happened to you?" he says crossly at me, looking at the swelling around my knee. I've never had someone angry at me before for being injured. The men here really know how to piss me off.

"So, you were told what happened, but not about the part when I landed with a hard thump? Well, Mr Mercurial, my knee got most of the impact of my fall apparently. I don't see why you're so pissed off with me for hurting, it's not like I did it on purpose!" I sulk. "Also, put me down, I'm quite capable of walking."

Reid just walks out of my room, holding me in his arms like a bride, ignoring my request to be put down. He walks over to the locked stairwell, where he presses his finger to a scanner under the door handle which then switches it open. That ends my resistance. I was about to see behind the proverbial closed curtain.

Up the flight of stairs is another door with the same lock mechanism, when the door opens I see to my left a giant window that's the entire expanse of the wall, looking over the entire garden below. I never even noticed that there was a window there. That's so strange, I'm usually more astute. In the room there's only a long boardroom desk with a locked door beyond it.

I'm taking in my surroundings as Reid places me on a chair at the head of the table closest to the giant window. He turns my seat slightly and brings another one closer to gently place my injured leg up onto it. Turning around he proceeds to say something into his earpiece, too quiet for me to hear.

It's not lost on me that not only did this delicious but strange man just carry me quite a fair way up many stairs, but he carried me like I weighed nothing and he isn't even a little out of breath. What do they feed them here? These guys must be ripped under their clothes, the thought of what he looks like under that uniform brings a nice warmth to my under-utilised core. *That's definitely not a healthy train of thought, Summer.* I realise pretty soon that I've been staring at him when Reid looks at me, literally catching me in the act of checking him out. Shame. With one side of his lips quirked up, he steps closer to me.

"You'll be meeting with the two guards that were on duty on your floor, the second in charge, and the head manager of Threshold, he's the overseer and is the only person with high enough clearance to speak on behalf of Boss." His voice takes a more serious tone. "You must respect both of their authority here, they have the power to make your stay here quite uncomfortable if they see fit to. Am I making myself clear, Summer? This is *not* a joke and you should take this meeting very seriously." I have a feeling that Reid is trying to stress the point as a kindness and not as an intimidation attempt, for that reason alone I'll heed his advice.

"Understood," I reply, just as the security doors directly ahead of me open.

Chapter Twelve

The first person through is the douchebag guard that caused this bloody issue in the first place. I stifle back the urge to give him the finger when he smirks at me and then sits down across from me.

Next, Mr Big enters the room, which is a surprise. He doesn't give me any notice and sits opposite the douchebag on the right side of the table. I look at him but he doesn't acknowledge me at all. Of course he was working with this wanker.

Then a fair-skinned guy enters, his black hair tied in a ponytail. He looks to be in his mid-twenties at the latest, with his boyish features, but carries himself with an arrogance which denotes either money or authority. His face takes on a pompous air and he strides in like he owns the place. I hope my life isn't in the hands of this man-child. Mr arrogant looks at me with disdain, like someone would a dirty dog on a clean carpet and I feel distinctly uncomfortable. My skin prickles at his clear distaste of me being here. He takes a seat on the right side of the other head seat at the table.

I look through the door as it's closing and see a small white room with another security door within, these guys are serious about their precautions.

I thought there was supposed to be another man joining us. In answer to my thoughts Reid says from behind me, "Where is, Blayze? He is to be a part of this meeting."

"Sit down, Reid, and know your place. We'll carry on without him," the young man of authority snaps, Reid reluctantly sits next to me. I get the impression that he's trying to get in between us.

Turning to me, the pompous prick begins, "Female, I am Leon. I'm the second in charge of Threshold operations. You won't speak to me unless I've asked you a direct question, is that understood?" I simply nod. "Good, now let us begin," Leon says without further discussion.

The door suddenly opens and a very tall, muscular, and frankly sexy as fuck guy walks in with gorgeous dark russet skin and my mouth drops open.

Hello, baby! I know it's wrong but I'd have to be blind not to rub my thighs together over this man.

Everyone turns to see who it is and all the men rise from the table immediately as he enters. I just stare in wonder at this magnificent creature.

"Rise, you despicable cretin," Leon spits at me venomously, slamming his hands on the table making me jolt in surprise.

I hold myself up in my seat and try to stand, Reid is by my side in a heartbeat gently helping me to my feet.

Leon shouts furiously going red in the face, "What are you doing, Reid? Leave the pet to stand by herself, she's not an invalid!"

"Enough, Leon!" The gorgeous man barks in our defence, his presence commanding complete compliance. "Why are you helping her?" He asks, directing his question to Reid.

Reid bows his head but doesn't let go of my arm. He explains what happened to me from what he understands. "Am I correct in assuming that I'm given permission to help her with her physical requirements until she's been seen by the physician?"

The good looking man who's obviously the guy in charge looks thoughtfully at me for a moment before saying, "Yes Reid, you've made an agreeable assumption. Please continue to assist her in her needs until otherwise informed by myself or the Doctor." He then looks around the table. "Well this certainly adds to the initial issue doesn't it? Sit down," he commands.

Reid helps me back into my seat with my leg raised while everyone patiently waits. It's a bit embarrassing actually, I'm not generally someone who likes help from others.

"Your name is Summer, correct?" Sexy Sir asks and I nod in response. "My name's Blayze. I'm the Threshold overseer and it's my duty to make sure that this facility is running smoothly at all times in accordance with Boss's house rules. Are you familiar with all of the rules at this point?"

I look into his chestnut eyes directly with confidence. "Yes, Blayze. I'm well aware of the rules here. I've also kept them to the best of my ability."

"Don't be an insolent pet. You'll call him *Sir* and you'll lower your eyes while speaking to him," Leon snaps at me from across the vast table.

"I believe I can speak for myself, Leon, and in the future, you'll wait until I'm present before you attempt to start meetings that I'm to be presiding over." Blayze tone flat while facing Leon before turning back to look at me. "You may call me Blayze, if you wish. You don't work for me so I'll not treat you as a lower rank and frankly it's refreshing to have eye contact for a change." He chuckles a little to himself and I can't help but smile at him. "Last night there was a curfew incident involving yourself, correct?" I nod in agreement. "I've received different accounts from both of the guards on duty to your floor at the time, Budd and Salvatore. Would you care to elaborate on the events of the evening in your own words, please?" Blayze's tone is professional.

Here is my chance to get this right, I go into deep detail about the events of the night, right down to the minute. Leon and the other guard, who's name is apparently Budd, look completely unaffected and in truth kind of bored. Salvatore doesn't move an inch and just stares at the table, but Blayze and Reid listen to every word with rapt expressions and the odd jaw twitch. "I'm truly sorry for having a shower so close to time, I won't be doing that again. I would have made it on my own if it wasn't for him." I curse, pointing at the dickhead in question.

Blayze sighs deeply. "Summer, how exactly was your knee injured?"

I wave my hand dismissively. "Oh, that just happened when I fell on my hands and knees, he didn't do that. I'm not really sure how that happened actually but I'll be fine, I just landed really hard that's all." Trying to make it sound like it's not a big deal,

I'm used to getting injuries so it's not a big deal to me.

I hear a loud cracking noise and notice that a very tense Mr Big has a crack on the table near his very tight fist. "Are you okay?" He just sits there completely still, ignoring me. I roll my eyes at him. What's wrong now? He's such a baby. "Whatever, Mr Big. Ignore me, I was just being nice," I snort gruffly at him.

Blayze raises an eyebrow. "Mr Big?"

I laugh out loud, accidentally covering my mouth with my hand, getting looks from all over the table, including Mr Big. "Sorry, we go way back, don't we, Mr Big?" I turn to Blayze. "I've been giving him a pretty hard time since I got here and he wasn't exactly hospitable either. It's all good though, we worked through it. Now we just have nicknames like old friends, I call him Mr Big and I'm pretty sure he calls me bitch when I'm not around."

Then Blayze starts to laugh. That's unexpected. Mr Big and Reid look uncomfortable, fidgeting in their chairs and frowning. *Whoops.* I hope I didn't just say something to embarrass him, it looks like I accidentally fell into a private joke.

After Blayze calms down his manner turns more serious. "I will not be rewarding you or your friends for this incident, Summer, rest assured. Though, perhaps in the future you should manage your time better. I will, however, have to take further action against any guards that came between the peace and harmony of Threshold and your injury will be taken as a serious offence."

"Oh no, that's not necessary. It wasn't his fault," I say, defending the thug because I don't like any injustice.

"I think you misunderstand me, Summer." Blayze looks at Mr Big and then back to me. "Salvatore was responsible for your injury, he's the person who pushed Budd out of the way, and you inside the cell, closing the door." There's a pregnant pause before he continues. "I would like to believe that he thought he was helping you and not acting maliciously, however in Salvatore's case it's quite hard to know his intentions, regardless of what they were. Reid will be taking you down to the medical centre for treatment and I'll have to reprimand Budd for his disobedience and Salvatore for placing you in harm's way."

I turn to look at Mr Big. "Were you trying to hurt me?" Feeling unsure of his intention, I know he doesn't like me but I don't actually feel threatened by him. He slowly raises his head so that his eyes meet mine, while mine searches for an answer, pushing his chair back he gets up and swiftly leaves the room without answering me, that's reassuring.

Blayze then stands. "This meeting's now over, all leave except for Summer and Reid."

Leon looks very put out by not being involved but does as instructed.

Once they leave the room, Blayze comes over to my side kneeling, next to me to take a look at my knee. He carefully moves his calloused hands over the area studying it, sending shivers up my legs and spine. "Does it hurt a lot?"

I nod despite myself, distracted from the sensual touching going on. "Sometimes," I whisper, my voice a mere murmur.

"I heard that you fell yesterday in the dining room as well and were experiencing stomach discomfort. How is that feeling now?" Blayze's voice husky, his tone sending tingles all over me, making me squirm and heat floods my core.

I chuckle, ignoring his effect on me. "Yeah I'm generally not this clumsy in life, I swear. My tummy feels fine now."

"You should take better care of yourself, Summer," Blayze rumbles deeply while taking my hand and leaning toward me. Reid remains still and silent through the whole exchange. "We can only do so much to keep you safe if you keep getting yourself into trouble." Then he stands abruptly and walks over to the door, before walking through he turns and states with a kind smile, "It was nice to meet you, Summer, next time I hope it's under better circumstances."

Smiling in return and apparently with no filter I reply, "Yeah, like maybe when I'm not a prisoner living in a glass hell." *Whoops.* That just slipped out.

Blayze scowls a little to himself, smile dropping off his face before closing the door.

Chapter Thirteen

I look over to Reid and find that he seems to be assessing my reaction to the whole situation before coming to some kind of conclusion.

"What?" I say, a hint of frustration lacing my tone. "Why are you looking at me like that?" Reid then stands and comes around to help me up, not saying a word but with inquisition in his eyes.

I get to my feet, Reid swings me up into his warm embrace and my arms slip around his neck. I smell the woods on his skin, an earthy smell of freedom, and I find myself subconsciously inhaling at the crook of his neck. Luckily he doesn't realise and he carries me effortlessly down to the medical centre with ease and care, holding me with an unimagined tenderness that I can't quite explain and don't really want to think about too hard. This whole situation is messed up and the last thing I need to notice are things like how strong his body feels against mine or how rich and woody his scent is, reminding me of his masculinity, which is alluring as hell.

We reach the medical centre and the doors swing open. Salem is holding them open so that we can go directly through, so I suppose he knew we were coming. He walks ahead of us and ushers us through the next set of doors to the Dr's rooms, nodding to me in quick acknowledgement before swiftly leaving the room.

Dr. Orion comes around his desk while motioning toward the bed. "Please place Summer on here, I'll take a look at that leg straight away," he directs Reid before turning to me. "My dear, I didn't expect to see you again so soon, at least not with a whole new injury. What have you done now? Another collision?" Smiling his bright grin and using a slightly jovial tone meant to lift the mood.

"Ha-ha-ha! Very funny, Doc. I'm not a bumper car." He raises his eyebrows. "In this case, it was just the floor and me. I toppled down, no other unsuspecting victims. The floor's fine by the way."

Dr. Orion laughs lightly at my sad attempt at humour, so I'll cut him some slack today and be a good patient. Meanwhile, Reid stands quietly at the back of the room observing our interaction. It's clear that he isn't going anywhere.

We discuss my fall and I play off my pain levels, even though I'm actually in a fair amount of it. He frowns and starts to feel on and around my knee, moving it in different directions. I manage to keep quiet but I cringe when it's too much to ignore. Deciding on further tests, he does an ultrasound to check for damage. I tried to insist on aspirin and rest, but he was having none of it.

Dr. Orion finishes up the ultrasound and looks at me seriously. "I suspect that you have damaged the tissue around your knee from the dislocation. So, I'm afraid it's a bit more complicated than you think, Summer. This kind of damage could take you up to six weeks of healing before it's back to normal. You really did a number on yourself and I'll be giving you some medication to help with the pain and healing, but you're going to have to use crutches for a while and not put any added weight on that knee," Doc explains.

I close my eyes and sigh deeply but I know that he's probably right, it's his job after all. I feel really frustrated, this puts my plans back. I'm going to need my knee in good working order if I'm to climb out of here. At least it gives me a bit more time to organise and get any plans perfected before I go ahead with them. I still feel bad for letting the girls down, maybe during this time I can come up with a back-up plan in case it's not as simple as climbing out of here.

With my appointment over, along with my new swanky crutches and medication, I head out to lunch because I'm not keen on missing another meal. These guys need to start doing room service since I'm a 'guest' and all. I shake my head at that thought. I go to catch the elevator because the stairs are clearly out right now and realise that Reid is standing there waiting with me.

"What are you doing?" I ask him.

Reid just stands there waiting for the elevator, not saying a thing. Of course that bothers me so I tap his leg with my crutch, he looks down at his leg and then slowly up at me. "Um, sorry! That wasn't an attack, I just wasn't thinking. Whoops," I stammer out, feeling a bit flushed at my own stupidity. I look over and he's still staring at me, all stoic and unreadable. *Ah crap, I'm in trouble.* Why did I hit him with my crutch?

The elevator opens and I hobble inside. Reid joins me, still not speaking. When the elevator door closes Reid leans forward and presses the emergency stop button and turns to me. I hesitantly peek at him and find his head tilted to the side with the same inquisitive look I saw on him earlier. "Who are you?"

I screw up my face and stare at him with a look of indignation. "Are you serious?" Feeling suddenly annoyed. "I have no idea where I am, why I'm here, who any of you guys are, or what on earth is happening to me, and you look at me weirdly and ask who *I* am?" My voice goes from reasonable to an edge of hysteria by the end.

Reid at least has the good grace to step back and look guilty. "My apologies, that was rude. It's just that you seem different from the other females, I was trying to discover why. It was an insensitive question under the circumstance."

I shake my head in bafflement. "Are you following me?"

"I was, yes. Perhaps it would be wise for me to shadow you for the day to ensure that there's no further damage to your knee, just until you become more fluent with your crutches. I'm also wondering if you're going into the dining room in your nighty? Don't you want to dress first?" He asks, scanning his eyes slowly down my body.

I feel belittled by this statement and hastily reply. "I think you've all done enough. I've been kidnapped, taken from my kids, trapped, drugged, probably experimented on, abused, insulted, injured, carried like a baby, and just recently you reminded me that I'm so insignificant that nobody who's stolen me knows who I actually am. So no, I don't think having one of you shadow me all day is going to be helpful to me at all. If anything, you should all just leave me alone or let me go. I don't belong here and I don't deserve to be here. I'll bet that none of these other girls do either. Do you care about that? Letting us go would be a great way to ensure our safety, if you actually give a damn. Also, I like my pyjamas!" My face feels warm from getting so flustered and I'd bet that I'm a nice shade of pink.

I lean forward and turn the emergency stop button off, immediately get off at my floor, and hobble away as quickly as I can without looking back.

I enter the dining hall and hobble straight for the food. Baine doesn't realise I'm there until he turns around and sees me at the buffet, waiting. He stiffens as soon as he spots me, taking me in, crutches and all.

"Holy Christ, lass." He goes white as a sheet and looks at me with guilty eyes.

"Baine, don't overreact, please. This is just temporary, don't fret. I just want a feed." I manage to get some colour back in his face. "Whatever you recommend will be fine."

Baine seems to come back to his senses before he snaps, "What happened? Did someone hurt you, lass?" If I didn't know any better I would've thought he just grew in size. Baine looks suddenly furious.

"Cut it out!" A deep baritone comes from the kitchen, it sounds like Hermes, but angrier. Baine instantly calms down though.

"Honestly, it's not a big deal, I just have some tissue damage from landing on my knee too hard in the dark," I mumble, waving it off flippantly. "Now feed me, please." I give him a winning smile, in the hopes it will speed up my food transaction.

I get a dazzling, full dimpled smile from Baine. "Your wish is my command, bonnie. Go and sit down, I'll bring over a plate. You cannae very well carry it safely now can you?"

I reluctantly agree before heading to one of the tables to sit down. Baine brings me over some lunch and a drink, then sits down across from me.

"Lass, I want to apologise. I dinnae mean to get you all upset yesterday, I felt really bad that you'd gotten yourself into a shite situation because you were so mad at me. You've got to understand that I dinnae ken what to say to make this place better for you." Regret is evident in his voice and I instantly feel bad for him.

"It wasn't your fault that I fell, but I'm not going to pretend that you aren't a part of why I'm locked up here. I'm angry at all of you, I don't deserve this and it's bloody confusing when half of you guys are awful to us and the other half act like you want to be our friends. You do know that it's wrong, right?" I stare directly at him, wanting to see a flicker of understanding.

Baine nods. "Aye, bonnie, I ken what you're saying. I dinnae want to be your enemy though, lass. I ken that it's not right but I'm just doing my job and trying to make this place as homely as I can. It's the least I can do, I dinnae mean any harm. Can we please have a truce? I think you're a fine lass and frankly I'd rather be on your good side, you can be bloody scary. I'm no walloper, I ken a strong lass when I see one. I've no doubt you'd give me an arse whooping if I mucked up." He chuckles deeply.

"We're good, Baine. I have to live here for now so I don't see why I can't be decent to you. I still don't want to be here but it would be nice to have a friend, especially one that feeds me." Taking a bite of my lunch for effect.

"That reminds me," Baine says, "from now until you're healed I want you to just wave at me that you're here and go to sit down straight away. Buck, Hermes, or I will bring your food to you, no need to be standing longer than necessary, then you won't need a bodyguard while you eat. There'd be no need for it, plus it's a wee bit weird don't you think?" Baine looks over my head.

I turn in my seat and low and behold, Reid is standing just inside the door scowling at Baine.

Interesting, why is he looking at him like that? I guess not all is as it seems.

Chapter Fourteen

"**B**itch, where the hell have you been? You were meant to meet us at the pool! Are those your crutches?" Bell all but interrogates me, plopping herself next to me as I finish my lunch, followed closely by Mia and Shylo.

I smile at them and say, "Sorry guys, I was called upstairs to have a meeting with the big honchos to talk about the incident last night. It's all good though, I'm not in any trouble, but it did take a bit of time, and then I had to go to the medical centre again to sort out my leg. Apparently, I'm on crutches for the next six weeks give or take." Sighing, I continue, "I feel like I've let you three down, looks like I won't be all that much help after all. I do still want to check out the cave though because swimming shouldn't be too much of an issue, and I'm going to keep my eyes open for any other possible leads as well."

Shylo reaches over and grabs my hand. "Don't worry about it, we wouldn't leave without you anyway. We've got your back, too. Are you in much pain?"

"You're a very good person, you know that?" I return, squeezing her hand. "It's not too bad, I'll be fine."

Mia clears her throat. "Summer, do you realise that Reid is over at the door staring at you? Should we be worried?"

Shaking my head, I groan. "Don't even get me starting on that shit." I stand myself up. "I'm going to go get my swimmers and try out that rock pool. Did you chickies go this morning?"

"Nah," Bell says, "we weren't sure if we should. I was keen but these two were freaking out. Honestly, it's fucking ridiculous how much I can't get done with these two in tow." She laughs.

"It's not funny, Bell!" Mia snaps. "It could be a trap. I don't want to be the first one in, besides you'd be on your own if it wasn't for us putting up with you."

I put my hand on her shoulder and speak before I head out. "It's no problem, Mia, I've got this. I'm happy to be the guinea pig but you two have got to lay off each other, we're a team now. Maybe when you guys are finished with lunch you can join me, your choice. See ya!"

I hear their confirmations grumble behind me as I walk away heading straight past Reid like he's not even there.

I hobble in my room thinking about how glad I am that I'm so fit because these crutches feel like a workout.

I go to get my bikini and turn to strip off my clothes just before I remember I had a shadow earlier, turning I see Reid standing at my door watching me. "Are you going to watch me get naked too?" I ask, my tone brisk.

Reid flushes slightly and his gaze drops to my body for a second before he catches himself. I smirk in response to that, ensuring that he sees that I noticed.

"Are you just changing there?" He looks around. "There are bathrooms."

"I know there are but isn't this my bedroom?" With that statement I grab the bottom of my nighty, balancing on my good leg.

Reid quickly turns around and I use the opportunity to take it off and my underclothes too, feeling rather frisky at my brazen behaviour.

I manage to put on my bottom half before I hear Reid snap viciously, "Not one more step, Summer isn't decent!" He emanates an almost animal-like growl which makes me tingle all over. What was that?

"Then why the fuck are *you* standing there?" I hear in return, the voice another deep growl.

I see Reid shuffle uncomfortably as I reach for my bikini top, this is just too much fun. I better get dressed though before I start a riot. I chuckle to myself loud enough for them to hear me.

"Don't laugh, it's not funny," Reid says, sounding a tad defensive.

Another growl. "And you better hurry the fuck up!" This time I recognise the voice as Salvatore.

"Why, is that Mr Big I hear? Am I making you uncomfortable?" I use my crutches to go through the door and look at him.

He stops dead and takes me in from head to foot, and so does Reid. You'd think they've never seen a bikini before.

"You can't go out like that!" Reid states simply, with fists bunched up at his side. What happened to the guy who's always in control?

I turn towards him, eyebrows raised and shock on my face. "I really hope you're kidding me. There are bikinis here for a reason and there's a rock pool. Why exactly can't I go out like this?"

Salvatore walks up to me, so close I inhale his woodfire and leather scent, my eyes flutter slightly at the surprise of what that smell does to me. He looks right down into my face, and swallows hard at our close vicinity. "Everyone will see your body, wear a dress or dressing gown over it."

I scowl. "That's not stated in the rules. I happen to be comfortable with my body and I don't care if you don't like it. You guys kidnapped a bunch of women, caged us in glass cells and yet never thought that you'd see our bodies? Is that right?"

Reid sighs and says defeatedly, "You are correct, I suppose, wear what makes you comfortable. Salvatore, take a step back."

Mr Big remains where he is and then he leans down and smells me, actually sniffs at me. "Does my odour offend you too? Why are you smelling me?" I snap.

Reid slowly steps forward before speaking with command in his tone. "You better step back right now Salvatore or we're going to have a problem, think about Summer! She's injured and needs protecting, not barbaric behaviour. You've done enough!" Reid sounds so angry with his last sentence that it makes me flinch.

I haven't heard Reid use any kind of force in his words, until now, but he sounds and looks super aggressive.

"I hurt you!" Salvatore says to me in a low deep voice that sends shivers through me and has me swaying slightly. "I didn't mean to."

Salvatore's eyes bore into mine so intently, leaning into my space more before turning and walking away.

I'm flushed all over my body, I feel the heat licking at my skin in all the best places, somehow he just made my body melt and get super wet all at the same time. *Whoa.* There's something about being in close proximity to Baine, Reid, Salvatore, and Blayze, that's getting to me. I'm not usually a horn bag, but I am now apparently.

"I'll walk you." Reid uses his sexy raspy voice. When I look at him I see that he's affected by my body as well, his eyes hooded and his hands clasped in front of him like I don't know what's behind them.

I decide to rock the boat because I'm me, that's why. "Are you going to carry me again?" I question, my voice heavy with desire as I get closer to him.

Reid steps back immediately. "No!" He snaps fast —too fast. "Uh, I think you should learn how to use your crutches better, I won't be here to catch you tomorrow."

"Don't worry, I was just kidding, you can relax,

tiger. I won't make you touch all of this." Indicating my generously curvy body. "You wouldn't know what to do with it anyway." I hobble off leaving a trail of laughter behind me.

I did manage to hear Reid grumble, "I'm not a tiger."

I finally get to the pool, drop my crutches, and slowly limp towards the water. It hurts a lot moving without my crutches and my body aches from all the extra effort I've had to put in to get here, not to mention I can't hop because my breasts are too big and they'll pop right out of my bikini top.

Just as my foot touches the water I get hoisted up and into Reid's arms again. "What are you doing?" A surprised squeal escapes me and I hold onto his neck tight, looking up into his clear blue eyes.

"You're in pain, I'm going to help you in and out of the water. You need to stay off your leg and you're getting tired," Reid explains as he walks himself down into the water, sploshing it messily as he goes.

I look around and see that we're all alone out here. "You're getting all wet. Your boots! Your uniform!" I shout, shocked.

Reid continues into the water up to his waist,

slowly immersing me in the cool water, it feels so nice on my skin and so does he.

"It's just water," Reid breathes down to me as he gazes deeply at my eyes. "I don't mind getting wet. In fact, I quite like it," he rasps, heat layering his words. I kind of sense a double entendre in that statement. Is he hitting on me?

I wrap my arms around his neck tighter. "Are you planning on swimming, too? It'll be easier if you take some clothes off."

I feel him shudder before he slowly puts me down, I slide my body down as close to his as I can because I just can't help myself. Oh boy, he feels hard, *all* over.

Reid grabs my waist to steady me. "Tell me when you need help getting out and I'll be here." His fingers linger on my skin, a firm hold on my body. His strong hands start to slide down smoothing over my bare hips, grip biting into my skin as he squeezes me.

I need to stop this, I can't think straight when he's touching me this way. "You're going to have to let me go if I'm going swimming," I say, reminding him that he's still standing here.

Reid instantly let's go and walks out of the water taking a seat on one of the boulders with his body angled away. Too late buddy, I saw and felt how hard you got, and oh my God, what a package to feel.

I turn around and dunk my head under the water, washing away all my dirty thoughts of the bad man. Something's seriously wrong with me.

I swim gently, only using my good leg and arms into the back of the cave, it goes way further than I realised. It's so beautiful here, the waterfall lights up from the sky and there are patches of rock floor that you can sit on. A perfect place for private meetings or even just to use as a getaway.

I swim close to the cascading water and look up, the ceiling is about fifteen feet up, but there's a large three by three foot cylindrical shaped hole right up to the surface where the water is pouring from.

I see the sky!

The beautiful, soft blue sky is right above me, with a little fluffy cloud passing over and butterflies fluttering about, and just like that, I'm in awe once more.

Seeing this little slice of the world outside is proof that I can leave, I can see freedom. In six weeks time I *will* get out of here and I *will* touch freedom again!

All I need to do is figure out how to get to the opening, how to climb up without slipping back down. I also have to make sure that I can take at least three others with me.

Together we'll get help and we'll free them *all*.

Chapter Fifteen

*P*erched on the rock edge inside the cave looking at all the beauty I hear Shylo call, "There you are!"

Three girls swim toward me with smiles on their faces, taking in the beautiful cave surrounding us.

"Wow! I've never seen anything so magical in my life, this is like something from a dream." Mia comes to sit on the damp stone edge with me. "This is incredible." She looks up and stares at the vast blue sky beyond the opening and her face slowly crumbles. Her eyes fill with tears as she whispers. "We're really trapped in this place aren't we? This isn't a dream at all." She faces me looking utterly defeated as one tear silently rolls down her cheek.

Putting my arms around her, I hold her as she

starts to sob. Shylo and Bell surround us still in the water at our feet with bottomless sadness in their own eyes, the sounds of Mia's sobs echo through the cave.

Taking this time to concede our fate and feel the grief and terror of being trapped, we find the support that we need with each other. Somehow, knowing that despite all of this we will be okay if we just stay together.

After we collect ourselves again, we sit and talk about all the plans we should make and agree that we'll brainstorm together every day in this cave after lunch. We'll use the time to keep our hopes alive and use the privacy to our benefit. As long as we keep our voices low, we should be able to talk without being overheard by the guards.

"Ladies, I don't mean to break our meeting up but I'm actually in a bit of pain and I think I need to go lay down for a while," I say lightly, knowing that I'm in desperate need of rest and pain meds, the ache in my knee throbbing badly. "You stay here and try to come up with some more solutions and brief me tomorrow when we meet again. Cool?"

"No probs, babe." Bell playfully salutes. "Take care

of yourself and I'll keep these two wenches out of trouble."

I laugh. "Yeah, because it's them I'm worried about." The other girls start laughing too.

Bell folds her arms. "Hey, I'm not that bad, I haven't even said anything about the soaking wet guard standing outside the cave. What did you do, fucking throw him in?" Bell asks smugly.

"I wish." I roll my neck and scoff. "He's been following me around all damn day, he reckons I'm gonna hurt myself."

"He's pretty hot though," Shylo surprises me by saying. "I can think of worse things to look at all day." She giggles, her cheeks reddening.

I nod. "Yes, he is. It's the main reason I don't mind so much," I say, pursing my lips in thought. "He smells good too, yummy!"

"Have you seen the other guard, Tyrese? Now he is gorgeous," Mia pipes up. "He can follow me anytime." She fans herself with her hand.

"Mia! Look at you, you horny girl. I know what you want for dinner." I wiggle my brows at her and we all laugh as I swim back out of the cave.

Coming through the other side Reid stares at me with a small smile on his face, his eyes crinkling humorously. God, I hope he didn't hear us.

I get waist deep and start hobbling out when Reid

comes trodding through the water to me. "I've got you."

"So you have," I sigh. "Were you ordered to do this or are you just being nice?" He lifts me up and I wrap my arms around his strong shoulders.

Wading out, dripping wet, he carefully places my feet on the soft grass before answering. "I'm doing the right thing."

Reid steps back putting space between us, breathes in deep and looks me up and down. "You're wearing white," he rasps out.

"Yes, very astute!" I'm confused by his statement until his gaze lands on my breasts, I look down. My bikini is see-through... of course, he's staring at my very visible large breasts and quickly hardening nipples. *Oh my*.

He takes another step back, his gaze moving lower, my breaths becoming fast and shallow as I feel his heated gaze taking me in. I feel a new wetness pooling in my bikini bottoms.

Reid raises his nose to the air slightly and sniffs, it looks like he's smelling the air and then retreats another step. "You need to pick up your crutches and start heading back." Reid's voice is breathy.

"What? Yes, right." I stammer as I try to shake myself out of my weird horny stupor. "Yeah, let's go."

I bend over, picking them up carefully and start

heading away from him toward the building again. I halt briefly to view the window above, but I'm startled to find that there's no window, just a big, sterile white wall. It has to be a one-sided window, my mouth drops open in shock. How many one-sided windows are there here that we don't know about?

Feeling shocked at what I see and what this means, I whisper horsely, "Reid?"

Close behind me, the feel of his warm breath moving on the back of my neck, Reid whispers softly, "Yes?"

Chills run down my back, goosebumps rising on my exposed skin, and I find myself leaning back into him before I correct myself, standing straighter. "How many one-sided windows are in this place?" Silence. "How many, Reid?"

His silence says all I need to know, I harden myself, my tone becoming cold without turning around. "I'll see myself to my room, I forgot who you were for a minute, but I remember now. You're the enemy. You're the person who steals someone while they're sleeping and locks them in a cage. This is a beautiful cage, but it's still a cage." I storm away, the best I can with crutches, and go back to my room. Reid doesn't follow me.

~

I shower, change into my comfy dress, take my pain medication and hop into bed before sleep takes me, the toll of today too much to fight.

I wake to Baine knocking on the glass.

"What's up?" I rub my eyes, feeling the pain in my leg almost immediately.

Baine shows me the tray of food he's carrying. "I bought you some tea, I cannae have you missing another meal, bonnie." A smile lights up his face.

"Thanks, Baine, come in. Do you have to leave straight away?" A sombre homesick feeling makes me not want to be alone right now. "I wouldn't mind some company."

He comes in and sits down on the side of my bed, giving me the tray to eat from. "Of course, I'm done for the night. Hermes and Buck said they'd take care of the clean-up, they wanted to make sure you were fed, too," Baine replies cheerfully.

I dig in, talking rudely around my food. "Thanks for being so thoughtful." I pause briefly pulling my fork down from my hungry mouth. "Will you tell me about the hidden windows everywhere?"

Baine shifts in his seat before saying, "No, lass, I cannae do that. You know I'm not allowed to tell you some things. I swear I'd tell you if I could." He drops his chin slightly. "I feel like I'm failing you every time you ask me a question that I cannae answer. I'll say though that you are one wiley lass, I dinnae think any of you ladies would notice a thing like that. How did you find out?"

In between chews, I speak. "When I was in the higher level having a meeting with Blayze, I..."

"What?" Baine stands abruptly.

I look at him confused. "What do you mean, what? I wasn't finished."

Baine frowns. "Why did Blayze want to see you? Why were you upstairs?"

"From when I got shoved down and hurt my knee last night at curfew. Reid took me up because Blayze wanted to see me and the guards to sort out who was to blame." I shrug my shoulders, confused but curious about his response. "Why?"

He just stares at me before growling. "Did one of the guards do that to you?"

"Yeah, but it was only to help me because the other guard wouldn't let me in my room and was trying to get me into trouble. They didn't mean for me to get hurt... I don't think." My voice is defensive.

Baine sits back down and leans over to place a piece of my hair behind my ear. "It's unusual for you to be above this level, I'm genuinely surprised you met Blayze at all. He can be ruthless and I'm glad you're okay," Baine says this to me with care in his eyes and it's sweet.

"I thought he was pretty decent, considering he kidnapped me. He was polite and I didn't get into any trouble. Leon was a fuckwit though," I scrunch up my face. "While I was up there I couldn't help but see the big freaking window looking out, but when I was in the garden swimming earlier, there was only a white wall, I just figured it out from there. I asked Reid about it but he just stood behind me and said nothing, so I'm pissed off with him now too. Thanks for talking to me about it, even if you haven't told me anything new."

"Bonnie, I learnt my lesson the first time, I won't be treating you with any disrespect again. Why was Reid with you? He was at the dining room for lunch as well, is he actually tailing you?" Baine steals a chip from my plate, chewing with a cheeky smile.

I shrug my shoulders. "I asked him why he was following me but he just said that it was the right thing to do. I think he was enjoying my wet bikini a bit too much to leave," I say with a laugh, remembering the look on his face.

Baine's head shoots straight to me. "Did you just say wet bikini? Why the heck didn't you tell me? I would've helped guard you too in that case," he jokes.

"I just bet you would," I mock.

"Look, this is getting way out of hand, lass. First, you go and neck with Salvatore, then you show Reid all of your goodies. What's left for poor wee Baine?" His voice drips with fake sadness. "It just won't do, bonnie, I demand recompense. Go and get your bikini on and get all wet for me, it's only fair." Baine puts a pout on his gorgeous mouth.

I can't help but burst out laughing. I laugh so hard that my mouth hurts. It feels so good to feel a bit of joy in a joyless time. I wipe the tears from my eyes and look at Baine who's staring at me in wonder, wide-eyed and mouth ajar.

"What are you staring at, wee Baine?" I put on a mocking fake accent.

He puts his hand on my cheek, a sweet smile pulling at his lips. "The bonniest lass I've ever seen. You're so strong, so ridiculous, so clever, and so *very* bonnie, but when you laugh it breaks my heart. I believe you've broken this lad. I'll never be the same now that I've heard that laugh and seen your eyes light with stars." Baine leans forward and kisses me so gently on my mouth that it feels like a whisper or a promise, his thumb softly caressing my cheek. "You've gone and ruined me for any other."

I'm speechless, this beautiful man just washed me with the most intimate sweet words I think I've ever received.

Suddenly his body tenses and he leans back to put distance between us but not without a smile and a wink. Two guards walk past, Simon the asshole from the stairwell and another man that I haven't seen before.

"What's going on here, Baine?" Simon enquires smugly.

Baine just looks over nonplussed. "Doing my job, Simon. How's Threshold looking today? Problem-free, I hope."

Simon sniffs hastily brushing his hand through his messy blond locks. "Of course it is. It's just a big pen filled with pets to feed, clean, and house. It's a disgusting job but someone has to keep those *things* in line."

I bristle at his comment. "Keep talking, dickhead, and I'll show you how *I* keep things in line," I spit, unable to help myself.

"Don't you remember the rules, pet? Or are you too stupid to process simple requests?" He's egging me on, waiting for me to give him a reason to punish me.

Baine puts his hand on my leg, with a small shake of his head, he looks back at Simon with a tight smile. "It's all good, Simon, just move on. Blayze has taken a personal interest in this one, best not to rock the boat."

"You aren't allowed to tell them names or information, they're like livestock, you'll be in deep shit when I tell upstairs," Simon threatens.

"Calm down, princess," I direct to Simon. "I've already met Blayze and Leon, I was upstairs this morning. Baine hasn't done anything wrong. Now go do some work and stop bothering me." Simon looks at me stunned, mouth agape.

Baine sighs. "I told you that Blayze had taken an interest in her."

After sputtering a few times, Simon goes back to his rounds.

Letting me know that he has to get back, Baine checks that I'm going to be okay. As he starts getting up, I grab his wrist to stop him because I have to know. "Why did you kiss me?"

He leans close to me with a gentle voice. "Because I felt like I'd die if I dinnae." He tilts my head up and gently kisses me again. "I don't own you, bonnie, but I'd like to win you over, if you'll let me try."

"I'm not beholden to you though just because you kiss me," I clarify, needing him to know that I'm no one's property despite feeling a little giddy. "Though I'm not going to say that I didn't like it."

With that Baine smiles and leaves me wondering what on earth I'm doing.

Chapter Sixteen

A few days later while everyone's still at breakfast I sneak off before anyone sees me. I can't help the excitement in my bones thinking about my long-awaited bath.

Filling the bath with warm lavender scented water, I swirl my hand in the hot liquid, mesmerised by the movement. My body really needs this opportunity to relax, but as I go to climb into the tub I snag a problem. My knee causes me a great deal of discomfort getting in, but I eventually maneuver into a comfortable position.

After giving my body it's much needed relaxation, my skin beginning to prune, I go to get out and realise I'm stuck. My bad leg is in pain from the effort it took to get into the tub earlier, and my good leg is stuck in an awkward position under me from my failed attempt to get myself out. I huff in frustration, deciding that I have to wait for someone to give me a hand.

An hour goes by but still no one. The once deliciously warm water is now freezing and it seeps into my body making me involuntarily dither. Enough is enough, I start calling out for help before hypothermia sets in, hoping to God that someone will hear me. The cold water makes the throbbing in my knee close to unbearable. After screaming out for a third time, my throat becomes hoarse and I'm about to give up when I hear a heavy knock on the door.

"Help me!" I cry out to my soon to be rescuer. "I'm stuck and I'm really hurting."

The door bangs open and a giant figure comes storming in. *Oh, hello Mr Big.* My shit luck would send him to me before anyone else. Salvatore freezes in his tracks, looks down at me in the bath, and drops hard to his knees.

"Yeah, that's not helpful!" Exasperation filling my words. "Could you perhaps get up and help me out?" He literally stares at my naked body through the water without any shame. "Oh my God! I'm butt naked, I get it. When you're quite finished staring at me, I'm in pain!" My voice takes on a higher pitch as

I throw my hands in the air in frustration, anyone would think he's never seen a naked woman before.

He snaps to attention and with that delicious deep voice says, "I'm sorry, what can I do?"

I lift my arms up. "Please will you pick me up carefully out of the water? I'm so cold and stiff, and my leg is aching. I've been stuck here for so long."

Salvatore leans over, looking at my exposed body as he touches the water. "It's freezing!"

"I just said that. Help me!" I all but growl at him, but damn, my teeth are chattering and my skin is turning blue, which deadens the effect of my words.

Raising his eyes to mine he says the strangest thing. "Do I have permission to touch your body?"

I look at him with exasperation. "Are you fucking kidding me? Pick me the fuck up *right* now!" This time I shout, chattering teeth be damned.

He smiles slyly, leans in and slides his arms under my legs before gently pulling me out of the water towards him. He holds me more gently than I would've thought was possible for such a giant, rough man. With only one very strong arm holding me flat against him, the other hand reaches behind and pulls his shirt off. Throwing it away, he holds me close to his warm muscled chest, surrounding me with his huge arms.

"What are you doing?" I'm shocked and don't

know how to react, but my freezing body doesn't protest.

He nuzzles my hair intimately, his beard tickling my ear. "Warming you, you're very cold and need body heat."

At that very second Reid stomps through the door and with one look at us, rage fills his face before he grounds out between clenched teeth, "Put her down and let her go. You can't just go around taking women out of the bath. What the hell are you thinking?"

My plump breasts mash against Salvatores hard pecs, and he encourages my legs gently around his massive waist so he doesn't hurt my knee, before wrapping me in his bulging arms again. "She demanded I touch her, I did nothing wrong."

My arms instinctively curl around my front as I shiver, shamelessly leaning into Salvatore's warm body, he's like a human heater. I'm straddled in his embrace and I let out an involuntary sigh as his warmth seeps into me. Reid seems to finally see that I'm shivering badly and steps forward asking Salvatore what's wrong with me.

"She was stuck in the bath, calling for help, and the water's turned ice-cold. I'm using my body to warm her." Salvatore's tone is a matter of fact, but I can feel a little more than kindness going on here.

Warmth hits my back, covering me all over. There's warm breath on my neck coming from behind and powerful arms wrap around my legs, one calloused hand rubbing my sore knee. Holy shit, Reid's shirtless behind me and I'm in a guard sandwich.

In my ear, Reid's soft, raspy voice whispers, "How does that feel? Better?"

I moan soft and deep because that's how my body likes to betray me. My arms wrap around Salvatore's neck to snuggle closer. I feel a small chuckle vibrate my back and a groan at my front. Salvatore's hands move from my hips around to where my ass meets my thighs, holding his fingers dangerously close to my pussy. My legs spread wide circling him, so he can feel my wetness pressing directly against his stomach. I clench my different aching muscles tight at the rubbing contact and hear him groan again, moving slightly against me, sliding me lower on his body.

Behind me Reid strokes up and down the outsides of my thighs and then up the sides of my body, grazing along the curves of my heavy breasts. I lean back into his sculpted chiselled body feeling his hard length press against my bare ass as I get lowered by Salvatore. My head lolls back and my breasts become slightly exposed.

Reid takes that as a sign to slowly move his hands

over my breasts, and hardened nipples, gently rolling them in his fingers making me moan again, this time louder.

Salvatore bucks his hips so I feel his rock hard dick through his pants rubbing against my core. Groaning as my hips start to rock back and forth over the hardness at my front and back, my pussy getting super wet and greedy to be touched, to be filled. It feels so good having them rubbing against me, straining to be free, and Reid's hands tormenting my aching nipples as he plucks at them with expertise.

"Oh God," I moan out, not able to help it any more, not caring at all if this is a good idea, just needing them to rub me, touch me, pinch me... fuck me.

Reid licks my neck and nibbles at a sensitive spot on my shoulder, growling sexy little noises as he goes. Salvatore watches me with his deep penetrating gaze as he holds my ass tight with one hand taking my weight while he slowly puts his other hand between us, looking for any sign that I want to stop. Instead, I thrust my hips forward to continue his movement. He deftly rubs his fingers through my soaking slit and gently circles my swollen nub with my own juices. The heat in his gaze is palpable, his touch is so good that I know I'm going to release quickly, which is so unlike me, but my body really needs this. I rock harder, wanting more, the chill in my bones long forgotten.

Between Salvatore's expert stimulation, Reid's sensual assault on my nipples while lapping at my neck, I feel my pussy clenching just before I get pushed over the edge. Laying my head back on Reid, I cry out in pure ecstasy, my climax rips through my body and my muscles shake.

Salvatore captures the last of my whimpers in his mouth as he ravishes me. Reid, meanwhile, gets down behind me and lifts my ass into the air before surprising me with his mouth behind me laving at my still convulsing pussy, licking up all my leaking juices, I hear a moan coming from his throat and it vibrates against my quaking centre.

When Reid starts working me up again I hear laughter outside, the men must have heard it too because Salvatore stiffens and Reid stops and gets back up. I turn around to see him licking his lips with a grin.

Salvatore sits me on the counter gently and the guys look at each other before Reid says, "I'll go and keep them out of the bathroom while you dress her." He then looks at me. "Is that okay?"

Sitting here bewildered and kind of confused with no idea how I got myself into this situation, wondering why they both look totally unaffected by what just happened, I reply, "Ah... yeah, sure." Apparently, I'm reduced to stammering.

Reid smiles at me again, comes over and kisses me deep, I taste myself on his tongue and I don't mind a bit. He draws back, puts on his shirt and leaves.

Salvatore gazes at me, then his eyes lower to my core causing my walls to clench again. Coming over, he drops to his knees in front of me and opens my legs wider, looking hard at my glistening pussy lips. *Fuck that's hot.* Leaning forward, he looks at me, then takes me into his mouth making slow, long licks with the flat of his sensual tongue, up and around my clit before delving his tongue into my slit. His beard brushes against my sensitive skin, as he watches me with fiery eyes the whole time, I've never been more aroused. He begins to really work me over with his talented tongue and I know I should tell him to stop because 'people outside', but watching him watch me as he eats me out is driving me over the edge so fast again that I can't bear to stop.

"Oh my God, I'm gonna cum," my quiet shocked voice squeaks. He keeps going, driving me fast to the edge. "Holy shit," my cries grow louder as I pant. Not able to stop myself, my head rolls back and his hand comes up and covers my mouth just in time to muddle my scream as I start to cum, squirting all over his face and beard.

"Fuck!" He growls as he licks it all up furiously. "I want you so damn bad that my dicks gonna rip through my pants," Salvatore growls in between licks, devouring every drop.

The door bursts open, startling me.

Reid orders, "Get the fuck out!" to Salvatore. "You were supposed to dress her, not make it worse." Reid looks at me panting, grabbing onto the edge of the sink, eyes hooded in post-orgasm bliss, legs wide open and wet as the sea. "Oh, fuck!" He growls with want.

Closing the door behind him Reid comes back over to me in two strides and slides his finger deep inside me with one hard thrust, I moan and rock my hips like a bitch in heat. I need him inside me, either of them, both of them, and I'm not above begging.

"Please!" I whine as he moves his finger inside me, curling it up in a come hither motion, his other finger gently working my clit at the same time. I moan again.

Reid puts his head against mine as Salvatore stays on his knees, his facial hair glistening from my juices. He's watching my core closely as I get fingered, and it's so sexy, there's something really arousing about being watched.

"Oh shit, we need to stop, this is so bad," Reid groans. "But I can't stop, I don't want to, I need to be deep inside you, I need to fuck you hard and fast. You smell and taste so damn good."

Salvatore grabs my inner thighs rough enough to leave a bruise, growling deeply while licking up the sensitive area like a possessed animal. Both of them look frazzled and about as desperate as I feel.

"Summer! Summer!" I hear Bell calling my name.

Wait, what the fuck am I doing? My name snaps me out of my lust-filled haze. I put my hand on Reid's chest and breathlessly say, "Stop."

He stops immediately, closes his eyes and slowly pulls his hand back. "Salvatore, she said stop." I hear a groan from between my legs and he slowly gets up. Joining Reid they both move to the back of the room with their hands behind their backs.

"You need to both go now." I use a surprisingly stern voice, under the circumstances.

They nod in unison. Salvatore puts his shirt on, picks me up and gently puts me down on the floor near my stuff. He washes his beard and face then they both walk out the door, closing it behind them.

I turn and look at myself in the mirror in shock. *Whoa. What was that?* I'm gonna need a shower after that, a cold one, I was so not done.

When I walk to my room after my much-needed

shower, Bell sees me and comes running over asking where I've been. Letting her know I had a bath, but I decided to leave out the rest because I'm not done processing that yet. She tells me that there's a rumour going around that some of the girls have been hooking up with the men here, and that everyone appears to be getting revved up, joking that something is in the water, but it makes me wonder if there is after my little bathroom experience. We talk for a bit more before I excuse myself, saying I need a laydown.

Leaving me to rest, I stare at the ceiling blankly, going over in my head everything that happened. In the end, regardless of everything, I can't deny that I loved it.

Chapter Seventeen

Mia sits on my bed the next morning waking me up, looking for advice. She shuffles around uncomfortably.

"The girls have been making fun of how horny everyone is all of a sudden and I'm a little bit worried about it because…" She looks at me, her eyes filled with shyness. "Because it's affecting me too, I can't stop thinking about Tyrese. I'm having all these dreams and he just smells so nice. I think he's feeling it too because I find him staring at me sometimes, but I can't approach him because of Bell and Shylo. Bell's being pretty hard on everyone and Shylo just says she doesn't understand why people are acting that way. Do you think I'm crazy for wanting him?"

"Why did you come to me? Did you think I thought differently?" I'm genuinely curious.

Mia smiles coyly. "I've seen how you look at Baine." She giggles. "I think he's not the only one affecting you either."

I laugh out loud. "True enough!"

"Do you think it would be wrong if I tried to act on my impulses? I'm not the kind of person to do that normally, I've only ever been with two people and it seems wrong, but he's like a really sexy magnet to me and a truly nice guy," she openly admits. "Technically they're bad people aren't they? So it wouldn't be right, maybe this is Stockholm Syndrome?"

"To be fair though, these are the hottest kidnappers ever!" I point out and we look at each other and laugh. "Honestly, I can't see the harm, except maybe it'd be a problem if there's no birth control. There's none here that I know of. I have the Mirena IUD so I'll be alright but there's still STD's to worry about and things like that."

Scratching her head in thought. "I wonder if it's rude to ask? I have a Mirena as well." She nods her head. "You know what? I'm gonna go for it, it's been so long since I've had a man's hands on me, I think I'm due."

I fist-bump her. "Go girl!" I cheer before she heads off with a skip in her step.

I'm not a stupid woman, I know that this level of horniness isn't normal and it's probably being induced somehow. What I want to know is why? And how? There has to be a good reason, but I don't think it's that big a deal because a little horniness never killed anybody.

"What are you daydreaming about, bonnie?" I hear Baine ask as he slips into my room.

I smile up at him. "Why, you of course."

He chuckles as he sits with me, so close our legs touch. "I missed you, lass. I've taken the morning off to spend some time with you, is that alright?"

"I'd love that." I agree with a kiss to his cheek.

Baine turns to study me before putting his hand on my jaw and guiding my lips to his. He kisses me with longing and devotion. Slow and deep, while burning my insides, I gasp as he stops to look at me.

"Do you ken that we share apartments in our quarters?" I shake my head. "Aye, and I happen to share an area with Hermes, Salvatore, Reid and two others." He stops to take in my reaction, which I carefully keep hidden, not because I'm going to lie to him, but I want to gauge how he feels before I tell him what happened.

I nod. "That's interesting, do you have your own bedrooms? Why were you put with them?"

"One's my twin brother, Derryn. Reid's with a

friend from the same village as him. Hermes and Salvatore knew each other well before we came here, both hermits with similar lives and all that. I cannae tell you more than that. Our beds are in separate rooms though," he explains before going on. "Anyway, yesterday Reid and Salvatore made an out of schedule stop together at our rooms when I was off shift and I happened to notice that they smelled a lot like you before they showered. I wonder why that would be, lass?" I get the impression that he has an idea of what happened by his expectant expression.

I must really smell for him to know that. I sniff myself inconspicuously and I sit quietly for a minute, deciding just to be honest and I explain to him, in not too much detail, what happened as he sat quietly and listened without judgement.

"I'm not really sure how it happened exactly. Most likely because I was naked and I've been so horny lately, but I haven't been able to do anything about it myself because of the hidden window in my room." I nod behind me at the big white wall.

Baine coughs a little and his ears go red before he turns his body to face mine with a hand on my good knee. "Does it matter if there's a window if no one's behind it? No one will use that room unless you're a danger to yourself or others."

"I disagree, somebody's been watching me, I can

feel it on my skin when they're there. I know what it feels like to be watched. I don't mind though because it doesn't feel menacing, it actually feels kind of hot. It's a problem for me because I don't know who it is. It's not you or one of the other two?" My voice sounds hopeful even to my own ears.

Baine looks at the wall nervously. "No, bonnie, only the people in charge here can go inside those rooms, we dinnae have access. Are you sure?"

I confidently nod. "I'm definitely sure. I know the moment they can see me, I can literally feel their eyes moving on my skin."

I shudder slightly, feeling wetness well between my legs. I've always loved being watched during sex and that's what it feels like when it happens. It's my own little kink and I'm not ashamed of it.

Baine tenses and leans forward, putting his nose right up to my neck, he breathes me in all the way down my cleavage. I groan and so does he.

My hand goes up to clutch at his unruly hair and he gently kisses and nips at my flesh above the swell of my breasts. "More," I plead and I slip the straps of my loose singlet off my shoulders exposing the top half of my heaving mounds, lust for my sweet, ginger Scot filling me.

Baine slowly moves his hand down from my neck to trace my collarbone and then lowers his head to take my still covered stiff nipple into his mouth. He bites down and I buck slightly, gasping at the intense feeling.

Baine pushes me back down onto the bed and lifts my sore leg up carefully, while keeping my legs spread slightly, as he moves his body on top of mine. I feel his hardness between my thighs and I shamelessly move my hips up and down his shaft, feeling him harden even more against my throbbing vagina.

"I dinnae think it's right that you're here like this," Baine rasps into my ear. "You should be free and I wish I could help you. You're everything to me, lass. I wish I could show you how much."

I nibble his neck. "Aren't you worried someone will see you?"

Baine kisses me hard on the mouth. "I dinnae give a fuck, I'm yours now, bonnie. I belong to you, fuck everyone else. I'd like to see them try to take me from you because it cannae be done. Tell me I can touch you, bonnie?"

"You can touch me whenever you want to, Baine, I like your hands on me. It doesn't bother you that I've let others touch me, too?" I get out in between frantic breaths, desperately needing to be honest with him.

"Nae, if that's what you wanted, if that's what you needed. Just because I'm yours, dinnae mean that I can tell you what you need. I may never touch another lass again, but you're free to make your own choices. Where I come from, you hold all the power and I'll worship you, every inch." And with that he takes my mouth again, kissing me so deep and so hot that I find myself grinding against his body in need.

My breasts come out of my shirt from all of the friction and Baine lowers himself to taste my nipple and lick every inch of them leaving me panting and moaning. He suddenly bites down sending my back arching and my wet pussy clenching.

"Please," I moan, not even knowing what I'm asking for, just knowing that I need *more*.

Baine pulls his shirt off and rips mine open at the front. I stare in wonder at the absolutely perfect man before me; his muscles taut and hard, his ripped abs flexing, and his chest heaving with desire. His deep green eyes focus on my breasts as he reaches down and caresses them, pinching my aching nipples, tormenting me.

"Well, fuck me sideways and call me Aunt Fanny!" Bell humorously sings from the doorway where she's currently leaning. "I would call that fucking excellent room service!"

"Fuck off, Bell!" I throw my pillow at the doorway, she's totally killing my buzz.

She laughs and heads down the hall shouting

back, "I'll be your sock on the door and yell out that I lost my shoe if someone's coming. Go get some, ho, I've got your back."

"Just kill me," I mumble into a chuckling Baine's chest.

"Do you want me to go, bonnie?"

I laugh before grabbing him, pulling him back down on me as he tries to get up. "Are you kidding? We just got a lookout."

Before he can react, my mouth is on his and my hands are clumsily undoing his pants. Thankfully he takes pity on my pathetic attempts and swiftly removes them himself. I lift my bum to take off mine and Baine helps me, gently removing them without hurting my knee.

I remember just then what Mia and I had talked about earlier. "I don't mean to be rude or anything, but do you have any protection? Or any STD's I need to worry about? I have the Mirena, so I'm not worried about getting pregnant, but you know it only seems right if I ask. I'm clean, just so you know," I bring up awkwardly.

Baine grabs me around the waist to pull himself back between my legs when he suddenly stops moving and tenses. I make sure to let him know that I mean well with my questions. "I'm sorry, did I offend you? I didn't mean to because I do like you a lot, Baine, but I think it's a reasonable question to ask, don't you?" Doubt begins to creep in my mind at what I'm doing.

Baine still doesn't move, I don't even think he's breathing. In a flash he abruptly stands up and steps back, picking up his pants. *Um... okay!*

Seeing the rising anger and shame in my face, Baine puts his hands up, voice shaky and Scottish brogue thicker than usual. "I'm sorry, bonnie, dinnae get angry with me. I just cannae take you like this, it's nae right."

"You seemed okay with it a second ago until I asked for protection. Have you got something and all of a sudden have found a conscience?" I blurt out suddenly furious. "I had a right to ask. Just go, Baine, this won't be happening again. Clearly I can't trust you to be honest with me even about this."

Baine flinches at my blatant hurt feelings, and at my words. He steps forward, obviously apologetic and regretting how he handled things, but I'm not interested. "I said get out!" I snap at his approach. I know I'm probably overreacting, but I'm feeling hurt and vulnerable.

I turn to the wall because I just know someone's been watching the whole time. "Grow some balls and come and see me in person. You obviously like watching and I clearly like to be watched, the least you can do is let me know who gets the privilege," I yell at it, my arms flailing about, face hard.

Baine pales considerably. "You knew they were there?"

"Of course I did. I'm curious to know why they didn't stop you from trying to fuck me though. I'd ask you, but apparently you're full of shit," I snap one more time, standing butt naked with one hand on my hip and the other pointing to the door, zero interest in even one more word.

Chapter Eighteen

Sitting in the cave listening to the girls laughing is just what I need after such an eventful morning. It's nice having good friends and we're lucky to have found each other here.

"You wanna know something really fucking funny? How about Baine this morning?" Bell bends over in hysterics.

My face crinkles up at the memory. "Oh shut up, it's not funny."

Still laughing, Bell manages to get out, "There I am being the proverbial sock when all of a sudden Baine comes almost running out, looking flustered as shit, he sees me and goes beat red because it's only been like two minutes." She's laughing so hard she can't breathe. "What a fucking disappointment, I had high hopes for the poor boy. Now that's a walk of shame."

Then they all crack up, hands slapping, knees laughing, I've changed my mind, they're all trolls.

"I'm telling you, Summer, you should've seen his face when I laughed at him. I told him next time he gets his dick wet he should try to last longer, it was priceless." Bell chuckles and even I have to laugh at that, I'd almost feel bad for him if I wasn't so unsatisfied.

"We didn't even have sex," I state, feeling like I should clarify. "He got all weirded out when I asked for protection. The whole thing suddenly felt wrong so I asked him to leave, he probably has something and was hoping I wouldn't ask." I shudder at the thought.

"As funny as this is, the movie marathon will be starting soon so I'm gonna go, I don't want to miss it. Hermes is going to make popcorn and put a coke machine in for the afternoon, I'm so excited. Anyone else coming?" Shylo asks in her sweet, chirpy voice.

"I'm in," Mia jumps back into the water. "Maybe I'll see Tyrese." She shoots a grin back and heads out with Shylo at her tail. Mia ended up telling the girls what she wanted to do and they were pretty good about it.

As Bell goes to leave she looks back and shrugs. "I love coke. Bye, bitch."

I decided to stay here for a while, the sun's directly over the hole in the roof so I lay down half on the rocks, my legs half in the water, to soak up its beautiful rays. I've missed being outside and in the sun so much.

I must've fallen asleep because the next thing I'm aware of is someone massaging my feet and another stroking my hair, wait... that can't be right.

Opening my eyes, I'm met with Reid's clear blue eyes staring down at me twinkling with satisfaction and a smile on his face to match. I look down and find that Salvatore is the one rubbing my feet. At the side of me Baine is sitting on a rock staring at the water, looking sombre.

"What are you doing here?" I tensely look in Baine's direction. "All of you?" Looking around at the others next.

"You were in here for quite some time and we got worried. Actually, Blayze noticed as well—he saw four of you go in and only three come out. I figured out who it was pretty quickly and thought maybe your leg was hurting too much to swim out and that you might need us." Reid gently strokes the side of my face with his finger. "Are you okay?"

I sigh deeply and answer honestly. "No, I'm not. My leg's the same but I'm not feeling okay. I'm tired of not understanding why I'm here and I can't figure out how to get out." I look at him hopefully. "Hey, can you guys get me out?"

A groan comes from Baine before Reid answers. "No, baby, I can't. None of us can, we're just as much a part of this as you girls are, we don't really have a choice." He looks unhappy about it and adds, "No one in this room wants you feeling locked up and trapped, you should know that. This is only temporary, Summer, but you can't go back home after this. You've figured that out, haven't you? You're too smart not to have."

"Do you have to say it like that? You're going to make her hate us too. Shut up Reid, you're just making it worse," Salvatore grumbles angrily. "You're safe with me—with us. We'll take care of you, and provide for you. We'll keep you safe."

I sit up on the edge of the pool. "I understand that if we get sent home we could talk about everyone and everything we've seen, I get that, but I *have* to go, I have kids that *I* need to protect and provide for. We can't stay here forever but the alternative is to kill us. Don't you get it?" I'm frustrated that they're only seeing one side of the story.

Baine gets up and punches the rock wall, making a large section crumble. Holy shit, how strong is this guy? He could probably punch his way out for me.

"Aye, we get it, bonnie. We cannae fix it, but if I could I would. I dinnae want to keep you from your bairns, nae ever, that goes against everything I believe in." Baine almost yells and then he turns to the boys. "Cannae you see? I dinnae care how much you want this, it's nae right, we need to stop this." I've found that whenever Baine gets over-excited his accent's so much stronger.

"Sit down!" Reid booms at Baine and he quickly does just that. "You can't talk like that, Baine, you know why we're here and you knew this would be wrong from the beginning but we have a job to do and a responsibility that's bigger than ourselves. Can we trust you with her?"

"Ha!" Pops out of my mouth. "You sure can, he won't even have sex with me when I'm throwing myself at him." I cross my arms petulantly, I know I'm acting a bit childish but I'm not perfect and I'm tired of feeling like a puppet in this game called *Threshold*.

Salvatore and Reid both gape at him in what looks like horror. "Are you fucking with me?" Salvatore's low menacing voice sends a shiver through me, raising goosebumps over my skin and an image of him drinking me down in the bathroom flashes in my mind, before I mentally shake it away.

Baine looks down while shuffling his feet before answering softly, "She deserves the truth and I cannae lie to her." Then he looked Salvatore hard in the eyes. "She asked me if I had protection against any disease because she knew she was protected against a bairn. I won't be taking her like that, it's deception and I can just feel that using deception like that will last forever for her. Dinnae you see that in her? I do, so I won't." Then he sits with a thump, head in his hands. I don't know how I feel about what he's said but my attention has certainly piqued.

Reid sits behind me, scooching in with one leg on each side of me so I can lean back into him. He strokes my hair to one side and kisses my exposed neck before whispering gently into my ear. "We don't want to lie to you but sometimes we have to, for your safety, and for ours. You need to know that all three of us have picked you. This is something that happens sometimes, even if some of us weren't expecting for sharing to be an option, but we're okay with it if you are. Please don't hold a grudge against us forever for things we might say or do while we're in here, we don't want to hurt you." I hear the pleading in his voice but I'm more focused on his strange words. What on Earth is he talking about?

"I don't understand why you talk the way you do, everything you say only gives me more questions instead of answers. What do you mean you picked me? I'm not a flower, I'm a person, and I don't like to be lied to Reid, and I won't forget when you do. Baine's right about that." I'm soft but stern when I speak. "If you have something that I need to know then you'd better tell me or I'll make you regret it."

I know it's a threat and so do they. I just hope they realise I don't make empty threats.

Salvatore comes between my legs in the water and brings his face up to mine. "You piss me off!" His voice stern, a small frown on his face. "I want to throttle you and spank you silly, female, but I also want to taste you again and again. You taste and smell like fucking heaven. You're the most infuriating, sexy woman I'll ever meet and I need you. Fuck what they say, if you want out, I'll get you out. I can't take you back home, though, because I don't belong there and I'm not fucking leaving your side." He takes my face roughly in his hand and devours my mouth, beard rubbing roughly against my face, dominating me lick by lick. I feel owned by him and I love it, his brutal passion is contagious.

Reid raises his hands and undoes the ties of my

bikini top stripping it from my body and kneading my heavy breasts from behind. Salvatore breaks free of my kiss and sucks on my nipples while Reid holds my breast for him and I hear Baine groan from the side.

"I'm going to taste you again, my kindred, and this time you're going to scream," Salvatore pulls at the ties on the sides of my bikini bottom, freeing my pussy to his hungry gaze. "Tell me you want my mouth to taste you? That you want my tongue on and in you?"

I tremble from his hot words and lean back into Reid, arching my pelvis further forward for him and opening my legs as wide as they go. "Yes, yes, I want that—I want you." I squirm, having no shame and I don't care, I desperately want his mouth on me again.

"Yes, what?" Salvatore asks me, his fingers brushing up and down my thighs as he greedily looks at my spread pulsing pussy.

"Yes, please, Sir." I moan the words making him groan loudly before lowering himself to my pussy and slowly laving around my clit and slit but never on it, driving me crazy with need. "Oh fuck, Mr Big, please."

He takes my clit in his mouth and sucks gently making me whimper and arch further. Salvatore slides his large finger up and down my soaking slit, sliding it in and out, finding my special spot and working it like a pro. He brings his head up to look at me as I rock into his finger before he adds another huge digit.

Reid reaches down and gives my clit VIP treatment as Salvatore pumps his fingers in and out of me, working me into a desperate state by rubbing and pinching my swollen nub. I lean on Reid's shoulder and look up to see Baine standing over me, staring down at me with a massive hard on, desire hooding his eyes.

I lick my lips seductively and he drops down and kisses me passionately, taking a breast in his hand and growling into my mouth. I reach over and palm his huge dick through his wet shorts and set that baby free from its confines to feel his soft, warm, velvety skin as I stroke his erection with care. I thumb the tip to feel the pre-cum already there waiting for me. I bring my thumb to my mouth to taste his saltiness between kisses before taking him back into my hand and stroking him just right, moaning into his mouth while the other two bring me closer to the ecstasy I crave.

The sensations are overwhelming and I feel my body tensing ready for release and it hits me like a freight train, my inner walls tightening around Salvatore's fingers. Baine catches my scream with his lips as he follows me over the edge before releasing my mouth as he cries out, *"fuck!"* into the cave, and his hot seed shoots all over my heaving breasts.

"I'm not done with you yet." Salvatore turns me so I'm slightly on my side uncaring about the warm fluid on my skin. "I want you to squirt all over me again, I like it when your body claims me as yours." He lays in between my legs, taking my pussy with his mouth again. I feel sensitive and try to squirm but he holds me still against his tortuous administrations, the brushing of his facial hair another layer of touch on my delicate skin.

Reid sits on his knees in front of me staring with hooded eyes as he palms his own dick watching me be pleasured by Salvatore. "Come here." I motion for him to sit right in front of me.

As he gets closer I lick my lips to let him know exactly what I'm after and he's in front of me in a flash. Reid guides his dick to my mouth as I lift up onto one elbow. I tentatively give his head a little lick and blow on it, watching him shudder with desire. I swirl my tongue around the tip and suck him in using my hand on his ass to guide him deeper.

Reid grabs the back of my hair and growls as he starts moving his hips, thrusting his dick in and out while holding my head still to take his member as far as I can, which to his delight is very far. I deep throat him all the way and he starts to fuck my mouth fast and hard as I gag on his length. Salvatore continues to fuck my pussy with his tongue and fingers, making me blind with lust.

I groan deeply around Reid's cock and feel myself getting closer, then Baine reaches around me to pinch my nipples, sharply driving me to the edge until I orgasm hard. My body shaking, my mouth and throat full of cock as I try to scream, my pussy squirting on Salvatore, once again driving him wild with need as he violently grabs my ass and licks every inch of me while moaning his delight.

My vibrating scream being choked around Reid's cock undoes him and I feel him tighten in my mouth as he watches me cum, before spilling himself deep down my throat, calling my name, and pulling my hair.

We come down from our orgasmic high and we all collapse on the rocks together. I think about how I should be mortified but it just felt way too good. I roll over to Salvatore and try to pull him on top of me. He gets in between my legs and settles against my core, still wet and pulsing for more. I need to be filled and Mr Big is very big indeed, his erection is over-flowing from his pants that are still on.

I undo his pants and pull out his very impressive cock, feeling it in my hand before sliding his pants down further. He grabs my ass and slides my dripping pussy up and down his super hard member, it feels so good, but when I try to grab him to guide him into my entrance he stops me, pulling his hips back. I frown up at him.

"Summer, we can't do that, for all of the reasons we just talked about," he states hesitantly to me, looking like he's fighting himself and his own needs, hard.

Reid sits up quickly. "Not you too?"

Salvatore sits up, lips swollen, beard glistening. He pulls me into his lap and holds me in his arms lovingly, kissing me on the side of my head. "Baine's right, she deserves more. Summer, we're going to go now and not because we don't want you but because we do. Please understand like a good girl and don't be a viper about it."

I sigh in frustration. "Well then at least help me get dressed so I can head back to the room and dream about all the sex I'm not getting."

In unison, they laugh and help me get cleaned and dressed before we all head off.

Chapter Nineteen

I'm laughing at something stupid that Baine just said, as Reid lifts me out of the water, when a guard standing there waiting for us near where the grass starts, clears his throat.

After Reid sees what I'm looking at he stops abruptly, followed by the other two men I seem to have ensnared.

"What's wrong?" Asks a visibly worried Baine as he steps forward.

Reid forces a smile. "Probably nothing, they're most likely just wondering why we took so long."

He takes me straight to the seat and hands me my towel and crutches. "You should go straight to your room and get dry and warm. Maybe have a hot shower, not a bath, please." Reid raises an eyebrow at me.

"I don't see why not, I had a great time at my last bath." I snicker at his serious face. "All right, all right. Gosh, anyone would think I got stuck in there."

Deep laughter erupts behind me and I stare in astonishment at Salvatore genuinely laughing, I think I've broken him.

The guard clears his throat again. "I apologise for the inconvenience but Summer's required for a meeting."

"What kind of meeting?" Reid's stern voice makes the other guard look nervous.

He puts his hands up in a defensive move. "Look, Reid, I'm just doing my job." Then he seems to think of something. "Why were you guys in there for so long?"

Baine looks down at his swim shorts. "Swimming you numpty, what does it look like?" Rolling his eyes he walks off, before calling back, "Late for work so I'll catch you later, bonnie."

Waving farewell to him, I turn to the other two. "You guys can head off too, I bet it's the medical centre again. Anyone would think I'm dying by the way they carry on."

"No, Miss, Blayze wants to see you upstairs." His statement, a matter of fact.

Salvatore instantly tenses up and comes to my side and Reid goes on to question the guard further, while I just look at where I know the window will be and find myself saying, "That's fine, I like Blayze, I'm sure it'll be nice to catch up."

All three of the men drop their jaws while I get up, straighten myself and say, "Well, let's go then"

"You know who I'm talking about, Miss?" The guard asks me, eyebrows raised.

I smile and nod. "Of course, we go way back. How is the firecracker anyway?"

The guy looks like he's going to die of a heart attack, I go and pat him on the back. "Come on, you'll be fine, I'll help you through it." I guild him away as I look back and wink at my two sexy men before hobbling off.

Wait... *MY* men. They're just two sexy men, talk about getting cocky, pun intended.

As we get closer the guard helps me up the last flight of stairs with a reassuring tone. "We're almost there, Miss."

"Ok... Firstly, my name's Summer, and you already know that don't you?" He nods. "Good, so use it.

Secondly, do you have a name or are you just not wanting me to know it? I won't bite you know."

He relaxes a bit. "Sorry mi... Summer, we're taught to be formal when at work, my name's John."

"Thanks, John. That's way better than not being acknowledged, don't you think?" I say as he opens the door to the big conference room.

As he goes to answer me, he sees Blayze staring at us and stands to attention.

I can't help but giggle as I hobble past him and up to Blayze, holding out my hand. "Hi, Blayze, it's great to see you again. I hope you've been well. I'm assuming there hasn't been any crazy uprisings since I saw you last?"

Blayze takes my hand but just holds it instead of shaking it. "Summer, it's a pleasure. I'm sure you're very disappointed to hear that no one has escaped as of yet."

I look up at him and feel heat rising in my body. God this man is delicious, he's by far the best-looking man that's ever been created; Strong and sexy with a natural smokey scent that I love.

"Summer?" Blayze asks as I stand there, realising that I'm just holding his hand and ogling him.

"Oh, sorry about that," I say, taking my hand back quickly. "You might need someone to clean up the drool I just left, not awkward at all." I chuckle slightly. "Do you mind if I sit? I'm still hurting quite a bit and I'm over feeling uncomfortable all the time."

Blayze gestures towards the seat closest to me. As I sit down, he comes to sit next to me, turning his chair in my direction. "Summer, I think that we need to talk... alone," Blayze starts, looking toward John, who nods and disappears through the door.

I smile at him and say honestly, "I'd really like that."

After a big sigh, Blayze leans back in his chair and takes me in from tip to toe. At that moment I realise I'm still in a wet bikini. "I'm so sorry, I didn't dry off properly and John said I had to come straight here," I give as an explanation for my appearance.

"You don't hear me complaining do you?" He smirks sexily. "I pay a lot of attention to what's going on around here and I notice almost everything. You've been eyeing every corner, every guard, and every shadow of this place, but you have yet to try to escape. Why is that? Is it just because of your leg?"

A little impressed with his honesty, I turn my head to the side, seeing him with more respect. "No, not really, I just haven't wanted to yet. You'll know when I'm trying to leave."

"How exactly will I know?"

"Well, I won't be inside Threshold anymore, obviously." Leaning back in my chair I pick non-existent lint off my bikini top.

Blayze laughs at that. "Are you really that confident?"

"Yes. Aren't you? Isn't that why I'm here?" I return, I can't help the sass that coats my words.

Turning his head to the side with his hand gripping his chin to study me he seems to come to a decision, "Do you know yet what makes this place different? Who we are? What we want? Why you're here? Why women?" He leans forward with one elbow on the desk, his chin still in his hand. "I really am curious as to what you've found out. What you yourself have come up with? I'm almost tempted to tell you a few things just to see what you do with it, do you know why those males of yours follow you around?"

I frown before answering. "I'm pretty sure they just want something from me but their feelings are getting in the way," I sigh and continue. "As for the rest, it's all just ideas for now."

"You're right about the guys, they do want something from you and they're desperate for it and not just for themselves. Your ideas have become quite fruitful though haven't they? Have you figured out who's been watching you?" Blayze's voice is curious.

I bluff my ass off. "You have been, obviously. Why would I think it would be anyone else?"

"You did ask them to tell you who they were didn't you?" I nod and he goes on leaning forward more. "I find you fascinating. I want something from you as well, much more than just to watch you Summer, though you're right on that assumption."

"Why? What do you want from me?"

Blayze puts his thumb and forefinger on my chin to look into my eyes before saying in his deep baritone, "You are what I'm looking for!" Simple, yet complicated, he leans into me and kisses me gently on the lips before trailing my bottom lip with his tongue. I open my mouth slightly and he nips at my lip gently. "I want to fix your leg and take you to my bed, you've been waiting to be filled for so long and I'm happy to help. If I take you and cure your pain though, things will be different for you, you'll know things that you can't unknow. Do you understand?" Blayze whispers to me sexily as he holds my face in his hand.

Trying to keep my senses, I breathe out. "What could I possibly do with any information that I learn? How do you plan to fix me exactly?"

"That's up to you, little bird. Now decide, do you want me to take you to my bed? I can promise you a very pleasurable time, one that you'll never forget,"

Blayze's voice and words send molten heat rippling through me, desperately encouraging me to say yes and just let him take me. Unfortunately, my brain doesn't work that way.

"Before I say yes or no, is it going to be pleasurable for you or me?" I point out and he chuckles in response.

He stands up with his hand out. "Definitely you, but hopefully both of us."

I take a minute to think about everything. He's hot and I totally want him. Plus, I can apparently get my leg better and get information out of him, this kind of seems like a win-win situation.

"What about the others? You're not trying to own me as just your own are you? Because I'm not okay with that." I want to make sure I know before I make a decision because nobody owns me.

I put my hand in his and he helps me to my feet. Blayze looks down at me with a twinkle in his eye and asks, "What if I do want you all to myself? I've never shared anything with anyone before, why should I start now?"

"That's a reasonable enough request but unfortunately for you, I'm going to have to decline. I'm not property, Blayze, and I decide where I put my body and whom I let touch it. It's a damn shame though because you're lickable and I'm worth it." I wink then I turn to leave.

Blayze comes up behind me and puts his hands on my hips to stop me from moving away, he whispers in my ear. "It's a deal. I'll share you for now, if I can have you as mine like you've been theirs. But you'll add no more to your harem of males, little bird. Do we understand each other? There's only so much sharing a man like me can take and when I call you, you'll come. That's not a demand either, you won't be able to help yourself." I feel his breath on me and his warmth at my back and I tremble in expectation as I nod. "May I have permission to touch you more, little bird?" His raspy heat filled voice tells me that he's just as affected as I am.

I turn around carefully and put my hands on his chest, raising my chin to meet his sexually heated gaze. "Touch me, Blayze, and set me on fire."

Chapter Twenty

Blayze meets my mouth halfway, with one hand squeezing my hip and the other one twisting in my hair to pull me closer. We breathe each other in as he ravishes my mouth with a lust that sets me aflame.

Our lips and teeth clash together with an undeniable need, my body folds against his and he pulls me in close. My tongue dances with his and I can't help but feel weak with desire. A desperate longing for more powers through my veins, one I've never experienced before.

Blayze grabs me under my thighs and I wrap my legs around him, feeling his strong body in between mine, his hard cock straining through his pants at my barely covered core.

He sits back on the desk, pulling me in tighter as I straddle him. I rock my hips back and forth, loving the feel of the friction between our bodies heating me and making me so wet for his touch.

I grab the hem of his shirt and go to work it over his head, but he stops me, panting out, "You don't want to wait until we get to my room?"

"You promised to fill me, didn't you? I've been teased so badly lately I'm losing my mind. Fuck me, because I need it!" I demand while continuing to take his shirt off.

Blayze chuckles deeply while nuzzling my neck. "I make the rules here, Summer, but I'll fuck you quickly to take the edge off. Then you're coming with me because I won't be done with you!"

Blayze reaches between us and pulls out his engorged and impressive member before moving my bikini bottoms to the side. He rubs his length up and down my swollen soaked pussy, making me moan at the contact.

"Oh God, more," I groaned with my head flung back as he rubs my sensitive clit with his engorged head.

He lifts me slightly while continuing to lightly rub my clitoris with his finger and breathing into my ear. "I'm no God, little bird, but you *will* worship me." He slowly pushes his thickness into my slick folds, lowering me down on to him.

The pain mixes with pleasure as he pushes his way inside me, stretching me as he goes. Thank God my pussy's so wet, giving him the slickness he needs. Bit by bit he lifts me up and then down, on to his big dick further and further, as one finger keeps up it's pleasurable torture on my throbbing nub.

The feeling's almost too much to bear, it's so good and I feel so full. My pelvis finally meets his and when I'm filled with all of Blayze, I come undone, clamping around him and clawing at his shoulders as I orgasm so unexpectedly, biting my lip and moaning.

He clenches his teeth, jaw tensing and holding me still for a moment before he starts to move me up and down the length of him, and the pleasure is astounding. Has anything felt as good as having this gorgeous man inside me?

I regain my senses and start to ride him on the table, up and down, harder and harder. "That's it, little bird, take everything you need," Blayze rasps through our increasingly desperate thrusts.

He moves his hips ever so slightly and then his dick hits me in the right spot, the one that makes my toes curl and my eyes roll in the back of my head. I feel myself getting closer again, riding the wave of ecstasy.

I feel him tensing inside me, trying to hold on until I find my release once more. I'm so close. He uses his fingers to strum my clit just right, throwing me over the edge. I scream out his name at the top of my lungs, riding my orgasm out as I feel him let go too, his cum spurting into me, deep, and warm. Blayze rumbles low from within his chest, grasping my hips tight.

Trying to catch our breath, we sit here holding each other, my pussy still pulsing from my orgasm and his member twitching inside me, still mostly hard.

"Wow," I breathe out. "I really needed that."

Blayze chuckles darkly before squeezing my ass tight enough to make me squeal. "Yes, you did. Now we can go upstairs so I can fuck you properly."

My jaw falls open. "Are you serious?" I stare in shock. "You have more in you?"

"So much more, little bird. Let's get going before we get an audience." Blayze lifts me gently to sit next to him on the desk.

I jump down and straighten my clothes and then freeze, *my leg!*

I feel completely fine. In fact, I can't remember the last time it hurt in this room. "What the hell, Blayze? Why does my knee feel so good?" I roll my leg around and lightly jog on the spot, it's amazing and doesn't make any sense.

Blayze is already getting his shirt on and smiles at me, looking ridiculously handsome. "I told you I'd fix it."

Hands on my hips, I splurt, "I didn't think you meant with magic jizz!"

Now he's laughing out loud... at me. I'm not trying to be funny, I'm freaking the hell out. "Why are you laughing?"

Blayze comes over and with a genuine smile tucks my hair behind my ear. "You're so beautiful when you're angry." He kisses the tip of my nose. "I don't have *magic jizz*, as you so poetically put it. I healed you as soon as you kissed me. Let's just say I have the gift of healing and leave it at that. Okay?"

"No, not okay, I have questions?" I'm feeling a bit shell shocked.

Blayze leans down and sweeps me off my feet. Holding me with my legs around his waist, he nibbles lightly on my ear giving me shivers. "You can ask me questions after, but right now I need your pussy wrapped tightly around my dick again and I want to hear you scream my name a few more times. It's never sounded better than coming from your lips as you cum on me," he whispers in my ear.

He takes me over to a stairwell door that I've

never been to before and opens it. Once we're inside he reaches over to the wall where there's an eye mask hanging and gives it to me. "Put this on!"

"Oh, I see what you're into now," I joke, hiding my disappointment at not seeing what's on the next floor.

I put the mask on as Blayze adds, "You know exactly why you're wearing that. Mind you, I'm certainly not going to say no to a little of that kind of play."

I can't help but smile, I'm a little surprised by how fun and relaxed Blayze can be. I know I shouldn't be doing this but right now I'm having way too much fun to care.

He carries me up the stairwell and through a few more doors by the sound of it and after a while he comes to a stop. I hear beeps like he's pressing buttons and then he places me onto something soft.

"You can take your mask off now, little bird," Blayze voice soft and seductive.

Complying, I see a large, bright white glass room with no windows, filled with white, soft, opulent furnishings and I'm sitting on a very large four-poster bed. I bounce my bum up and down, the bed feels soft like a cloud.

"This room's luxurious but it seems just like a different kind of cage," I say, turning to Blayze as he takes off his clothes and places them on the back of a couch. My mouth goes instantly dry. Holy cow, he's hot! In this well-lit room, I see every gorgeous, hard line on his body, and he has many.

Blayze clears his throat at my inspection of his body, a sexy smirk on his handsome face. "We all have our roles to play here, Summer, whether we like it or not." Blayze walks closer to me stopping just far enough in front of me that I can still take all of him in. "Do you like what you see?"

"Is that a trick question? I pretty much just wet your bed with my juices looking at all of that." I wave my hand up and down, indicating his naked body.

Blayze comes to stand in between my legs, making me look up at him or stare at his dick right in front of me.

"Good, because I'm going to need you all wet to take me over and over again." Blayze's sexy rasp excites me further. "Do you think you can handle that, little bird?"

I feel myself squirming and heating up. Taking matters into my own hands, I lean forward and lick his cock from base to tip slowly, making sure to flick the tip slightly when I reach the top, tasting my own sweet juices from our last session. Blayze jerks his hips in response, obviously wanting more. I look up to see his eyes are hooded and filled with desire.

I lean down slightly and lick his heavy balls before taking one in my mouth and sucking lightly, his knees almost give out as I hear him moan and he grabs the bedpost next to me. "Fuck! What are you doing to me?" His deep voice shakes.

I smile up at him, "I thought you said you wanted me to worship you?" I whisper sultrily.

Then I take his other ball into my mouth and grasp his penis while sucking harder, slightly pulling on it and stroking him at the same time. Blayze growls and moves his hips in time with my hand.

"Do you want more?" I lick my lips and continue to stroke his velvet cock.

He just groans in response and I take the tip of my tongue and swirl it lightly over the tip before gliding his swollen head into my mouth, tasting us from earlier. I suck him down slowly and come back up again, I increase my tempo, taking him faster and deeper.

Blayze grabs the back of my head with both of his hands and starts to fuck my mouth. I open my throat to him and take him all the way to the hilt, letting him fuck deep into my throat. He groans and cries out, "Holy fuck, you're amazing."

Starting to harden even more he pulls out of my mouth and lifts me partly by my hair, Blayze throws me into the centre of the bed, crawling after me.

He pins my hands down above my head by my wrists and I open my legs to him. Blayze pushes his cockhead at my core and glides it into my soaking tight sheath in one swift move.

"You are so fucking wet!" Blayze grinds out, as he pushes in as deep as he can. "I'm going to cum inside you and then I'm going to flip you over and fuck you again."

Blayze holds my wrists with one hand and my hip with the other and begins to pound into me hard and fast. His pelvis rubbing against my clit as he does, driving me wild. I move my hips, matching his rhythm, driving myself and him to the edge again.

"Cum for me!" he demands as I start to tighten around him and just like that a gush of release is unleashed. I scream out bucking my hips at the overwhelming sensation of him still fucking me hard while I orgasm all over him. Unable to take it anymore Blayze pushes deep inside me, arching his back and crying out my name, as I feel him spurting deep inside.

We lay here panting, I look up at him and say smugly, "Now whose name sounds good?"

With an arched brow, Blayze leans down and kisses me hard. "Challenge accepted."

He abruptly pulls out of me and flips me over, pulling me up to my knees and pushing my head down, "Ready for round three, little bird?" Blayze slaps me hard on my ass.

"You can't be seriously ready to go again?" Incredulously, I turn my head to face him. He gets up on his knees to show me his fully erect penis, glistening with the remnants of both of our releases. "Holy shit, fuck yes." That's all I can say and I assume my position with enthusiasm.

This is going to be a long, wicked afternoon and I'm going to be sore tomorrow.

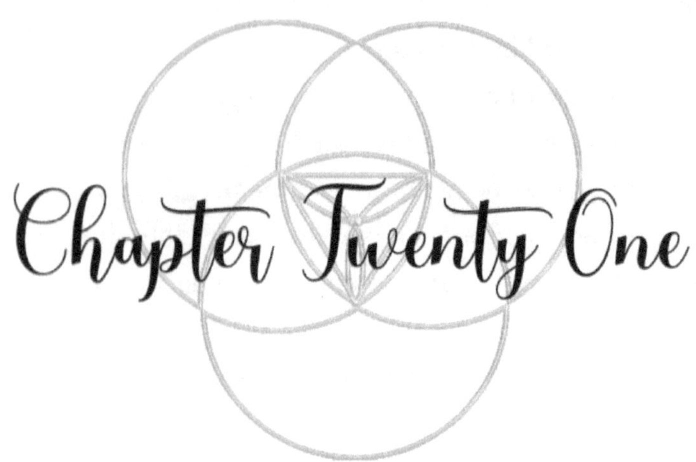

Chapter Twenty One

I wake up to somebody lightly stroking my hair and the first thing I think is that my snatch is aching bad, then I remember where I am.

I snap my eyes open to see Blayze smiling and looking down at me, already dressed and clean looking. I wonder how long I've been asleep.

"There's some dinner here for you to eat but you're going to have to munch it down pretty quick because it'll be curfew soon and we need to get you back on time." Blayze points to the table with juice and an omelet laid out for me.

Just like that, I'm reminded of my place here and where I stand. "Right, because I'm a prisoner. I don't know how that slipped my mind. I'm not hungry," I lie because I'm starving but I'm angry at myself and don't want anything but answers from him.

"Really? Because I was starving after our eventful afternoon. Don't be like this, little bird, you know the deal in this place." Blayze pulls at his sleeves.

I give him an obviously fake smile. "You owe me some answers, I believe."

Blayze flinches. "Is that what it was to you? Payment for answers I'll give you?"

"Like you give a shit, Blayze, we had a deal, starting with my leg. How did you do that?" My voice cold, I sit up in bed, not bothering to cover myself.

Blayze laughs and sits down. "I have healing abilities with some of my bodily fluids. Before you ask again, it was *not* magic jizz, I used my saliva to heal you when we kissed. I'm not human, Summer."

There's silence as I look at him waiting for a punch line and then I realise I'm not getting one. "This isn't a joke is it?"

Sighing deeply, Blayze grabs my hand. "No, it's not."

"What are you? If you're not human then you have to be something, right?" This is weird, I'm not sure I even believe him but how else do I explain my leg?

Blayze purses his lips like he's deciding what he's going to tell me. "I'm a shifter. Like the kind of things humans put in books, but we're different. This is very real, I can shift my shape as a man into one of an animal. Do you understand?"

I get up from the bed, my face hard. "I have to shower." I need some space because otherwise I'm going to freak out.

Blayze walks over to a door next to the bed and opens it. "There's a shower in there but you have to be fast, curfew is only getting closer. And, little bird..." He goes quiet before saying, "I don't want to hurt you. Please try to relax, there's a bathrobe in there that you can use to go back with if you want it."

I walk into the bathroom to shower, fully aware that he said he didn't *want* to hurt me, not that he wouldn't.

After washing myself clean and putting on the dressing gown, I try to wrap my head around this crazy situation. *Shifter?* I can't believe this is happening. Well, that made the confinement a little scarier, we need to get out of here as soon as possible. No wonder he's in charge here, he's not even human. It makes me wonder if the guys that work under him know.

I walk out of the bathroom and straight to the bedroom door, I turn and look at Blayze.

"Where is the eye-mask? I want to go now."

"I thought you might want to ask me some more questions, we could probably take five more minutes." Blayze takes a few steps toward me.

I sigh heavily, feeling exhausted.

"What more do I need to know? Will it change the fact that I'm locked in here as a prisoner? Or that I slept with someone who isn't human? Or that I'm probably going to die here and I can't help any of these girls escape the same fate?" I use my anger to hide the rising fear I feel at him being a shifter, my heart beats fast with my rising panic.

Blayze steps back again, apparently not expecting me to be as blunt as that. He opens and closes his mouth like he's looking for something to say.

I hold my hand up. "Don't bother!" I glare at him. "I don't want to hear it, let's go."

Facing the door I wait patiently before I feel a hand on my shoulder, his other hand goes around me to hand me the mask and I put it on immediately, not interested in looking at him again.

"Summer." Blayze squeezes my shoulder gently. "It's nothing personal." I stay quiet, not moving. "Do you want to know what kind of shifter I am?"

I reply simply, with ice lacing my words. "I don't care!"

I feel his head lean against the back of my head and he sighs in my hair before straightening. I hear the door open and he grabs me, lifting me into his arms, this time cradling me like a bride.

I keep my eyes closed, my body and face tense, I squeeze my jaw together and focus on the tapping of his feet as he walks, *click clack click clack,* down some kind of hall, through a few doors and down the stairwell.

As he opens the stairway door I hear someone inhale sharply, Blayze stops and places my feet on the ground. "Reid will take you from here, remember to walk fast, time's running out." Blayze removes my mask.

I keep my eyes closed and jaw tight until I hear him retreating back up the stairs. When I open my eyes, I see an angry Reid staring at the stairway door.

Not too nicely, I snap, "Get me the fuck out of here now!"

Reid swings his head to me, nods and guides me to the door, opening it and takes me down the stair-well. At the bottom I wait for him to open the door but he just stares at the lock. "What did he do to you?" He asks in a very scary and menacing voice.

I flinch, for the first time Reid frightens me, my

hackles rise all over my body. I get the feeling I should run but I stand my ground.

I put on the bravest voice I have. "Let me out now! You don't get to corner me like this, Reid. I don't care who you are, I'll fight you."

His head snaps up and turns around with shock on his face. He breathes in deeply before saying in a more normal tone, "Fuck. I apologize, I didn't mean to scare you." He shakes his head, rubbing his hand through his hair. "I was worried about you, that's all."

Reid steps towards me but I reflexively back up a step, he stops and puts his hands up, "I'm sorry."

"It's fine. Let me out!" I use a monotone voice.

He nods and opens the door. I all but run past him, push open the doors and speed walk to my room. I make sure to sit directly on my bed facing away from the door, which honestly is against my better judgement but I can't look at anyone right now.

"Summer? Please? What happened?" I hear from my doorway but I don't reply and I don't look back, I just lay down and close my eyes.

Eventually the doors close and the lights turn off but I know Reid's still standing outside my door staring at me. I'm too tired to care and in time I drift off to sleep.

~

I wake to the unbeatable fragrance of fresh coffee, that's the smell that dreams are made of. *Yum!*

I open my eyes and see a mug of fresh coffee right in front of me and it's attached to an arm, Baines arm, with a happy, ever-smiling Baine at the end.

"You know, a girl could get used to this view in the morning." I reach for my coffee with one hand and pull him down for a kiss with the other.

Baine gives me a sweet, soft kiss and a beautiful beaming smile in full dimple mode. "Bonnie, it would be my pleasure to give you this view every morning." The tip of his ears blush.

I pull him down for another kiss. "You're such a sweetheart, Baine, and you treat me so good."

He sits on the side of my bed and watches me sit up and drink my coffee but there's something dark in his expression.

"What's wrong, honey?" I sip my coffee and release a satisfied sigh.

His eyes light up at another endearment. "Nae a thing, my love. I'm just worried about you. Reid told me that Blayze took you yesterday and then returned you last night nae looking good. Did he hurt you, bonnie? I'm here for you, you ken that!" Baine has real worry in his eyes.

I look down into my steaming mug. "I really don't want to talk about it, Baine. Can we just drop it, please? Actually I wouldn't mind a bit of space from you guys for a couple of days, I'm feeling a bit overwhelmed by everything."

For a moment Baine looks panicked before he closes his eyes and breathes out. "Okay, if that's what you want I'll tell the others, but if you change your mind, please come and get me. I'll miss you."

"Yes, I know. Off with you then." I shoo him, he stands and starts to walk away, "Baine, thank you for my nice wake-up."

Baine smiles back at me. "Anytime." And with that he's gone.

I see Bell watching us and I wave her over with my finger to my lips to be quiet.

"Let's go to the bathroom," I mouth and walk past her.

We meet in the back, I go and whisper in her ear. "I have a plan now but you guys might not like it. We have to get out though, it's worse than we thought here. Tell the girls that we're definitely meeting after lunch."

Bell smiles wickedly. "Fuck yeah, bitch. I'm in, whatever it is."

Chapter Twenty Two

I watch as everyone goes down to breakfast before I head back to the bathroom, I need a bath to soak my aching body. Yesterday left me feeling sore all over, especially in the tender parts.

Soaking in the bath with my eyes closed I go over my plan in my head, refining what needs to be done. It has to be seamless and I can only hope that the girls are going to agree to this plan because it'll be a lot harder to pull off without them.

Next thing I know I feel my arm being washed gently with soapy hands and I open my lids to find Reid kneeling next to the tub, washing me tenderly.

"What are you doing?" Not sure if I'm angry that he's here or softened because he's being sweet. He continues down to my hand and takes it into his, washing it gently and lovingly. I snatch my hand back before he softens me further. "Stop, Reid. I asked for space," my voice snaps like a whip.

He leans over the tub with one hand on each side, hovering over me unaffected by my harsh words. "I'm not giving you any. Why should I?"

Sitting up, I put my face close to his. "Because you guys have taken everything from me and I don't belong here, none of us do. I'm so over feeling defenceless. I trained myself to always have my own power and to never let someone squash me down. Yet here I am trapped and sometimes I might want some fucking space!"

"What did he do to you?" Reid almost yells at me.

I duck under his arms and rise up so I'm standing in the bath. I put one leg up, placing my foot on the side of the bathtub. "He fixed my knee!" I shout pointing to it. "Wanna know how?" Reid flinches and I continue. "Wanna know why?"

Reid grabs my knee with one hand and my waist with the other, keeping me open so he can see all of my body. "Did he hurt you? Did he force himself on you? I could smell him on you!"

"Why would he hurt me if he healed me?" I spit back, "Why do you keep talking about my smell? I don't bloody stink! He did fuck me, though, over and over and over again. At least somebody did for a fucking change!"

With that Reid grabs my face and kisses me hard. "What, do you think I don't want to fuck you, baby? Is that it? Well I do. I want to fuck you so God damn hard that you scream like a bitch in heat. I want to cum deep inside you, claiming you as mine, as he did." He snarls into my mouth. "Is that what you want? Huh? You want me to fuck you? Do you want to be my bitch, Summer?"

He grabs my thigh and puts it over his hip as he lifts me by my ass out of the tub, turning me around and flattening me against the wall.

He kisses me passionately and bites my lip, hard. "Well, baby? What do you want? Fucking tell me." He grinds his clothed dick against my body.

"Fuck me, do it now! I'll be your fucking bitch, but you better fuck me hard, Reid. I need it!" I'm desperate to not think anymore and badly turned on by his take-charge attitude.

Reid pulls his pants down so fast that I barely register it and with one leg still over his hip, his dick is filling me in a heartbeat. It fucking hurts but I don't care.

"Summer!" Reid grinds out between his teeth. "You're *my* fucking bitch now, say it! Tell me you're my bitch. It's what you want, isn't it?"

Thank God he makes me so wet because he starts to pound his dick into me with a fury, fucking me so hard that my teeth chatter and I can't catch my breath. "Oh yes, fuck me, Reid. Hard!"

"Tell me! Say it!" He demands as he fucks me with ruthless, unforgiving thrusts. It's so delicious.

I grab his shoulders and tremble in his arms from the onslaught of pleasure. "I'm your bitch, don't fucking stop!"

Reid grabs my thigh and squeezes it so tight as he rams into me, I know I'm going to bruise. He reaches up with the other hand and pulls my hair, tilting my head to the side.

Breathing up my neck Reid licks me, tasting, nipping, and growling as he goes. I'm so overwhelmed with sensation and he's driving me crazy, my eyes roll into the back of my head and my cries of ecstasy increase.

I feel Reid thickening inside me, becoming more frantic and he growls low and loud, "Mine!" He bites me fucking hard where my neck meets my shoulder and I scream out as the shock of it gives me a mind-blowing orgasm.

Reid cums deep inside me again and again like his sperm will never end, raising my orgasm to new heights. How is he doing that?

"Holy shit!" I say shaking in his arms, his mouth

still clutched to me. If he wasn't holding me I would've fallen, my legs giving out from the pleasure.

Reid's mouth lets go and he licks where he bit me carefully as both of our orgasms subside. "I've got you," he whispers in my ear. "I won't let you fall."

He pulls back and strokes my hair to one side before turning me gently in his arms. I'm completely jelly as he places me gently back into the still-warm water while softly washing the sweat from my face and body.

"Are you okay?" His forehead wrinkling with worry. "I didn't hurt you?" He washes my shoulder where he bit me and it feels a little tender. He didn't break the skin, thankfully, but it will bruise.

I sink in deeper feeling pretty satisfied. "You bit me pretty hard but apart from that I'm fine."

He looks down regretfully. "I'm sorry, baby, I never wanted to hurt you."

"It's fine, I like rough sex anyway. That orgasm was fierce, my legs might never work again," I chuckle.

Reid looks up and smiles at me warily. "So it was worth the bite?"

I laugh. "Hell yes!"

He looks relieved now. "Lean forward and I'll wash your back."

Doing as he says, he uses my sponge to soap up

my back in smooth circular motions, carefully kneading my back muscles as he goes. I sigh. "I really do need some time though, sex or not, but thank you for not denying me anymore. I don't know why you guys were being so mean to me."

Reid stops what he's doing and gently kisses my back. "You'll find out sooner or later." He sighs, sounding slightly forlorn.

"Sooner would be better, Reid," I return.

He gets up and comes around to where I can see him. "For you, maybe," he mumbles. "I have to go back to work, baby. Can I just ask you one question?" I nod. "He didn't force you? You did want Blayze to do that, right?" His face genuinely concerned for me.

"Yes, Reid, it was consensual. Is that going to be a problem?" I ask with a small smile on my lips to reassure him.

Reid looks utterly relieved, his shoulders dropping as they relax. "No, baby, I just wanted to make sure that you weren't taken advantage of. You know where we stand with sharing you. I would've preferred Blayze not be a part of this but I'll respect your wishes. We just want you to be happy."

"Let me be very clear, I agreed to have sex with him but he's not a part of whatever it is that we have going on. That was a one time only deal and it won't be happening again... ever again," I exclaim vehemently, creasing my head and tensing my jaw.

Reid tenses again. "Why, what happened? What am I missing here? Am I kicking his ass or not?"

I'm warmed by his protectiveness. "I don't think you can kick his ass." I laugh.

Apparently that was the wrong thing to say because his eyes go dark again, he steps back and grinds out between clenched teeth, "If he hurt you, just watch me. Don't ever belittle me or my ability to protect you. It's highly offensive to someone like me, Summer, and I won't have it. I'll have to fight him to prove myself to you."

I sit up fast, splashing water out of the bath, panic rising in me because I know that Blayze isn't human and I don't want Reid to get hurt. "That's not what I'm saying, I know you're super strong and can protect me. It's just that he's your boss and I don't want you to get into trouble."

"Why are you afraid?" Reid's eyebrows shoot up.

I shrug. "I'm not." I lie.

"Yes, you are. Are you afraid of me or him?" Reid's clearly angry. "Either one is unacceptable."

"I'm afraid of this place, Reid. I'm afraid of getting rewarded because you do something in my name. I'm afraid of you losing your job. I'm afraid I'll never go home. I'm afraid that I'll never see my kids again." I stop there as I start to sob, unable to keep it inside anymore. "Why is this happening to me? I want my kids back, I want to see them, and hold them, and know that everything's going to be okay."

I look up at Reid through my tears. "I'm human, Reid, not a robot. I can't hold all of my hurt in forever and I *am* hurt. I'm hurt and scared and tired and angry." Burying my face in my hands, I cry my heart out. *I have to get out of this place.*

Reid rubs my back while I cry, standing naked in the bath. He makes soothing noises and tells me that he's here and that it'll all be alright but I know it won't.

"Oh my goodness." I hear Shylo shout from the door. "What's wrong? Should I call someone?"

Reid turns to Shylo with his hand still on my back. "Can you please take care of your friend? She's having a hard day."

"Okay." Shylo looks at Reid warily like she thinks he might be somehow responsible for it.

Getting out of the bath and covering myself with a towel, I convince the two of them that I was just feeling overwhelmed. Wiping the lingering tears from my wet cheek, I smile weakly, insisting that they both go on with their day. Shylo reluctantly leaves me here to get dressed.

Reid comes over and kisses me softly on the neck.

"Whatever you say, baby." He walks out the door with one look back and a heart-melting smile. "Summer?"

"Yes, Reid?" I say with one brow up and my head to the side.

"You are *mine* now." Just as he goes to leave again he stops and says before he disappears out the door. "I love you."

I must look ridiculous, wrapped in a towel, tear-stained cheeks, staring at the door with my mouth wide open.

He just said *that*. I barely know the man. Where the heck did that come from?

Well, that just adds another layer to my already fucked up life, sure no problem. What's one more mind fuck?

Chapter Twenty Three

After lunch I meet with the girls in the cave, as usual, to tell them my plan and get them up to speed with everything.

"Before you start with this escape plan that you've hatched, you have to tell us what on earth is going on with your leg?" Mia finally blurts out. I knew she was struggling to contain herself. "You told us to wait and we did, now what's the story?"

I nod and it's fair enough, they've been super patient up until now. "Somebody healed it. I need to prepare you because this isn't going to be easy to hear or accept, it might sound crazy but it's real. I even thought about lying to you guys so that you didn't panic," I say, my arms wide and going for complete honesty.

"Just tell us, Summer, we can handle it. Is this why you were crying earlier?" Shylo asks me sweetly. She places her arm around my shoulder for comfort, I lean into her slightly in appreciation.

I sigh knowing this is going to suck. "Partly, yes. I went to see Blayze the Overseer." Filling them in on why I was there and that Blayze healed me after the two of us got carried away, and how he proceeded to tell me that he wasn't human but a magical shifter instead.

The cave is quiet for what feels like forever until Bell bursts out in laughter. We all look at her like she's crazy.

"Why on earth are you laughing?" I look at Bell wide-eyed.

She calms herself down before chuckling out. "I'm sorry, I thought it was something way worse, I can work with a shifter. So what? We're being run by a freak. I don't know if you figured it out but Boss sounded pretty freaky to me, too. Human or not, they're all nuts."

I shake my head, unable to stop a smile from forming. "I worry about you sometimes." Smirking at my odd but brave friend, I continue, "My issue is that it makes this place a touch more dangerous, don't you think? I don't know about you but I feel a real urgency to get the hell out of here."

All the girls agree, even crazy-pants Bell.

"The next thing I want to talk to you about is the only plan I've been able to come up with for escape." I take a moment because I don't really want to tell them about it. "I don't think you guys are going to like it, because I know I don't."

"Consider us warned. What is it?" Mia's impatience was showing.

"I know how to get through there." I point to the hole in the roof of the cave. "I need you to be honest when I ask you this, really honest. Would you be capable of climbing a rope all the way to the top without any assistance?"

Bell replies without delay. "Nope, not a chance."

"No, I can't do that," Mia adds.

Shylo just shakes her head.

"Yeah that's what I thought. No offence, because it would be too hard for most people. This is the part where you might not be so happy with the plan," I start. "I know how to get a rope made up to get out of here and I can climb out, but I'll have to go alone. You guys will have to trust that I'll get us all help. I know that's asking a lot, and I hate the idea of leaving you guys behind but it's the only way. I won't be able to do it without your help and support though.

"I know how to navigate, I'm fast, and I'm capable of doing this, but I'd like you guys to be on board with it." I finish, hoping that they'll be okay with it.

"Absolutely," Shylo answers immediately, nodding. "I would've slowed you down anyway, I think this is a much better idea."

Bell throws her arms in the air dramatically. "Well shit! Who knew my fat ass would leave me in an actual hole one day. You better move that tight ass, fast as fuck, bitch."

Mia wrings her hands nervously while pacing. "I guess I don't have a choice. I really want to go home, Summer. I know you'll come back for us. It's just going to be hard watching you leave us behind." She breathes in deep. "We'll help you. What do you need?"

I feel so touched by their faith in me. "Group hug, ladies, we need it." We all come in for a squeeze.

"There are a few things we need and a few things we're going to have to do to pull this off." Getting back to business, I focus. "Shylo, you're the tallest so I'll leave you in charge of the branch. Have a look around the trees, in them and on the floor, see if you can find one that's about one and a half metres in length and about the thickness of the centre of a toilet roll. Be careful that you aren't seen. When you find one, bring it in here and hide it at the back, just in case someone else comes in. Do you think you can do that?" My gaze directed right at her to make sure she understands.

Shylo nods and smiles. "Yes, I can totally do that!"

I turn to Mia. "Would you be okay being the lookout or guard distractor for each of the mini-missions? You can watch out for Shylo and then watch out for Bell and myself when we try to pull off ours."

"Not a problem, that seems easy enough." Mia smiles confidently.

Looking at Bell with mischief in my eyes, I ask already knowing what her answer will be, "Are you ready to steal some shit?"

"I was born ready." Bell laughs boisterous. "What are we stealing?"

We all laugh at Bell's enthusiasm to do dangerous shit.

"I fucking love how excited you are." I chuckle. "We need seven towels. I can use mine as one, maybe we can find the rest left behind in the bathrooms. I think it's best to leave yours alone so it doesn't look like you were involved."

"Pish! That's easy," Bell says.

I nod, scratching my head. "True enough but we have to make sure nobody sees us between where we find them and the cave, that's where it'll get more interesting and Mia will have her hands busy keeping us as clear as she can."

I pace while I continue. "We need to get all the pieces, bring them back here without being seen and then we have to make shit. What I was thinking is that we do one thing a day so we don't raise suspicion and we aren't rushed. Day one- branch, day two- steal towels, day three- make the rope, day four- attempt escape. What do you guys think?"

Bell shrugs, "Yeah, sounds good."

"How do we make the rope?" Mia taps her chin in thought.

"Good question, you know the edges on a towel? We need to pick away at the stitched edging until it's weakened and then strip the strong edges off. The rest of the towel will be too weak but the edges are strong enough to make a rope out of and I'm really good with knots so I can secure them properly. Does that make sense? I'll be showing you on the day anyway. I'll do the first one so you get the idea," I explain to the girls.

Shylo claps happily. "This is really exciting, it's a solid plan and you'll be able to go for help. Yay!" It's sweet that she has so much faith in me and I really hope that I don't let them down.

"Wait, wait, wait!" Bell throws her hands up, "Don't get too fucking excited. We have no idea what's waiting for her up there. Be careful and don't do any stupid shit, Summer."

"I've thought about that, too. I'll do my best to get to help but there's always a chance something could happen to me. I'm pretty hard to catch though." I smile reassuringly, putting my fists up and throwing some pretend punches for humour.

Mia comes over to me and hugs me, not convinced by my bravado. "Be safe, please."

"Why don't we all go and do something fun in the games room, take our mind off what's next and just take a day to do some fun things together, we've earned it," Shylo suggests tapping our shoulders in a friendly gesture.

Agreeing, we take off to have some no stress time before shit gets real again.

Chapter Twenty Four

Day one went without a hitch; Shylo found the perfect branch, no one was around and it was just out of view of the big hidden window. Success!

Today is day two, we've decided to hit up one level at a time. Level's two and three we'll check during breakfast, four and five during lunch, and then we're going to get anything left during dinner.

In level two, Bell and I find two towels left lying in the bathroom, we grab one each and casually head to the waterfall, like we're going swimming, no one stops us or thinks anything different about it.

After that, we go to the level three bathroom but it's spotless, nothing's out of place. Apparently, they have an OCD girl on this level. I'm not going to touch anything because it'll be noticed.

Then we rush to the dining hall for a quick breakfast. So far, so good.

At lunch we check our bathroom first and find two towels left behind. I grab mine as well and give one to Shylo, one to Bell, and one to Mia. "I'll go check the fourth level and meet you there."

"Are you sure?" Mia looks concerned about me going on my own.

"Yeah, it's fine. I can make two towels look like one if I have to. I will just scrunch one inside the other," I say, reassuring her. We all head off in our chosen directions.

I only find one towel when I get to the fourth floor bathroom, but we only have one left to get, which we can pick up from anywhere at dinner time.

As I start walking towards the exit of the accommodation area, Salvatore walks in, stopping dead in his tracks when he sees me.

"I'm not following you," he states defensively, his hands up in a submissive gesture and I smirk at him. "I'm just doing my rounds."

I smile at him and approach, I get up on my tiptoes and pull him down to give him a soft kiss on his cheek. "I know, Mr Big." My soft voice and hand that caresses his jaw and tugs gently on his full beard, has him relaxing.

His arms wrap around my waist and he lifts me up, kissing me properly on the mouth, tasting me. "What are you doing here?" he asks in his low baritone voice as he puts me down.

"Stealing a towel." Figuring it doesn't mean anything to him, I go with a half-truth. "Mine was too wet to use and I found this one just lying in their bathroom. Got a problem with that, Sir?" I smile defiantly.

He slaps me on the ass, hard, groping my left cheek with a tight squeeze. "Mmm... I think I do." His sexy low baritone full of mischief.

"Really? Well, Sir, what are you going to do about it? Punish me?" I jokingly taunt.

Apparently the joke is on me because he bends over and lifts me over his shoulder, carrying me further into the room.

"What are you doing?" A happy squeal peels out of me.

He slaps my ass again but harder this time. "Showing you what I do to naughty girls."

Oh boy, do I get wet fast at that. I feel my pussy clench at his words.

Salvatore carries me into the meditation room

and puts me down before turning and locking the door behind him.

"Are you worried I'm going to try to escape my punishment, Sir?" I decided to play along with the sexy new game.

He chuckles darkly, turning to me. "This will give us a little privacy."

Salvatore goes over to the mat, turns to me and sits down with his legs in front of him. "Come here and get on your hands and knees across my lap so I can give you the spanking you deserve!" He demands, stroking his beard, eyes dark and hooded.

I sashay over to him and assume my position. "Good girl, now open your legs a little bit wider," he instructs and I do. "That's it."

I feel his large hand move my bikini bottoms to the middle of my ass cheeks like a G-string and slowly, tenderly rubs my ass in steady circles. *Slap*, I flinch and squeak as he shocks me with a stinging spank to my ass.

"Quiet, don't move!" Salvatore commands me.

He goes back to rubbing me softly before, *slap*, another one, *slap*, again, *slap!*

My nether regions pulse and soak my bikini bottoms as Salvatore's hand glides them down to my knees. Slowly and softly he brushes the insides of my thighs; up and down, up and down. Getting so close to my pussy but not directly touching it.

Slap! "Oh!" I cry out, unable to keep quiet any longer, my juices sliding down my inner thigh. "Please!" I beg.

"Shhh... quiet and take it like a good girl," Salvatore coos in my ear and I hear in his husky voice that he's affected by this. "I like watching your ass go from white to red, my handprint on you, smelling your sex as it gets wetter and wetter for me." *Slap!* "That's it." *Slap!*

I hear him groaning deep in his chest and the next slap has his fingers tapping hard on my swollen pussy. I shout out, not in pain but in ecstasy. I know if he does that again I might cum, the mixture of pain and pleasure too much.

"You like that huh?" *Slap!* Right on my wet folds and my clit, making me arch my back and moan loudly. *Slap!*

"Oh fuck, don't stop!" I scream loudly.

He stops and whispers in my ear. "Don't stop, what?"

I arch as far as I can, opening my legs more, pussy pulsing. "Please, Sir, don't stop." My voice is no more than a moan now.

Slap! Slap! Slap!

"Fuuccckkkk!" I scream as I cum hard. He keeps tapping my clit over and over, and I squirt through each tap. "Holy shit!"

Next thing I know Salvatore's behind me, slipping his fingers inside, scissoring and stretching me. It feels so good to have his fingers deep within my tight sheath.

"I want more, Sir. Please fuck me, fuck me hard! I need you inside me." My tone desperate and needy, rocking my hips up and down.

Salvatore growls behind me and then thrusts his huge dick hard into my pussy making me cry out in pain at the huge size of him impaling me. "Take it!" He snarls in my ear. "You want it, so you'll take it!" Then he thrusts again, pushing that monster deeper inside me, again and again until he reaches the hilt.

Thank God I'm sopping wet because I need that lubrication, his dick is no joke.

Salvatore gives me half a minute to adjust before he pulls all the way back and then thrusts in deeply again. This time it feels fucking amazing, pleasure taking over. His dick touches areas of my pussy that have never been touched, it's so big and hard.

His hand reaches around to grab my throat, choking me with enough force that I can barely breathe. With the other hand he grabs my hip as he thrusts hard, every time! Hard and deep, lifting the front of my body so that I'm arched off the ground as he owns my body and takes what he wants from me.

His heavy balls slap on my clit as his dick rubs my g-spot and it drives me over the edge again, but I can't scream because he has my throat just tight enough to stop the noise from escaping. I clamp around him, cuming and moaning while he continues with his relentless thrusting and I can't get enough.

Two more times I cum like this before he pulls me to his body, turning my face and kisses me hard. Salvatore bites my lip so hard it bleeds and says between fierce thrusts, "You... are... fucking... mine! Do you hear me?"

I nod weakly as he grabs my nipple and twists making me cry out in a mixture of pain and pleasure.

Salvatore starts to become more frenzied as my pussy spasms again, making more of a mess on the floor. He cums so hard I can feel the spurts burning my insides as if it's hot, searing me in a delicious way. Shot after shot his seed fills me while he holds me against his body, both of us shaking and panting, our sweat mingling and the musky scent tickles my nose.

We collapse, laying down on the ground in a spooning position with Salvatore still deep in my body. It's intimate and kind of nice, considering how rough and animalistic that was.

Salvatore nuzzles me behind my ear, his arms wrap around me tight and pull me in as close as I can get. I feel him smelling my hair and breathing me in. It's really touching that this giant, tough man can have this little moment of intimacy and tenderness.

I get a strange feeling coming from him. "Are you vibrating?" I ask, a purr-like feeling coming from his chest, a low soothing noise.

It stops immediately. "No! What do I look like, a sex toy?" He immediately stopped himself. "Don't answer that."

I giggle because I can't help myself, he already knows me too well.

"As much as I'm loving these cuddles, and I *am* by the way, this is a nice side of you. I have friends waiting for me at the rock pool." My tone light-hearted and satisfied.

With a devious chuckle from Salvatore he says, "I didn't hear you complaining about being punished."

I move so that he's out of me and I turn to face him. "That was good too, I'll have to make a note to be a bad girl on occasion." I give him a sweet kiss.

"On occasion? When are you not doing something naughty? I should've punished you a long time ago, back when you gave me cheek in the beginning!" He snorts.

I laugh. "You couldn't because this beauty slayed that angry beast with a kiss." I smile and wink.

Salvatore's face turns serious and he just stares into my eyes, stroking my cheek with the back of his giant hand. "Yes, she did," he simply states with his heart on his sleeve, then gets up and fixes his clothes.

"Can I ask you a question?" I look at Salvatore as I fix my own clothes. "Are you guys the reason that the jerk guards have been leaving our floor alone?"

He sighs deeply. "Partly, but also because, unfortunately, they found easier targets to deal with. We can't protect everyone, but we try. At this place about a quarter of the workers are anti—." Salvatore stops suddenly.

I frown at him with my hands on my hips. "Anti what, Mr Big?"

He looks at me. "Women." Somehow I feel like he was originally going to say something else.

"Pfft! Fuck those losers, I wish I could stop them. If I see them I will." Grumbling, I pick up my towel.

Salvatore puts his hands on my shoulders, frowning down to me. "You'll do no such thing, I want you to stay away from any woman-haters, okay?"

"Are you actually asking me or telling me?" My eyebrows raise at him.

"I'm asking you, but there's only one answer I'll accept," he says with a smirk on his gorgeous face.

"Ha ha ha, very funny. We'll see. I gotta go, Mr Big, give me a kiss and wish me a nice day." I bat my eyelashes at him sweetly.

He smiles, shakes his head, and kisses my temple before unlocking the door and strolling through.

Chapter Twenty Five

The next day we find out that Bell took Mischa's towel because she thought it was super funny that she wouldn't have one for the day. They'd become unfriendly with each other during our time here, which is unfortunate but it'd be impossible to expect forty confined women to all get along with so many different personalities.

I show the girls how to strip the towels properly and do all of the knotting myself, making sure I secure it very carefully so that it'll support my weight tomorrow. We all leave feeling super confident about our plan.

"Ladies, I'm going to do this during lunchtime and I want all of you to be in the dining hall when I try it. It's important that none of you gets incrimi-nated in the breakout when I'm gone. Alright?" My tone grave as we leave the cave.

"You can't be fucking serious? What if you fucking fall and break something else? No bloody way," Bell protests.

I look at her dead in the eye. "I need to concen-trate so that I don't fall. I need to be alone and I need to know that you guys are safe or I'm not doing it. Do I make myself clear? While I appreciate your concern, now's not the time to be stupid."

"Fine. Fuck off, then, but you better not fall." Bell sulks, I know that she's rough around the edges but I also know that her heart is huge and she means well.

I pat her on the back. "I'll be fine." Then I look at all the girls. "I promise to do the best that I can."

They all nod, wish me luck, and then we go our separate ways for the rest of the day.

I wake, feeling nervous but excited, I always loved going on task. There's a hype that fills my veins before a mission that's addictive. The only thing that's slowing down my excitement is knowing this is the end of the boys and I. While I know they're technically the bad guys, I can't help but feel something for them. They were there for me many times when I needed them, but this is for the best. I have to get home to my kids and protect the lives of these women first.

~

Lunchtime comes and the girls gather together to leave, all turning to look at me as they go, showing their silent support.

I'm wishing that we had shoes at this point but I have tough feet and a strong will, so I know it won't slow me down too much.

I get to the pool and take my clothes off, leaving me in only my bikini, I hold my clothes above my head and wade into the water, making sure to keep my clothes as dry as possible in case I'll be stuck outside overnight once I'm out. I have no idea what the weather's going to be like out there. I'm hoping sunny and warm because the hole always shows nice weather.

Getting to the other side of the cave, I pop out and dry myself with the leftover towel pieces before getting dressed again. It's time.

Looking up, I re-measure in my mind the angle

that I need to throw the stick. It shouldn't be too hard, this kind of thing is child's play for me.

I pick up the branch, aim and throw. *Boom!* First time, piece of cake.

Grabbing the makeshift rope tight in my hands, I use my legs, wrapping them around the towel to hold my weight. The trick is to use my strong thighs, not my arm strength. My legs start to push me up toward the top, the water from the waterfall strengthening the fabric even further, helping my ascent.

It doesn't take me much to get to the top and I pull myself up onto the stick and out of the hole. Not a problem at all, just as I expected.

I look around, taking in my surroundings. This isn't good.

Looking towards the facility, there's an empty helipad next to a massive glass observatory room and below that is the roof of the garden, which I can see into. Behind the facility is an island which is just a big pointed mountain with nothing but sea around it.

I move to the side and look down at the right of Threshold, it's an upside-down, triangle-shaped building, just like I thought but it's over the sea and built in between two islands. The rock walls I've seen inside the building are the sides of both the islands, there's one in front of me... and *fuck it*... the one I'm standing on.

I'm on a fucking island!

I look around. Maybe if I climb to the top of this one I'll see something different.

I run and I climb with all my might, desperation fuelling me to the peak of the island. I stare in wonder and horror at the vast empty ocean beyond.

The only thing I can make out is an oddity to my left, it's an isolated storm raging out at sea, on an otherwise clear blue day.

My stomach drops and I heave my breakfast onto the ground. My life is fucked. What the hell? I gasp deeply and wipe my mouth, my breath panting and shallow from fear.

Obviously the only way on and off this fucking place is by helicopter. Luckily, I know how to fly one. Unluckily, there isn't one here. They would probably just shoot me down anyway. There are big turrets coming from the glass tower and an anti-aircraft gun on the top of the building.

Rubbing my hand over my mouth, head wrinkled with worry, I walk over to look at the storm and drop to my knees, defeated. *What now?*

Suddenly, I hear vicious growling coming from behind me and turn to see a large rusty coloured Wolf and a huge Grizzly Bear staring me down.

"Oh good, I'm dinner too!" I mumble, trembling

and deflated. "Just fucking eat me and get this over with," I snap at the snarling Wolf, with zero fucks left to give.

The Bear behind him just huffs and sits on the ground with a heavy thud.

Growling more, the wolf slowly prowls toward me, lips peeled and teeth bared, salivating from the mouth. I'm scared out of my mind but I have nowhere to go and there's no way I can fight them off. "Hurry up will you, I'm over this fucking shit," I grumble and squeeze my eyes closed. I wait and wait...

"Lass, are you seriously just going to sit there and let a Wolf eat you?" I hear in an unfamiliar Sottish brogue.

My head pops up and a naked red-headed man is staring at me with his hands on his knees and his head cocked sideways like a dog. He looks kind of like Baine, only buffer and neatly trimmed, with a tattoo of a Wolf on his chest.

I gape at him and stutter. "W..w..what?" I feel confused. "Where's the Wolf?"

The Bear gets up and swipes at the back of the man's head, but he ducks quickly to miss it. Turning around, he says to the Bear, "Oh come on, get off it. As if I'd stay like that. Look at her. She almost wet herself." His hand pointing in my direction and I'm instantly offended, I thought I took being eaten pretty well.

"I did no such thing," I quip to the deranged man's butt that's currently in my face. "Where are your clothes? You're winking at me!"

He turns, stunned. "I'm what?" Horror written all over his features making me scoff in amusement.

"Your ass is fucking winking at me, put it away or face it somewhere else." With an attitude I flare my hands to shoo him away, feeling disgusted.

He laughs. "Oh aye, you can look at this instead then," he says turning around and showing me a clear shot of his limp dick. I grimace.

The Bear then starts huffing and rolling around on the ground.

"Is that Bear laughing at us?" I point, stunned.

Naked guy snorts. "You better bloody believe it, he thinks he's some kind of comedian. It's nae funny you numpty, get off the ground or I'll send you to the circus where you belong. We have to take the princess here back to her castle."

"Ha!" Pops out of mouth loudly. "If that's a castle then I'm a fucking raccoon."

"Whatever you say, love, you could be for all I care. Now get up and let's go, my willy's getting cold," he demands, walking off and kicking the still laughing Bear as he goes. "Fucking numpty!"

I can't help but bite back at that. "Is that your excuse for the size?" I get up, brush myself off and walk over to the Bear hesitantly. "Are you trained, Mr Bear?" Bringing my hand up to touch him.

He stops laughing and stares at me abruptly. I freeze and he moves toward me so quickly that I can't move. *Smack!* The Bear gives me a high-five. What the fuck?

The Bear goes back to his huffing laugh sound and follows the naked guy, I sigh and go along with them because we all know that I have no other choice.

We approach the glass observatory and the naked guy turns back to the Bear. "What do you think they'll do to her? She kens too much now."

I turn to look at the Bear and instead see a large sun-kissed God of a man with shoulder-length dark blond hair and sapphire eyes.

"Not sure. Hopefully it's not too bad, she's hilarious." He laughs while patting me on the back.

I stop. "Wait!" They look at me. "You guys are shifters too?"

"Too? What do you mean *too?*" The Bear man asks, with a lot less humour in his voice.

I put my hands in the air with a huff. "Well Blayze told me he was a shifter but I just assumed it was only him." I'm super frustrated. "How many people here are shifters?"

"You hear that? Bloody Blayze knows the lass. What's your name?" The Scottish naked guy asks.

"I'm Summer, who the fuck are you guys?" Frustration layers my words.

Scottish guy steps back shocked. "Did you just say, Summer? Baine's Summer?"

"Yes." I'm a little more excited now. "Do you know him?"

His hand wipes down his face slowly like he's drained. "Aye, I'm Derryn, Baine's twin brother."

"Shit is getting real!" Bear guy says excitedly, grabbing my hand and kissing the back. "I'm Kenneth, pleasure, my lady. So you're the girl who has his brother all in knots. Well, I'm not disappointed, he's got good taste. Strong, sexy, independent, and fearless. You thought you were going to get eaten back there and you just said *'fuck it, eat me'*. Ballsy! I like it. It does make your self-preservation a bit low though."

I look at him in astonishment. "Who are you people?" Then it hits me and I look at Derryn. "If you're a shifter than that means Baine can turn into a Wolf too, doesn't it?"

Oh my God!

They both look uncomfortable for a minute.

"Do you think we're in trouble now?" Kenneth asks Derryn with a worried frown.

He shakes his head, still looking tired. "Dinnae ken but we need to go inside now and see Blayze, he's going to want to talk with her." Pointing to me regretfully. "Let's go."

Chapter Twenty Six

Derryn and Kenneth take me past a bunch of gaping males, whom I now assume are all shifters, which makes me very uncomfortable.

We head to some stairs and go down one level and to the end of the hallway where there's a large recognisable door.

Kenneth knocks hard and steps back. The door opens to show me a surprised, and not at all happy, Blayze.

"What have we here? Is there a reason that Summer's walking around without a mask on? The windows are all open." Blayze gruffly faces Kenneth.

He shuffles his feet uncomfortably looking for words when I cut in. "I've already been outside so I don't care about your fucking windows, Blayze.

You've got some explaining to do!" I shout out, pointing my finger at his chest.

I feel a hand on my shoulder. "Lass, you had better calm down, you cannae talk to Blayze like that." Derryn sounds strained and tries to pull me back.

I push his hand off and turn to give him a filthy look. "Don't fucking touch me, Derryn. I don't care if you're Baines brother, I *will* kick your ass if you do it again."

I hear Kenneth chuckle under his breath which he stops the second I look at him. "Don't you start, chuckles!" My finger now pointing in his direction.

"Put your finger away, little bird, before you hurt yourself. Come inside and tell me what happened." Blayze's calm voice is directed at me, before saying more sternly to the boys. "All of you!"

We enter the room and I instantly notice that the white walls are gone and are replaced with a wall of windows as I stare out at the vast, beautiful ocean.

"I see your cage is more open today, Blayze. How nice for you!" I spit as he comes up behind me.

Blayze tries to put his hand on my lower back but I quickly move out of the way and turn to face him with a scowl, making it pretty obvious that he's not to touch me right now.

Blayze sighs. "So that's how it's going to be today,

is it? Fine." He turns to look at the boys before asking them, "Tell me what happened?"

They both look at each other and then look at me before Kenneth steps forward. "We found her on top staring out at the ocean. When we approached her while we were shifted she told us to eat her. I've never seen anything like it."

Blayze turns slowly back to me with his eyes narrowed. "Why in hell would you do that? And how exactly did you get there?" He sounds both pissed off and shocked.

I put my hands on my hips. "What the fuck else can I do? I'm going to die in this fucking place anyway, why wait? You're never letting me go, I can't get off this God forsaken place and I'm never going to see my kids again," I huff out my frustration. "I went through the hole at the top of the waterfall, it was easy enough."

"The waterfall? Of course, that's why you've been spending all your time there." Blayze looks out the window thoughtfully. "How did you get up?"

I roll my eyes at him and blow out a breath. "I made a rope from towels and climbed out, obviously. It's not like I flew."

I hear a snort and both Blayze and myself turn to see Kenneth covering his mouth and looking down.

"Is there something funny, Kenneth, that you'd

like to share with us?" Blayze addresses him with a scowl.

Kenneth shakes his head and then quietly apologises. "I'm sorry, Sir. I've just never imagined a female like this and I've never heard anyone talk to you like that before. It just shocked me. I'll keep myself quiet now, Sir."

I look over to see Blayze's hard eyes on mine. *Uh oh.*

"Summer, was your intention to do that as soon as your leg was healed? Did you use our interaction to get out of here sooner?" His tone reeks of warning.

I shake my head. "I was always planning to escape, but that's not a secret around here. I did tell you that myself, you guys just didn't think I would or could. I wasn't, however, planning on trying so soon because I would've liked to get all of the girls out with me."

"Why did you decide on leaving earlier than planned, after I healed you?" A curious glint in his gaze.

I look him dead in the eyes and say with conviction, "Because I found out that you were a shifter and I wanted to get the fuck away from here as quickly as possible to get help for the girls. I was scared and the threat in this place increased exponentially, in my opinion." I look at the other two men in the room and back. "And on top of that I'm now aware that all of you are shifters. We're just fish in a bowl here, we have no way to leave, and are at the mercy of monsters. What am I supposed to do with that? What the fuck do you want from us?" The last sentence sounds a bit hysterical, even to me.

All of the men flinch at my use of the word *monster*. I should feel bad but I don't. This is screwed up.

"What are we, food? Entertainment? Did you just feel like culling some of us for fun? Some of the guys have been calling us pets, are you going to try to train us and turn us into your fucking puppets?" I shout in outrage. "I am no one's goddamn pet. You might as well kill me now and get it over with because I'm not playing your fucked up game!"

Blayze steps towards me with his hands up and cold, harsh eyes looking down at me. "We aren't going to kill you and you aren't our pets. You need to calm down now or I'll show you just the kind of *monster* I can be," Blayze grinds out at me. He's obviously enraged by my outburst.

Suddenly, there's a hard knock on the door before a voice shouts in, "It's Leon, I've been made aware of the situation."

Both Kenneth and Derryn turn towards me, a

look of worry creasing the corners of their eyes and their lips flatten out. What's that about?

Blayze sighs deeply, looks down and says to me quietly, "You knew the rules." Before walking to the door and opening it, showing a smug-looking Leon on the other side.

"Why are you here, Leon?" Blayze's stoney voice is cold and uninviting.

Leon looks past him and straight to me with a malicious smile. "I was informed of one of the pets escaping and being led here. I was sure that you'd want me present for the interrogation," Leon replies with a feral look in his eyes, licking his lips.

Blayze raises his posture higher. "There's no need for that, she's being escorted back downstairs momentarily. While I appreciate your observance, in the future you'll wait until you're summoned by me, understood?"

Leon's smile drops from his face. "Of course, my apologies. May I ask how you'll be dealing with *its* disobedience?" *Its!* Like I'm nothing more than a scrap of meat to him.

"I'll be following protocol, as instructed by Boss. Anything else, Leon?" Blayze positions his body to make sure Leon can't enter his room.

He shuffles uncomfortably. "No, not at all. I look forward to this evening." Leon nods his head slightly at Blayze and then looks at me one last time with a shine of excitement in his eyes and a sneer on his face before turning and leaving.

"What does that mean?" Suddenly I feel nervous from the look Leon gave me, making my blood run cold, and freezing my veins in fear.

Blayze turns to Kenneth and Derryn while pointing at a pile of towels. "Cover yourselves and then take her to the boardroom, call for someone to escort her to her room." He turns to me. "You'll be confined to your quarters for the remainder of the day. Don't fight this or it'll be worse for you all. Do you understand me?"

"Are we going to be rewarded?" I feel fear trickle down my spine at the way he's avoiding eye contact with me.

"Do you understand?" Blayze repeats in a very scary tone.

I nod, and he moves aside, gesturing to the door and looks back out the window.

"Come on then, lass, let's get you back." Derryn's tone sympathetic, with his junk now thankfully covered.

I walk over to them and as we leave through the door Blayze grabs my arm firmly and says to me in a low voice, "You did this, not me." With that he lets me go and closes the door behind us, his words leaving me shaken to my core.

I look at Derryn with questioning eyes but he avoids my gaze and guides me down the hall with Kenneth at our backs. The boys are quiet the entire way to the boardroom. When we enter Kenneth says something quietly into an earpiece and before long Simon comes through the doors.

"Hello, pet," he sneers down at me.

I look back at the other two and see them leaving through the door without looking back. This doesn't feel right, my heart starts to gallop against my ribs.

"Come on, I don't have all day," Simon snaps when I continue to stare at the now-closed door.

I turn to him with cold eyes, sauntering past him and down the stairs, trying my hardest to not let him know of the turmoil of emotions riding me. Simon takes me to my room and locks the door behind me, chuckling to himself as he walks away. Nausea rolls in my stomach. I have a *really* bad feeling about this.

Chapter Twenty Seven

My day ticks by relatively uneventful except for the deep well of anxiety in my stomach. The longer I sit in my room the worse it gets. As time passes and nothing happens to or around me signifying 'rewards', the more nervous I feel. I don't know what's going to happen or when, but this quietness isn't right. I just know there's more.

About an hour before lights off, people start filtering into their bedrooms and eventually I see Bell, Shylo, and Mia.

I knock on the glass and Bell turns to look at me

with an audible, "Fuck!" escaping her lips before the others see what she's looking at.

They all come running over. "Are you okay, what happened?" Shylo cries through the glass with her hands pressed against it. I can see a mixture of fear and worry in the girl's eyes.

"I'm so sorry," my voice breaks from the emotion filling me. "There's nowhere to go, we're on an island in the middle of the sea. They caught me quickly."

Mia chokes out a fearful sob. "Rewards?"

The others look at her with a renewed fear and then look back at me.

"I don't know what's going to happen, but Blayze said he'd follow protocol. I've let you guys down and there's nothing I can say but I'm sorry." I try to hide my own fear and show them just my remorse. "There's more, I found out that all of the men here are shifters. I saw a man-bear and a man-wolf so far. None of them are men, they're something else entirely." I make sure my voice is low so that no one else overhears me.

There's a silence between us that stretches much too long before Bell claps her hands with a 'that's enough of this shit' face.

"No fucking worries, mate! We'll be fine, it's not your fault, so stop your whining." Bell tries to change the mood. "It's all good, let's just carry on like normal. Maybe the toss bags will just enjoy our fear of the unknown, I mean the man-imals haven't actually hurt us yet, so I'm sure it'll be fine. They wouldn't know what to do with a pussy in a pussy buffet, let alone us lot. Unless some of them are actual fucking pussy cats, that'd be a hoot. Come on, cheer up and let's fuck off to bed." She chuckles at her own joke and I can tell by her face that she's picturing a man-cat.

The girls nod at her with fake smiles and slowly go to their designated cells. Fear still permeates the air.

I go to bed feeling nervous but exhausted from the stress of today.

Bam Bam Bam!

I'm blasted awake after what feels like minutes of being asleep by the loudest, heaviest music. The lights are strobing on and off, on and off, endlessly. What the fuck is happening?

It's so loud and bright that I cover my head with my pillow but it doesn't help. I can't even hear myself screaming.

Then it hits me! I know what this is, I've been through this before. *Shit!*

This is an interrogation technique that intelligence uses to torture people, breaking them down emotionally, psychologically, and mentally.

Bam Bam Bam!

This is going to be a long night.

The sound and lights go on and on, screaming in my ears so loud that I feel like my ears will bleed and my head will explode. My skeleton shakes from the bass and force of the volume, the lights are unending torture for the senses. God, please make it stop.

After what feels like ages the room goes dark and quiet with the only sound being the screaming inside my ears and the whimpering of women all around.

"Summer!" I hear Mia cry out between her sobs, the buzzing in my ears making it hard to make out.

I squeeze my eyes shut and shout loud enough to get to quite a few girls. "This will go on all night, we'll get through it, hold on."

The wailing of women all around are saying things like, "Please, no!", "Why is this happening?", "No more!".

My eyes fill with tears and they stream down my face, this is all my fault. I did this; just like Blayze said.

Looking at my watch's light glow it says 10:08 pm and I know I need to sleep as much as I can, whenever I can, because I'm almost positive that they're not done with us yet.

Just as I feel myself slipping into sleep, I'm once again assaulted by sound and light.

Bam Bam Bam!

I usually like death metal and heavy music, but this is too loud—too hard. The screaming of Alex Terrible digging straight into my mind, shoving into every corner of my consciousness until I can't hear myself thinking anymore. My jaw is so tense that it hurts, my eyes squeeze shut, desperate for relief, and my hands hold my ears, rocking my head back and forth.

One sound bleeds into another, the light blasting into and behind my eyes. There's no escape from this, there feels like no end, just light and sound and *eternity*.

Blackness surrounds me once again, my brain is throbbing with tinnitus and it hides any true silence from me. *Buzz!* How did I get through this last time? I look at my watch and it's 10:31 pm. Please, no!

I close my eyes feeling my body shaking, my back sweating, and my breathing laboured and forced. My closed eyes still see the remnants of flashing lights as I squeeze them shut, hoping, praying for sleep.

I'm too wired to try to sleep now. Fear overriding my senses, keeps me awake and trembling. My adrenalin is spiked so high that my body feels foreign to me. After half an hour of staring at my watch and trying to calm myself from the rising panic, it starts again.

By the fourth round, I no longer care about the cries of the people around me. I've rolled into a ball. I'm a shaking, sweaty, exhausted mess. My body isn't sure if I should pass out or be hypervigilant.

I've never been religious but I find myself praying. Praying for silence, darkness, peace. Praying for it to stop. Praying for help.

I can't handle this anymore, why isn't anyone helping me? Where are the guys? Why would Blayze do this to me? Can this kill me?

I know that logically I can get through this, but as the night goes on I find myself doubting everything I once knew, everything that I once was. Logic no longer exists, only sounds, lights, and fear.

Time becomes irrelevant. I start to pass out after each torture, my body not being able to handle it anymore, my mind shutting down. At one point I urinated on myself without even realising it.

The torture goes on forever with no end in sight and only madness for company.

The lights turn on and stay on, there's only silence and our doors click unlocked.

Nobody moves, not a soul, the silence lingers on with only the ringing in our ears surrounding us. I remain in the foetal position, twitching and feeling like I'm going to vomit. I want to die.

Footsteps are heard banging down the hall in a run, heading closer towards us and then Baine is flying to my doorway. I squint my eyes against the bright lights above with no expression on my face or in my heart. He stops frozen in his tracks, staring at what's left of me, with his hand on the doorknob.

I slowly look up at his face and see his eyes fill with unshed tears. He slowly steps towards me as if not to frighten me and then kneels at my side.

"Bonnie…" Baine's voice trembles. "I'm here now, I'm so sorry. We were locked upstairs."

He places his hand on my shoulder and I flinch at the contact. I'm still so shaky, so tired, I can't think right.

"It's all over now, there's nae more, it's just me and you." He keeps his hand on me for reassurance.

I know I stink, I know I look like a mess, but I don't care. I don't care about anything, not anymore. I should never have had to go through this again, every time feels worse than the last. It's not something you get used to, the trauma just multiplies. It's my mental hell.

Arms slide under me and Baine starts to carry me somewhere, I don't know where. My eyes are closed and I just flop in his arms, weak and tired.

I hear a sharp intake of breath and Baine says vehemently, his voice holding a terrifying edge that I've never heard before, "I dinnae care who or what you are, if you touch her right now I'll kill you." A deep, menacing growl vibrates through his chest and he stalks me away from whoever it was.

I must have passed out again because the next thing I know both Baine and I are in the bathroom. He lowers me onto a seat in a shower stall, I sway slightly but manage to lean on the wall as he turns on the shower.

Baine faces me and quickly undresses me, his gaze filled with love and regret. He pulls me into his arms and we're both under its warm spray in seconds. He's still fully dressed and doesn't seem to care. Baine washes my hair gently and soaps my body from head to toe with delicate movements that I didn't know the man was capable of making, as I just stand there, leaning against the wall, eyes glazed over.

After he's done, Baine disappears for a moment, reappearing with a towel and dries me off with care. He then cradles me in his arms and carries me back to my room where he sits me down on a cleanly made bed. I don't question who made it because I don't care.

Baine precedes to dress me in silence, puts me into a clean nighty and tucks me into bed. He gets in behind me and wraps me protectively in his arms, feeling his breath on my cheek and temple as he peppers sweet kisses there. Baine's chest rises and falls with his steady breathing, his arms tight and warm around me, he falls asleep and finally I'm safe.

Chapter Twenty Eight

I start to wake and feel warmth flooding my back and a hardness pressing into my ass. Baine. I open my eyes and turn to face the gentle, loving man at my back.

Blinking a few times to clear my head, a heaviness settles on me that I can't shake. I look at Baines relaxed face as I take in every beautiful feature, the laugh lines etched around his eyes, his unruly hair of fire, and his shapely lips that are slightly parted as he breathes lightly in his sleep.

The corners of his lips start to curve into a smile, flashing me his sexy dimples and I look up to his now open eyes staring at me with love and adoration.

His features start to fill with concern as he takes

in my heavy expression and his arm tightens around me, turning me fully into his embrace. "Are you ok, bonnie?" Baine talks quietly, not wanting to startle me, which I'm grateful for because my head pounds and my ears are still buzzing inside my head.

I don't want to talk, my mouth doesn't want to move, so I just stare at him hoping he'll understand.

Baine leans forward and kisses my forehead lightly, breathing me in deeply. "I've got you now and I won't let you go until you want me to." His whispers meant to reassure me.

I snuggle closer to him and breath in his musky, manly scent. I feel him shudder under my nose as I gently trace his neck. I kiss him softly, needing to be closer to him, feel him, taste him. A sudden desperate desire to feel something other than what I do right now fills me.

Baine seems to see this and he lowers his head to mine, hesitantly taking my mouth with his, brushing his lips against mine.

I let my tongue slide out of my mouth and softly trace his lips with it. He parts his lips slightly and I suck on his bottom lip, nipping it and nuzzling my body as close as I can to his.

"What are you doing, my bonnie lass?" Baine looks down into my eyes, searching for something, an answer he needs. Instead of giving him one with words, I lean up to his mouth again and kiss him harder, more demandingly.

It seems to be all the answer he needs as he meets my demand with no hesitation. Baine kisses me back hard and sure, filling my senses with all he feels in that moment; love, desire, regret.

I wrap my arms around his neck and lift my leg over his hip, deepening the kiss further with a hint of the desperation I feel.

Baine grabs my ass and grinds himself against me, showing me just how much he wants this.

I pull him over me, hoping he'll understand and he does. Settling himself between my legs, he rests himself against my core, allowing me to rub myself on him shamelessly.

I go to unbutton my top button when Baine stops kissing me and places his hand over mine. "I dinnae think that's a good idea, we should stop. It's been a big night for you and you dinnae want to make a decision you'll regret later." He's giving me an out, but I'm not interested in an out. I want an in. I need to forget for just a moment.

I lean up and kiss him again, resuming the task of unbuttoning my nighty. He lets my hands go and groans into my kiss, grinding himself even harder on my core, finally giving in to the temptation that is *me*.

Pulling my arms out of the nighty, I'm totally

exposed, except for my underwear which Baine helps me shimmy off.

He looks down at me with reverence and fire before taking off his own clothes and slipping the blanket over us both, resuming his place in between my thighs.

Kissing me deeply, I stroke my hands over his bristly cheeks and wild hair, really feeling this man in front of me. Needing to be as present as I can to get rid of the memory of the night before.

I tug his hair lightly and he pulls back to look down at me, our eyes meeting in a way that feels soul deep.

"I love you, lass, with everything I am, I do," Baine lovingly says to me before taking my mouth passionately, stroking his cock up and down my folds, my core fills with wetness.

His cock glides over and in my wet lips, rubbing my clit as it goes. I moan and rock my hips, working myself up until I'm consumed by a deep need to be filled by him. Baine teases me, letting the head of his cock put pressure on my opening without breaking through, before sliding up to my clit again. Never entering me, just driving me closer and closer to the edge.

I groan deeply, turning my hips up towards him as

far as I can, trying to get him to impale me, pleading with my body for more. Baine reaches down with his hand to stroke my clit and then positions himself, slowly pushing inside me, driving me crazy with need.

He moves his fingers to cover my swollen, throbbing nub with my own juices, circling it and working it in a way that makes my pussy clench around his cock as he maneuvers it inside me.

"Fuck, you're so tight and wet, it's like heaven and hell." Baine groans as he slides deeper inside me, filling me to the brim with his thick pulsing cock.

Holding himself still inside me for a moment, feeling me twitch and throb around him, he continues to work my nub closer to climax.

Baine rubs my clit in a rhythmic circling motion driving me further and further to the edge. My hips tipping up and my toes curling before I feel the coiling release and my body quiver with ecstasy around his dick.

Baines thick cock starts to slide in and out of me, deep and slow, while I ride my orgasm out, stretching it out to a whole new level.

When I start to come down from my high, Baines thrusts increase in tempo and force. My legs wrap around his waist, he guides himself in and out, so deep and hard that he feels like part of me, all the while kissing me passionately. Our bodies push hard into the mattress, filling the room with the rhythmic creaking of my little bed.

Baine brings his kisses to my neck, laving me with his tongue, and whispering sweet nothings into my ear. Making love to me and holding me in a way that I haven't felt in a long time.

He moves deep inside me, his pelvis rubs along my clit bringing me back to that ecstatic state of being, that edges me to and from another orgasm. Baine starts to thrust more erratically inside me, his cock thickening and stretching me even further.

Lowering his fingers to my nub again to increase the pleasure, bringing me so close to orgasm that my body shakes. He whispers in my ear, "Cum for me, bonnie. Cum on my cock." And I do. So fucking hard that I cry out.

Baine leans down and bites my shoulder, hard, increasing the pleasure with pain. He fucks me harder until I feel him squirting his juices inside me, over and over again, filling me up with his seed.

His mouth let's go of me and he licks delicately at where he bit me, just like Reid had done. Kissing me tenderly on the neck, jaw, and then mouth. "You're mine now. I'm never leaving your side as long as I live," Baine vows and then kisses me deeper.

I'm so satisfied that we stay like this, with him still inside me, until I drift back off to sleep.

I wake up screaming in the dark. I sit straight up, confused and shaking. Looking around me I can't see anything, am I blind? My eyes search for anything else in the darkness, panic rises inside me, memories assault me, and I take deep breaths to calm myself.

The faint light of my watch catches my eye, it reads 2:00 am. I slept through, it was just a nightmare. I'm okay, it's okay, I tell myself over and over again.

I hear tapping near me but I don't know where it's coming from. Muscles tensing I look around, frightened again.

"Calm down, it's me." I hear from the dark in a man's deep and familiar voice. "You're alright, you have to be quiet though, go back to sleep."

Who is that?

I stare into the dark, my heart still beating fast. I can't think straight, my fingers grasp at my face in fear.

"It's Reid, baby, please calm down and go back to sleep or you'll get into trouble." Reid's voice is quiet, worry threading his words.

"Please, baby, lay down. We're not going anywhere, you're safe. Shhh, now sleep."

That voice was different from the first one...Mr Big? They're both here, I'm alright, I sigh and lay back down.

They'll keep me safe. With that last thought, I drift back off to sleep.

Chapter Twenty Nine

"Good Morning, ladies." Blasts from the speakers in my room, rousing me from slumber.

"As I am sure you are aware, the day before yesterday there was a breach in one of our house rules and rewards were given to remind everyone to please refrain from trying to break those rules in the future," Boss starts in a polite and friendly tone, one that instantly rubs me the wrong way.

"However, my lovelies, I have come to the decision that because of this unfortunate event where somebody left Thresholds walls momentarily without permission, it opens up an opportunity for a new development that I am sure you will appreciate. I will be introducing large windows around Threshold to help open the atmosphere in the hopes of further cooperation in the future. I am positive that all of you will enjoy the new view that you'll receive of the lovely ocean that surrounds this island getaway." Obviously I've ruined his plan of our isolation being a secret. Now that I have seen outside, there's no need to hide it anymore, I suppose.

I hear gasps from some of the ladies, which isn't really surprising. I'm sure I wasn't the only one hoping to run away.

"As there is only one form of transportation off the island, there is no need for you to leave the safe confines of Thresholds luxurious walls. I hope that going forward we have a more stable, and calm, cooperative nature being spread throughout the accommodation, filled with all the luxuries that I have very graciously provided to you."

This is a fucking never-ending nightmare. I'm never going to see my kids again, this is our lives now. We're pets... in a cage... kept by monsters.

"Continue enjoying all of the wonder and luxury that Threshold has to offer and I will be in touch. Remember, the house rules are provided to you for a reason and it would be unfortunate if you were to ignore such reasonable requests. Have a glorious day."

With that, he's gone and nothing but silence remains.

I choose to stay in my bed with my body facing away from the glass wall, the people behind it and the world remaining to me. I have no need to leave or communicate this time, and plan to stay in bed whenever I can. There's nothing for me here.

I ignore the people that come and go, keeping my eyes shut from the world and my mouth empty of words.

Baine, Salvatore, and Reid visit with no avail. They bring food and drink, I consume the bare minimum that my body requires. I'm not hungry, I have no appetite or need for anything but rest.

Staring off at nothing with glazed eyes, my mind replaying my life on repeat. My soul feels heavy, heart empty of all but sorrow, the pressure of my reality pushing me down with it's bulky weight that I can never lift. Honestly, right now I don't have the energy to try. Mental darkness is a scary place, an insatiable well that devours any room for light. Depression is a strong foe when you have no more will to fight.

Sometimes I feel Blayze standing behind my wall, watching me. I ignore him too. I don't know why he's there, bathing in my misery. He's an animal, a monster, they all are. Just watching their pet, wounded and tortured, what entertainment I must be.

I don't care, I just want to rest.

Three weeks roll by with nothing exciting happening. All the girls are quiet, joy and laughter are gone from this place. All that's left are shells of former women, walking around and doing their basic needs. They pushed us too far and the illusion of freedom is dead.

I've remained in bed most of the time and haven't said a word since that night, not because I can't talk but because I have nothing to say, and nowhere to go.

I'm broken, I'm betrayed. In hindsight, I don't know why I adjusted so well to begin with. I suppose it was surreal in the beginning, we were given all these normal things to do and no negative aspects except for not being able to leave. We could kid ourselves that it was all okay, all just temporary, but that's different now. We've changed. We know just how stuck we are and that monsters hold us. That we'll never leave, that they'll hurt us, that we'll probably die here.

Now it's real, now we can see.

I wake to feel someone picking me up. Turning my face I find Reid, straight-faced and not looking directly at me. When he turns me I see Baine, and Salvatore in my doorway, they're looking anywhere but at me as well.

I lay limply in Reid's arms, I have no desire to hold him, to even lift the heavy stumps I wear. I close my eyes again hearing Salvatore swear under his breath as Reid carries me somewhere, I don't check to see where. I don't care.

Reid stops and drops my feet down unceremoniously, I guess I have to stand. I open my eyes and see we're in the gym. What used to be two white walls are now two big, clean, transparent windows looking out at the endless sea, making the room look open and dazzling.

Reid lets go of me and walks away to lock the gym door. I watch him nonplussed as he comes striding back, eyes hard and narrowed, as he takes hold of me to shake me roughly, my head tumbling from back to front.

Grimacing, I try to step out of his grasp but he holds my shoulders tight and states firmly, "Snap out of it, Summer!" I look up at him as my head rolls. "It's been long enough now, no more. You're better than this."

He stops shaking me, still holding me in a

punishing grip but I don't really know what he wants me to say so I just stare at him, eyes wide, feeling numb.

"Let her go, Reid." Baine steps closer to us. Reid turns to growl low at him, baring his teeth, and Baine takes an involuntary step back.

They stare at each other for a moment before Reid growls again and Baine lowers his eyes, it's then I remember that my men are animals too. I wonder why I'd never noticed it before, their behaviour has always been predatory one way or another.

"What are you?" My voice barely rasps out from lack of use. They all snap their eyes at me in shock. I clear my dry throat and try again, staring up at Reid. "What are you?" It comes out clearer this time, my mouth downturned and clearly unhappy.

Reid's startled by my question and looks away from my penetrating gaze. I turn to look at the other two, neither of them able to face my question directly either, following Reid's example.

"I asked you a fucking question," I try to shout but my voice comes out as a croak. I raise my hand to stroke my sore throat. "What the fuck are you? Because you're not like me, I don't know what the hell you are." I raise my voice, anger growing within me for the first time in weeks. The betrayal of what they've done to me, seeping into the core of who I am and raging inside, setting fire to my heart, to my words, and to my very being once more.

I step back out of Reid's hold, shrugging him off. I look around at them with accusation in my eyes. "Let me guess, chicken or pussy?" My voice is now a yell. "Because none of you had the balls to tell me that I was *fucking* an animal."

Reid's head snaps up at that, enraged, "I'm more than an animal, Summer, and you know it. I'm a shifter and I'm proud to be one. I'm an honourable male and you're lucky to have me," he growls out.

"Holy shite!" Baine mumbles, shaking his head at Reid.

Reid shoots him an angry look too. "No, Baine, fuck this. I'm an Alpha, a Chieftain of my people, and the female of my choosing should be proud of me." He shoots off throwing his hands in the air. "Instead, here I am pleading with a woman that hasn't talked to me for three weeks and then calls me an animal."

I look at him blandly, untouched by his rage. "Was I misinformed? Do you not turn into a type of beast? Did you not just growl like one?" I ask, straight-faced and without sympathy. "Was I told wrong that you shift into something other than a man? Or am I confused about you telling me about it before you became intimate with me? Please enlighten me with the mistake I made."

I stare into his eyes, one eyebrow up waiting for him to correct me, and knowing that he can't. He just stares back, swallowing hard, his Adam's apple bobbing with the action.

Baine steps up closer to me. "Bonnie, you met my brother Derryn and ken that he's a Wolf shifter, as am I. I dinnae want to lie to you about anything and you ken that too. I also dinnae make love to you until after you ken it," Baine addresses me softly with his arms open and eyes sad. "I will tell you anything that you want from now on, I swear it. My allegiance is to you, bonnie, only you. I swear to never lie again, you have my word."

"Baine!" Reid snaps at him.

"Fuck off, Reid. You may outrank me but she's mine and I'll nae bow down to you when it comes to her, nae ever again." Baine moves to my side, he turns fully to look at me, placing his hand on my waist warily and I let him. "What do you want, lass?"

"I want to go home!" My words are simple but deep.

Baine nods. "Aye, then you'll have it. I'll find a way to take you home if that is your heart's desire."

Salvatores deep voice fills the room. "It's not that easy Baine and you know it."

Baine doesn't take his eyes off me while replying.

"I ken that, Salvatore, and I dinnae care. I'll get her home even if you two dinnae help, I'll find a way."

I put my hand on his stubbly cheek and he closes his eyes at my touch, leaning into my palm. "You would really do that for me?" Incredulously, I gaze at him.

Baine smiles, eyes still closed with his dimples popping out. "Aye." He kisses my palm softly and looks back into my eyes. "I love you, dinnae you hear me when I told you that? I only say what I mean."

I wrap my arms around his neck, grateful that I found somebody who really does care what happens to me. I promise myself that I'll give us a real try, regardless of how weird this is, because I owe him that much. "Thank you," I whisper in his ear.

Hearing a huff I turn to see Reid with his hands on his hips, eyes furious.

"If you have a problem with me, Reid, then leave because I never deserved this and you bloody know it. You have no right to get shitty with me, I've done nothing to you. If your pride is too big for your heart then bugger off because I'm not here to stoke it," I say moving towards him with my finger pointed at his chest. "Clearly you're not who I thought you were. Now unlock this door, it's time I got my shit together."

Salvatore stays back for most of the conversation

and doesn't influence me one way or the other regarding him, which is surprising because he's usually full of opinions. Not today though apparently. Seeing that Reid isn't moving, Salvatore comes over and opens the door for me, standing in front of it just before I leave to block my way out.

I look up at him with a deep sigh, waiting for another fight. "Yes, Mr Big?"

"Reid's an Alpha Wolf and a Chieftain of the Wolves, that is why he's a high ranking guard here. Baine's an Omega Wolf, that's why everyone likes him and he usually tries to keep the peace. I'm a Dragon and I don't live with a pack, I live alone in the mountains and I like my solitude. I came here because I wanted to find my Kindred, but never thought I actually would, not really because it seemed too good to be true. You *are* my Kindred, Summer! It might not mean much to you but it means everything to me. Dragons don't share and yet here I am. I am a Dragon of fire, one of the fiercest of the Mhanu race, and I'm feared by everyone here, except for Blayze. Yet you have brought me to my knees," Salvatore says all of this loud and clear, giving me eye contact the whole time. Shocking me he gets down on his knees in front of me and when he speaks it's even deeper than usual, while bowing his head. "I *am* an animal. I can't change that, but please don't leave me alone again. I promise to be a worthy male for you."

The room is silent and my mouth is agape, staring at my giant man, brought to his knees in fear of losing me. I don't know what to say but I'm truly touched by his gesture. Of all things, he's a Dragon, I suppose in a weird way that makes sense.

Getting on my knees in front of him, lifting his chin up until he looks at me again, I search his eyes before leaning forward to kiss him softly. Salvatore groans into my mouth and kisses me back; a kiss adorned with love.

Pulling back and catching my breath, I say, meaning every word, "Let's figure this out one day at a time, but you've got to help me get out of here."

Chapter Thirty

he girls and I are lining up for lunch, we talk and catch up after me being M.I.A for a few weeks.

Mia and Bell were the first to start trying to go back to normal, with Shylo not far behind. My guilt for being responsible for their torment had kept me from socialising for fear of seeing their pain, as well as my own, mirrored back at me.

"At no time have any of us thought of you as being responsible for what happened," Shylo explains kindly with her arm around my shoulder. "This would've happened eventually, one way or another. Please stop taking all of the blame for it. It's not your fault, it's their fault for doing this to us."

We all have a group hug and move up in the line

until we're at the buffet. Baine sees me and comes around to take me in his arms. We are no longer hiding what we have with each other, there is no point. Plus he brings me joy in this joyless place.

"Hello, my bonnie lass." Baine crushes my lips with his.

The girls hoot and holler at us, with Bell saying a crude comment or two.

I shove him off playfully, his dimples in full sexy mode. "Get back to work, Baine, and get me a feed." I use a fake stern voice, earning me a gorgeous laugh.

"Aye, I'll get right to it," he says with a salute and a slap on my ass.

We're all laughing still as we take a seat and Mia just looks at her plate with a green face.

"What's wrong, babe?" Bell rubs her back gently, concern in her voice. "Are you feeling crook again?"

We turn to look at her and she nods her head slowly, rubbing her stomach.

I grimace in agreement. "I haven't been feeling well either. Plus, I'm exhausted all the time and just can't get my energy up."

"Oh no!" Shylo cries out with her hands on her cheeks. "That sickness we were told about, what if you two caught it? Have you been taking your pills every day?"

I grumble. "Yes, the boys would come and force

them down my damn throat every night. You could be on to something though. I did go out on the surface and we spent a lot of time in the cave where the local air would have gotten in."

I look at Mia. "We should go down to the Doc just in case, don't you reckon?" I ask, a bit worried about how awful we feel.

She nods looking even more green than she did before.

"Alright, we'll go after lunch. Try to eat something to keep your strength up." I take a bite of my lunch.

We all decide to go to the medical centre together.

"Hey, Salem," I wave as I walk through the door and see the gorgeous blond standing there.

He turns with a big smile. "Hi ladies, what can I do for you on this lovely day?" Salem uses his usual cheerful voice.

Bell goes up to the desk. "Here's how it is, pretty boy. We think that Summer and Mia have caught that sickness you keep warning us about so you had better fix them with something because I'm not dealing with this place without my bitches in it."

Salem just looks at her for a minute like he's trying to decipher what she just said, so she clicks her fingers in front of him. "Chop, chop, we haven't got all day!"

"Uh... yeah, sorry. So you're not feeling well?" He turns to us looking a bit confused.

I smile at him. "Yeah I'm feeling pretty shit and Mia's feeling worse than me. Is there any way we can see the Doc together?"

"Well, you both have the same doctor." He scratches his cheek thoughtfully. "Let me go and ask."

Salem talks to Dr. Orion and comes back to us saying that it's fine. While Bell and Shylo stay in the waiting room, Mia and I go and see the Doc.

"Good day to you ladies," Dr. Orion greets. "Take a seat and tell me what's going on with you both."

Mia starts. "I haven't been feeling well. I've been throwing up and just can't keep any of my food down."

"Hmmm, that's not good. What about you, Summer, are you the same?" He faces me.

"Not exactly. I feel a bit sick, but for me it's more that I'm really run down and super tired. I've been sleeping non-stop but I don't seem to have any energy, no matter how much I rest." Feeling frustrated, I release a huff of breath. "I was wondering if it could just be my depression, or something like that, because the rewards really did a number on me, but our friend Shylo reminded us that you guys were worried about that weird sickness. It's better to be safe than sorry. Is there a way we can rule that out? I'm mostly worried about Mia though because she really doesn't look good."

Dr. Orion nods as I talk and takes it all in. "The best thing I can suggest, if you want to be 100% sure, is by having a blood test done. We have all of the stuff here so it'll only take about an hour to get the results. How does that sound? Then you can come back, we can look at the results and go from there," Dr. Orion suggests.

"Sounds good to me. Mia?" I look at my pale friend who nods meekly.

We get our blood taken and head off for an hour. We go out to the garden and look out of the windows and up at the beautiful blue sky. The walls and roof in here are now completely transparent except for the back one with the hidden window to the board room.

It really is a mixture of beautiful and terrifying at the same time. All the vast ocean ahead of us, going into a seemingly endless horizon.

The only thing to note out there is the same crazy storm that I saw when I was on top. How is that even possible?

"Has that storm been there the entire time?" I ponder aloud.

Bell snorts. "Yeah, it's weird as shit right? And no one will tell us fucking anything."

I think about what Baine said to me earlier about answering my questions. "Come with me."

When I arrive in front of Baine in the dining hall he was just heading out. He gives me one of his heart-stopping smiles before he takes in the look of determination on my face. "What's wrong?"

I take his hand and squeeze it. "I have some questions, are you ready to be honest?"

He looks at the girls and then at me. "Aye, I said I would."

"What's that storm?" I don't waste any time and jump straight into it.

He flinches and then hesitantly says to me, "It's the Bermuda Triangle, lass."

We all gape at him in shock.

Bell steps forward. "What the fuck? We're in Bermuda?"

He looks at me without saying anything. "Baine? Are we in Bermuda?" I question on a hunch that it's not that simple.

He shakes his head. "Afraid not, bonnie," Baine

sighs and then continues. "We're on the other side of it, the side that the planes and boats pop off to, lass."

"What like a black hole of sorts?" Shylo's voice is filled with wonder. She's not looking scared, just fascinated.

"It's nae that simple. I'm going to get into trouble for telling you this, just so you ken," Baine quietens, obviously hoping I'll tell him to stop, but I won't because I want to know, I need to know. He sighs even deeper, rubbing his free hand down his face. "This is a parallel world, lass, and that's the door. You can only get through a certain way or you get lost."

I put my hand to his prickly cheek. "Be very clear here, honey, what are you saying? We aren't on Earth anymore?" The words come out very slowly, my mind rebelling against what he's trying to tell us.

Baine looks at me apologetically, turning his face to kiss the palm of my hand. "That's right, welcome to Rathe!"

We all look from him to each other before Bell breaks the silence. "Holy shitballs! I didn't see that one coming!"

All of a sudden I'm feeling sicker than I did before and right on cue Mia vomits on the ground.

"Oh shite, I'm sorry, lass." Baine put an arm around Mia. "Come and sit down, I ken it was a bad idea to tell you."

After sitting Mia down, Baine calls Buck over to clean the mess as he rushes to get her some water. Returning with a cold glass, Mia sips at it and rests the cool drink on her head, just as Tyrese comes around the corner.

When he sees Mia he comes rushing over. "Are you okay, peach?" He gets on his knees in front of her.

She mumbles a "No" and leans on him for support, his arms encapsulate her and he tenderly rocks her from side to side. "You need to go to the Dr," Tyrese purrs in her ear.

"We took her before," I interject, noting how sweet they are together, I guess I'm not the only one that picked up some feelings while I was here. "We have to go back soon to get our results, actually." I look at my watch. "We should get going now."

Baine looks at me confused. "What do you mean *our* results?"

"No big deal, we're just checking to see if we caught any illness since being here. I guess it makes sense now that we could catch something unusual since we aren't on Earth," I consider in deep thought.

"What?" Tyrese almost shouts looking at us.

Baine groans and Tyrese looks at him with wide eyes. "You told them?" Tyrese blasts Baine.

"Aye I did, I'm not keeping anything from

Summer. If she asks me a question then I'm gonna tell her the truth." His explanation is steadfast and unapologetic.

Tyrese whistles low. "Ballsy!"

"Alright, fellas, enough chit chat we've gotta go." I get up. "Are you alright to walk?" I look at Mia.

Tyrese leans down and picks her up. "I'll carry her down," he says, without hesitation, before she can answer and starts to stalk swiftly away.

I laugh lightly. "Bye, sweety." I put a soft kiss to Baine's cheek before I scurry off behind them.

Entering the medical centre Dr. Orion is already out at the desk waiting for us, he smiles until he sees Mia being carried in.

"What happened?" He comes over to us, concern written all over his face. Fuck, this can't be good.

"She's not well at all, Dr. Orion," Tyrese's voice has a slight tremble, eyes wide.

"Put her straight in my office on the bed. Summer, you follow me as well," Dr. Orion states, quickly moving into his room.

I follow them in, feeling a little bit nervous now because of all the worry and tension in the air.

"Did she fall?" The Doc asks.

I shake my head. "No, she just vomited after hearing some pretty full-on news."

His face takes on a serious mask as he sits behind his desk, "Tyrese, is Mia your Kindred?" Doc looks at him hard.

"Yes, Sir, she is." What is this Kindred thing I keep hearing?

With a knowing look shared between them, Dr. Orion nods slowly. "Right, then you'd better stay too."

"Oh my God, what's wrong with her? Is she alright? Am I alright? Please get to the point straight up," I plead, starting to panic, my legs jiggling up and down anxiously.

I hear Mia whimper and look to see Tyrese rubbing her back and telling her it'll be okay.

"Calm down please, everything will be fine. I need the both of you to stay as calm as you can from now on, no panicking," Dr. Orion slowly states, like we're children.

I stay quiet and wait, leg still jiggling wildly.

Dr. Orion starts, "Both of your test results have come back saying the same thing. We know what's wrong and know what to do." He pauses and looks at us both. "You're pregnant."

Like hell I am!

Chapter Thirty One

"What the heck did you just say?" I stand abruptly, my chair falling to the ground.

I stare at Dr. Orion with hate and fire in my eyes and say vehemently, "You had better check again!"

Dr. Orion slowly moves his chair back, making more space between us as I lean over his desk aggressively, pointing my finger at him accusingly.

Then I hear a cry from behind me and turn to see Mia sobbing in her hands and a very pale-faced Tyrese by her side.

Tyrese turns to look at her and drops to his knees in front of her chair holding on to her legs and his shoulders start to shake as he silently cries at her feet, head laying in her lap. It stops Mia from crying and she looks down at him sniffling, eyes in wonder. This massive tattooed man sobbing on his knees, groping at her legs like she's his life vest.

"Are you okay?" She sniffles out to him, patting his hair.

Tyrese looks up at her in awe, with damp eyes. He stands quickly pulling her up with him and takes her mouth with his, desperately. "I love you, I love you, I love you, I love you," he says, kissing all over her face. "Whatever you want in the world, it's yours."

I turn my shocked face to look at the Doc who's smiling from ear to ear, unshed tears in his eyes.

"What the fuck is this?" I direct to him in a low, dangerous voice.

Dr. Orion turns to me, steeling his features at the look of my increasingly bad mood. "What do you mean?" He asks, clearly full of shit.

I sit down with a plonk. "Oh fuck, we were stolen for breeding, weren't we?" Shock and horror at my statement is making me want to vomit. I turn to the Doc again. "I don't have a Mirena anymore, do I?" He at least has the common sense to look away guiltily.

Looking back at Mia, her and Tyrese are kissing happily, she might be giddy about this, but I am fucking not.

I get up and walk out, stopping in front of Salem. "You had better answer me honestly or I'll jump over this table and fucking attack you." I point at him with a heated glare.

"Whoa, what the fuck happened, babe?" Bell gets up, standing at my side.

I continue to stare at the nervous-looking Salem. "Does every man or shifter or whatever, know that we're here for breeding? And don't you dare lie to me!" I grind out between my clenched teeth and snarling face.

He steps back before nodding very slightly.

"Excuse me?" Shylo's shocked body joins us, staring in horror.

I look at Bell and she looks red with rage. Shylo, however, looks white as a ghost.

"Don't sleep with anyone, Shylo, it's a fucking trap. They took out our contraception when they stole us. If you do sleep with them, you'll end up pregnant like Mia and me." The room is crickets.

I do, however, notice Salem's mouth turn into a smile. "Do you think smiling right now is going to help you get through this alive?" I stare at him coldly.

He stops immediately.

The girls are staring at me with mouths wide. "Yeah, that's right, Mia and I are pregnant. We've been knocked up without our permission by animals."

"Fuck me sideways!" Bell rubs her face hard in shock.

I shake my head. "No Bell, no fucking, thank God you're a lesbian." I turn to Salem. "Made a mistake there didn't you? Because she's not fucking any dick."

"Sing it, sister," Bell cheers as she raises her hands in the air. "See, I told you team pussy was the best one, but *no* you guys had to pick the roosters. Sucks to be you, cum-dumpster."

I put my hands on my hips in frustration. "Is now really the time for that, Bell?"

"Well, frankly, if you'd listened before you wouldn't be in this mess. I'm telling ya, team pussy all the way." She chuckles.

Salem clears his voice. "I couldn't agree more." We turn to look at him and he starts to fucking *purr*.

That breaks Bell and she cracks up laughing and they give each other a fist bump. I stare at them incredulously. "Seriously? You honestly think that now's the time to joke? You both suck!"

They both laugh, hard. Shylo even tries to stifle a giggle.

Tyrese and Mia come through the door at that moment smiling from ear to ear, his arm wrapped lovingly around her.

"Well, apparently I'm the only one with an issue here," I say, huffing unhappily as I cross my arms over my chest. "Salem, what was in the pills you've been giving us?"

Salem looks around sheepishly. "They're to help with multiple ovulations and strong egg growth inside the ovary, to encourage the future probability of shifter babies. We're a stronger breed and therefore your bodies need to be prepped for insemination."

"You son of a bitch!" I yell at him while throwing his stapler across the room and smacking him in the forehead. "I fucking hate being lied to. How dare you do this to my body without my permission."

"Summer, you don't understand, we very rarely have female births and therefore are a primarily male world. If we don't reproduce with human females we'll die out," Salem protests, rubbing at his head and squinting. I hope it hurts.

I stalk out of the room like my ass is on fire, get ready Blayze because here I come.

I stand at the stairwell entrance banging on the door. "Let me in, I need to talk to Blayze," I scream, looking a little bit crazy.

"Baby, what are you doing?" Reid comes up behind me.

I whirl around. "Don't you dare call me *baby*!" I push his chest. "You made your choice, Reid, and it wasn't me. Now, take me upstairs because I need to talk to Blayze. It's important."

Reid stops in front of me grinding his teeth. I watch his jaw clenching as he deliberates what I've said.

"Fine, I'll take you to the boardroom but I can't guarantee that Blayze will see you." He finally opens the door and lets me through.

I stomp up the stairs. "Stop looking at my ass," I snap at him.

He laughs quietly behind me before he passes and lets me into the boardroom. Reid talks quietly into his earpiece before he tells me, "Sit and wait, Blayze is on his way." He sits two seats down from the chair that I chose.

Blayze opens the door only moments later looking flustered. Did he run here?

I glare up at him with my arms crossed but he doesn't seem to notice. "You're out of bed today?" Coming around to where I am and sitting across from me.

I squint my eyes at him. "Obviously." My words are ice cold.

"Are you well? Can I get you something?" He looks me over, for what I'm not sure.

I roll my eyes at him. "Don't pretend like you give a shit, Blayze, because we both know you don't." I look at him stiffly, thinking of what he put me through.

Blayze reaches over to grab my hand but I pull myself back in a yank. "Don't fucking touch me," I spit, moving further away.

Sighing and rubbing his hands through his hair, Blayze cracks his neck. "What is it you want then, little bird? Is Reid needed for this?"

"I'm not going anywhere," Reid's knuckles turn white as his hand's fist on the table.

Blayze looks at Reid for a moment and the tension rises, so I get to the point. "So, this is a breeding prison?"

They both snap their heads to look at me.

Reid throws his hands in the air. "Fucking Baine."

"What's Baine been saying?" Blayze questions me, looking tense all over.

I bang my hands hard down on the table and stand up in a flash. "I'm pregnant, you fucking buffoon! Oh and news flash, I'm not fucking happy about it."

Both of the guys lean back in their chairs, mouths agape. They look like they're in some weird euphoric haze, with their eyes all glassy and gooey, it pisses me off even more.

I slam the table again, snapping their attention back to me. "Snap out of it!"

"Baby..." Reid leans over like he's going to touch my belly and I slap his hand away.

"If you touch me ever again I'll kill you!" I tower over the table at him. "I don't care that you're half-Wolf, I'll make you into my bloody coat, you piece of shit! That goes for both of you," I shout, moving my gaze menacingly to Blayze.

I take a few steps away from the table and turn angrily. "You kidnap me, pretend to care for me, knock me up, torture me so badly that I can't get out of bed for three weeks, and then think you can touch me?" I stare them down. "You're legit monsters! What kind of disgusting being would ever do this to someone?"

They say nothing because there's nothing they can say to make this better.

"There's a baby inside of me and I don't even know if it's a Wolf, a person, or a Dragon. I never asked for this. How *dare* you do this to me?" My voice breaking into a sob at the end.

Blayze stands up slowly. "I know this is scary but you have four Kindreds that'll protect you and look after you, you don't need to be scared."

"Really?" I scoff. "How does that figure? One of my *Kindreds,* whatever the hell that means, tortured me while the other three let it happen. That's not my idea of safety."

"I didn't have a choice, little bird. I work for Boss and he's ruthless. To him there's no harm if you're not touched, but I didn't agree with it. If Leon hadn't gotten involved then I could've dealt with your escape differently, I had no choice!" He coos to me softly, as he approaches me cautiously.

I hold my hand up to keep space between us. "Stop! Don't come any closer. How could you do this to me?" My tears silently stream down my cheeks. "You all betrayed me and broke me down, and now I'm supposed to have one of your children. I have my own children waiting for me, needing me at home. Their father won't care for them like they need. He moved on and left them. They need me and I'm here. How could you? I want to go back to Earth where I belong, where my babies are." A loud sob escapes me.

"Baby, please stop crying." Reid comes up to me from the other side. "I can't stand it when you cry."

"Deal with it, Reid, you did this to me. These are the tears that you've earned," I return, my bottom lip trembling as I speak.

I close my eyes, cover my face, and cry deep, heart-wrenching sobs as I think about how big this is and how powerless I really am.

Before I know what's happening I have two sets of arms surrounding me, holding me tight and telling me that it's going to be alright.

"I promise I'll never do that to you again," Blayze whispers in my ear. "It nearly killed me having to do it, I was up all night dreading what you were going through. I'm so sorry, little bird."

I stand here and cry in their arms until I can't cry anymore, but I'm too lonely and scared to push them away. Regardless, the damage is done.

Chapter Thirty Two

"We should call Salvatore and Baine up and let them know what's going on because the baby could be any of ours," Reid calmly states after I've settled down and am sipping on a cup of tea.

I scoff. "Yeah because that doesn't make me feel like a slut at all."

"It's normal for a lot of shifters to share Kindreds. Less so for Salvatore and myself, but we knew what we were getting into." I scowl at Blazye because not everyone did. "We'll worship you, little bird, it's our duty to. Females are so scarce here that you're sacred to us, from now on we'll make sure you feel that way."

I screw my face up in thought and ask Blayze,

"Are you a Dragon too? You've never actually told me. Is that why you're the head here?"

Blayze laughs under his breath. "No, my dear, I'm a Phoenix. A very rare and very powerful being, there's no shifter more powerful than I."

"A Phoenix, a Dragon and two Wolves, sure, no problem. That's really easy to deal with," I say, sarcasm dripping from my lips while taking another sip of my tea. "So, Rathe, hey? Interesting, is this a big place?"

Reid calls up the other guys while Blayze answers my questions. "It's an almost replica of Earth, we are parallel from one another. A trick of the Gods I'm afraid, we're their never-ending amusement I'm sure." Blayze leans his elbow on the table. "Here our people as a whole are called Mhanu. There are many types of us and we all have our place, but unlike on Earth, here the Celestials interfere whenever they like. It can be a cruel world but we have wonder and magic, and many beautiful things that are just not allowed on Earth."

"What does that mean?" Feeling a bit overwhelmed with this amount of new crazy information.

"Well, when both worlds were created by the Gods they decided that an experiment would be fun, a *bet* if you will. They created one world to be filled with equal parts male and female, weak and power-less. The people will get sickness and die young with a century life cycle but they can breed easily. They will have no magic, no power, and no assistance from the Celestials or their Guardians. These beings called Humans would know so much death, disease, and heartache, but would be able to find comfort again in love and family," Blayze goes on.

"Then they created an opposite world of power, magic, and the ability to seek guidance and help from the Guardians and Celestials; for a price. They will live for thousands of years and be immune from disease and disabilities. They will be strong and true, and be able to find the deepest form of attachment and love with a Kindred spirit, far beyond a human bond as it's everlasting. However, they are doomed to barely ever have the opportunity to find one as the females are rare and few between, making the contin-uation of their species difficult to maintain. While the Mhanu people are powerful and long-living, they're ravaged with loneliness and loss. War is as common, as love is sparse.

"You see, little bird, we're chess pieces in the Celestials game of life. We're here to entertain and amuse as they watch us from above, seeing what we'll do next," Blayze continues with a heavy sigh. "Three thousand years ago a Phoenix shifter, who was a leader like myself, struck up a deal with the Gods to help with the low population of females. They agreed to bring forty fertile human women every one hundred years to Rathe to breed with the Mhanu male's. The agreement is that the shifters work at Threshold, helping to prepare the women for Mhanu procreation and follow the rules set out. It is a done deal that we cannot back out of because if we don't breed, we'll die out. Forty women is not a lot for an entire world of males, little bird. Not all of the Mhanu are good, some will want to take the women to breed in a very uncivilized way and this is here to prevent that. I know it all seems cruel but you need to think of it from our perspective, we have no other choice," Blayze lowers his head into his hands. I haven't moved an inch since the story started.

Just then the doors open, Salvatore and Baine walk in, confused by the tense atmosphere.

Baine strolls over and picks me up, sitting down and placing me on his lap. Nuzzling into my neck he breathes deeply with a satisfied growl in his chest. "My bonnie, why are we here?"

Salvatore comes over and places a kiss on my temple before taking a seat across from me.

With a big breath, I just lay it out there. "Hey guys, um... So I'm pregnant."

"The fuck did you say?" Salvatore chokes in a

shocked voice at the same time that Baine whoops loudly, turns me to face him, and lifts me so that my stomachs in his face. Baine pulls my shirt up and starts kissing my belly like a crazy person.

"A bairn, holy shite, a bloomen bairn. Come here you sexy lass of mine." He pulls my lips down to his mouth and in between kisses he says, "I... fucking... love... you... bonnie!"

I can't help but giggle at his outburst and then I'm lifted right off his lap and swung around in Salvatore's arms like I weigh nothing.

Salvatore looks into my eyes as his chest vibrates on mine with a rumbled purr. "Who knew that little hellhound of a woman would be my Kindred and carrying my baby. I never knew I could have such good luck and I wouldn't want anyone with any less fire. You're mine and I'm yours." He kisses me hard. "I'm sorry I didn't say this sooner but I'll protect you from here on out and nobody can stand in my way women, nobody! You want to leave then we'll leave tomorrow."

Blayze clears his voice heavily. "She's not going anywhere."

"That depends entirely on what she wants. I'll deny her freedom no more." Salvatore places me behind him protectively and my heart swoons a little.

"Okay, time out, guys. Let's just sit down and talk about this calmly." I go over to the head of the table and sit down.

Baine immediately sits to one side of me and Salvatore on the other, with Reid sitting next to him. Blayze looks at our group and slowly moves to sit next to Baine.

"Right," I start. "Firstly, I don't know who the father is, so you should all calm down."

Baine puts his hand on mine and says to me before I continue, "We need to be clear here, none of us care who the father is. We'll love that bairn regardless. We only care that you're the mother and that we're there for the bairn. The type of shifter it turns out to be is irrelevant."

All of the guys surprisingly nod at his statement.

"How can it not matter?" I huff exasperated.

Reid answers smiling. "Children are a blessing here, there are no words to describe how much we want to help you raise this baby because we already love it. This baby is your gift to us and to our world, it's a beautiful, pure part of our Kindred, that's all that matters. New life is a wonder to behold. Thank you, Summer."

I put my hand up to him. "Reid, I'm not just going to pop it out and hand it over, this is my baby too." Fear filling me at the idea of them taking it away.

"We know, little bird," Blayze reassures me softly.

I breathe in and out deeply. "I already have children, they're this baby's brother and sisters. If children are so important to you then why are you not remembering my other ones?"

Baine leans over and kisses my cheek with a beaming smile. "Let me go for them, Derryn and I are some of the only shifters with a pass to enter the triangle. We were brought up there in Scotland because of our Da, he's stationed there as a type of embassy for the Mhanu that need emergency shelter. We can slip through and get them without being noticed, if that's what you want. If you'll just think about agreeing to stay with us. Will you think on it?" Baine questions me hopefully.

That's something I never would have thought of. "I can bring them here?" I ask, wonder filling my voice.

Blayze sits up straighter. "No, it is not in the rules." I give him a hard angry look.

"Fuck the rules, we need new ones anyway. We need to make the path open for more than just the travellers, I've always said so, just ask Derryn," Baine puts in, still beaming like the cat that caught the canary. Hope that I might stay with them, filling him.

"If only it was that simple," Salvatore points out, tapping on the table in thought.

"Well, why can't it be?" I lean back in my chair and cross my legs. "Why not try to come up with a new deal? Like maybe once a year a certain number of Mhanu can go to Earth for a month to find their Kindred and see if they'll return with them, or something like that. It's much better than kidnapping a bunch of people. How unreasonable can the Gods be?"

They all make various scoffing noises.

"Is Boss a God?" I inquire thoughtfully.

"No," Blayze replies immediately. "Boss is a dick-head of an Angel that likes power and has zero fucks to give about the people in either of the world's. He's the Guardian assigned to Threshold, the gate between your world and mine. All of the Guardians have different assignments whether they're Angel or Valkyrie."

"You have Angels and Valkyries too? Wow." My hair falls in front of my face and I tuck it behind my ear. "This is nuts, wait... Valkyries are women. Why not breed with them?"

Salvatore turns to me. "They're sterile, another of the Celestials cruel jokes."

"This is a lot to take in right now." I rub my temples, tension giving me a headache.

Blayze speaks up. "It's important that you know I want you to accept me as your Kindred, my beast chose you for its own and will never take another. I know that you might not like me very much right now and I don't blame you, but please don't block me out entirely. I give you my word that I'll only treat you with the worship you deserve." Then looking at me harder, he says more sternly, "You should be careful of Leon and a few of the workers here. Leon's a very powerful Leviathan shifter, also known as the water Dragon. There's a different belief that some shifters hold, believing that humans should be treated as pets and bred like animals and he's one of its propagators. You really need to avoid them if you can, they're very dangerous and on the mainland, there are many wars between the factions. These types of men are unnecessarily violent and will stop at nothing to get what they want."

I nod, silently agreeing to steer clear of them. I can't talk about any more of this stuff, it's all been too much for one day. "I need to go now. I'll think about everything that's been said and if I have more questions, I want them answered, no more lies. Do I make myself clear?" I exclaim, leaving no room for argument.

Baine replies with an enthusiastic smile and kiss to my cheek.

I get a hand squeeze from Salvatore. "You have my word."

I look over to Blayze and he nods in agreement, while he stands to leave himself.

All the while Reid just stares at me blankly. "I take that as a no from you?" I return his stare.

"You have my loyalty, Summer, you always did. I may be hard but that's because I'm in a position in my life that requires me to make the tough choices." Reid puts his hand through his thick black hair. "I will now put myself in your corner. I will defend you and I'll do what I can to help you if you'll let me, but I cannot leave Rathe. I have a duty to my people here. I help them keep the peace and I lead them the way they deserve to be led. I can't leave my responsibilities. I want to make us all work as a family, but will you please consider staying?"

He's being honest with me so I'll return that honesty. "I won't live here without my children, Reid, not for a day longer than is necessary. I'll fight every single day of my life until they're by my side. If there's a possibility of them being here with me then I'll think about it, but you all need to find a way to get my kids to me and every single one of the girls out of this prison as soon as possible. These women deserve a right to choose to go home, so you figure it out."

With that I get up and move to the door where

Salvatore's waiting for me. He puts his arm around me and leads me back to my room. When we get there he lays down with me on the bed, spooning me from behind as I quietly contemplate my weird reality.

Chapter Thirty Three

"Wow!" Shylo shakes her head in astonishment as I finish getting the girls up to date on everything I found out. "Do you think Baine could get Jett for me too?"

I turned to her in shock. "Don't you want to go home?"

"Honestly, there's nothing there for him or for me. We have no other family, and no real ties in my life. Plus, I think it's kind of important to help these people and I certainly wouldn't mind being loved again, my son would benefit from a strong father figure... or two," she giggles at the end.

I grab her soft hand. "I'll ask, but I can't see why not. It'll give me more reason to stay too, I could use a friend."

"Fine, fuck. You don't have to be a bitch, no begging is necessary. I'll stay and babysit you and your spawn," Bell chimes in, leaning on my shoulder.

We all laugh.

"Bell there's no women here except the chicks already in Threshold. What are you going to do for fun? And for love?" My head furrowed, I want her to be happy too.

She scoffs loudly. "Clearly you weren't listening, I heard you say Valkyries. Everybody knows they're hot as fuck, so I say, challenge accepted."

Now we're laughing harder, I don't know what we'd do without Bell. She's a rude SOB but she's a keeper.

"What about you, Mia? What do you want to do?" She seems more reserved than normal.

She smiles weakly, eyes downcast. "I'm sorry, guys, but I have a lot of family and we're really close. I've talked to Tyrese and he's agreed that if we can he'll come back with me to live. He's a Shark shifter and they don't travel in packs, so he has no one that he's worried about leaving behind. I don't live far from the sea and we can always move closer when we go back to Earth. I'm happy you guys want to stay, but it's not the life I want. I just want to go home."

I hug her close. "Don't even worry about it, Mia. We'll miss you but you have to do what's right for you. And might I say how happy I am for you and Tyrese, that man only has eyes for you."

She giggles low with a happy faraway look in her eyes. "Well he was telling me that once the Mhanu find their Kindred and they consummate their bond for the first time, from then on they can't have sex or orgasm unless it's with them. It's like the ultimate faithful partner, they literally can't get hard for anyone else, so I'm not complaining."

"I didn't know that." I rub at my neck. I guess it makes sense, now I know why they only ever seem to look at me.

Shylo sighs looking off into the distance. "See, that's what I'm talking about, I need that kind of devotion in my life."

"There's something I should tell you," Mia starts, "Tyrese and a few of the other shifters here are prepared to start a riot and try to take over. He's hoping that they can get Salvatore and Hermes on board because they're Dragon kind and will give them a fighting chance. Do you think Salvatore will help fight for our freedom?"

I do a double-take. "Did you say Hermes is a Dragon too? But he's so mellow." I'm kind of shocked. "I mean, it would explain his size, that dude is a giant. Salvatore said that he'd get me out if I wanted to so maybe, but I want to see if I can convince Blayze. He's coming around, I think. Let me see what I can do."

We all go about our day, our heads and hearts filled with hope once more, a different hope than we started with, but hope nonetheless.

That night when I'm lying in bed, my wall started to turn transparent and was soon a window with a low light shining through. There's an outline of a large man standing on the other side, looming just beyond the glass, I'd know that man anywhere.

I quietly get out of bed and walk to him, I place my hand on the glass and he mirrors my actions, bringing his face down closer to mine.

At this moment Blayze seems more like a desperate man reaching out than a tyrant holding us against our will and it chips away some of the ice around my heart. It can't be easy to be in his shoes and I don't envy his position in all of this.

Just then his hand lowers from mine to where my stomach would be if he could reach it and I uncon-sciously lean forward. These dangerous but lonely men are fighting for survival and somehow along the way, they've caught feelings. I see it in the way they look at me, I feel it in the way they touch me. I'd be lying if I said I was unaffected. I don't exactly know how I feel about them but I know it's more than it probably should be. I care for each of them in different ways because they each bring something different into my life, into my heart.

Blayze leans back up to his full impressive height and looks at me, he pulls a piece of paper out of his back pocket and unfolds it before leaning it on the glass. It's a note, I can barely read it but I work to make it out.

'Don't be scared. I have a plan! Trust me.'

I look up at him and nod, showing him that I read it and I'll try to trust what's to come.

He nods in return and reaches out to my face before the glass window is no more and I'm enveloped in darkness again.

I make my way to the bed carefully and lay myself down, hoping for a restful sleep to tackle whatever it is that Blayze is going to throw our way.

Chapter Thirty Four

"Mmmm," I groan, stretching out my body. My head feels solid and dopey, my limbs are heavy, like I didn't sleep well or I drank too much. I feel terrible.

Opening and closing my dry mouth, my tongue clicks in my mouth uncomfortably, I really need a glass of water.

Slowly I sit up, rubbing my eyes before opening them. Shock hits me and I instantly go on guard.

My back goes up against the wooden wall behind me as I look around the foreign room, where the hell am I? Not this again. I huff out a breath and push my hand through my long loose hair.

The room I'm in looks like something that you'd find in a little wooden cottage in the middle of bum ass nowhere. Wooden bed, wooden cupboard, wooden floors, wooden door. Jeez, I better not think any hot thoughts or this place is going to catch on fire.

I hear people outside walking around and distant chatter. Lots of movement all around, even men's laughter fills the air. Is this real, a dream, or what?

The thought enters my mind that maybe I'm back home or perhaps I never left and it was all a coma or something. My kids... my eyes instantly widen and my pulse races at the idea of seeing them again.

I touch my stomach and feel the familiar pang of ickiness that pregnancy brings before I acknowledge that it isn't a dream, not at all. But that doesn't answer the nagging question of, *where am I*? And if I'm back on Earth, does that mean I'll never see my men again?

A pang of sadness fills my tummy, joining the sickness I already feel at that idea. Shaking my head a small *no* escapes my lips. Was Blayze saying goodbye?

My eyes cloud with unshed tears and a lump forms in my throat, the feeling of regret and heartache etching my insides. Why didn't I tell them how I felt? I would've stayed with them if they found my babies, I really would have.

The tears start to silently stream down my face and a deep wrenching sob escapes me.

The big wooden doors abruptly thrust open as a wide-eyed Reid stares down at me. "Baby, what's wrong?"

Pulling myself out of the bed I run to him and jump up wrapping my legs around his waist, my arms around his neck, and kiss him hard on the mouth. My crying turns into a constant sobbing as I kiss him all over his face.

"I thought I was never going to see you again. I thought you'd left me," I sob, taking his mouth again.

A chuckle takes root deep in his chest as he holds me tight, letting me lavish him in desperate kisses.

I sniffle and look into his eyes with a pout that doesn't suit me. "It's not funny, I was scared. Where are we? Are my babies here?" Anticipation I feel at seeing them again clings to my words.

Reid reaches up and wipes my tears away with his thumbs before kissing my still damp cheeks. "This is a village on the way to my home, baby. I'm taking you to where you belong, my bed." He smiles tenderly at me.

"But my kids, I can't leave them Reid, I told you that," I counter shaking my head, my stomach dropping again, lips trembling.

Reid puts his finger on my lips to quiet me. "Baine and Derryn are already on Earth looking, baby. We've got your back, but you should know that Tyrese and

Mia went with them, love. I'm sorry but she's gone, as well as a couple of the other females. Baine will bring your babies home to you, or should I say, he'll bring our babies home to us. We're a family now and we'll love them as though they're ours, I swear it." His devastating smile undoes me and I cry my heart out in his arms, unable to hold my emotions in any more.

He strokes my back and whispers in my ear, "Isn't that what you wanted? Why are you crying? They're even getting your friend's boy, Jett. Don't be sad, whatever it is we'll fix it. Just tell me what you want me to do." His voice comes out frantic and rushed, clearly concerned about my overly emotional response to everything.

All I can say in his embrace is, "Thank you." I sob in between words. "I need them so much, thank you."

Reid sits on the bed with me straddling his lap, rubbing my back in gentle circles, cooing in my ear that he's got me. He lets me cry and cry and get out all of my pain, confusion, fear, sadness, and anything else I've been bottling up over this crazy ride. Before all of this happened, I'd never been much of a crier but this whole thing has really taken it out of me. Add in a dose of pregnancy hormones and I'm screwed.

After I've calmed down and got in the best cuddle

ever, I turn my face to Reid's. "Where's Salvatore and Blayze? Are they with us? Did Blayze just let everyone out?"

"It's not that straight forward, Summer. Blayze and Leon have gone against Boss's rule and they're trying to negotiate with him as we speak," Reid explains calmly.

My face scrunches in confusion. "I thought Leon only wanted to breed us?"

Reid's body tenses underneath mine, his hand suspending its movements. "Yes, this is a plus-minus situation, baby. In order for you all to have gotten released into Rathe freely, you're all at higher risk because of the conflicting factions. They'll try to hunt the women down now and take them as their own pets. While females' choices mattered on Threshold, they won't if they're captured in Rathe. That's the deal that had to be made with Leon to set you all free, and before you get all pissed off..." His hands rise defensively when he sees my face getting angry. "We've spread the females out all over with trusted allies, to prevent easy capture. Once each woman gets a Kindred they're no longer a target and will receive full protection by having a male. In the meantime, the unmated females will be watched by different breeds from all over, and until they're part-nered we'll be constantly moving them to keep them safe and out of the wrong hands, as well as increasing their chances of finding their Kindreds. There's a maximum of three unmated females per area to help ensure their safety. We actually have three others here at the moment." He kisses my temple. "Also, there's going to be one opportunity every year for the females to return home if they so choose."

I sigh deeply, taking in the information that I've just heard. "This isn't ideal but at least they'll have more choice over their lives. What kind of shifters are there?" I never really cared to ask before.

"Other than what you already know about, there are Griffins, Serpents, Lions, Panthers, Polar Bears, Stags, and Cheetahs. Honestly there's a whole heap, you do know that there's more than just shifters though right? We were just the species of Mhanu that were chosen for Threshold duties."

I think back, squinting my eyes in thought. "Blayze did say something about that. What else can there be though? I know there are Celestials and Guardians." I scratch my head trying to think of anything else I may have heard.

"Well, there are the Downworlders, Sorcerers, and the Fae," Reid says as a matter of fact like it's not at all weird to hear that sentence.

"Um, okay then. So, Sorcerers are like witches right and Fae are Fairies? I mean, that's what it sounds like." My eyes popping out of my head in disbelief that I'm having a real conversation about this.

Reid laughs out loud. "I would love for you to call them all that!" He laughs even harder before going on. "You are pretty close with the Sorcerers, but there are different groups of Fae. They're divided by what you'd call elemental forms. The Air Movers are Fairy, but not the others."

"This sounds complicated, what the hell are the downer things you said?" I ask, an overwhelmed feeling settling into my bones.

He strokes my cheek gently and says with a smile, "You do love your questions, don't you?"

I scoff. "No shit, Sherlock. I always have questions, now gimme them answers," I playfully demand.

"You should steer clear of the Downworlders. They're called that because that's where they were made, the world beneath both of ours but there are no doorways into your world. They're mostly creatures of darkness; Demons, Vampyres, Gremlins and the such," Reid supplies, as his forehead wrinkles with a look of concern.

"That's not ominous at all," I shiver involuntarily. "Now where did you say my Dragon went?" I ask, pushing for a nicer subject because I can't dwell on extra things at the moment.

Reid laughs, his mood light again. "I'll take you to him, he's sitting outside the village watching over in protective mode. He doesn't like open areas like this for his Kindred, it's against everything Dragons believe in. Come on, let's go and bring your Dragon inside." His eyes twinkle with mischief. "Wait till you see him."

Reid stands up, puts me down, holding my hand lovingly in his as we turn toward the door, I can't help but feel excited to see new land and my brooding Mr Big.

Walking through the cottage and out the door, I'm surprised by what I see.

Everything looks totally normal, a little rustic and medieval perhaps, but otherwise there doesn't seem to be anything peculiar. The sky is blue, the grass is green, the sun warms my skin with its rays, and everyone in the village is walking around getting on with their lives. It feels almost surreal.

A giant *roar* fills the air, I tense and freeze to the spot, sucking in a sudden breath.

I look over the vast green hill before me to see a colossal Dragon. Large black and red wings spread wide, two twisted sharp horns adorning the head, and it's roaring bellows into the wind.

The Dragon then turns it's large ferocious face my way and I swear it's big scarlet eyes look right at me. Fear takes hold within me, the hair on my body rising.

Holy crap! I take an involuntary step back into the cottage and I feel an arm wrap around my waist. A hard, warm body presses against my back, and I inhale the familiar scent of male and woods.

"Baby, calm down, I can smell your fear. It's just Salvatore, you're safe," Reid reassures me, rubbing his hands over my arms.

Of course it is, but it still takes a second for my brain to come to terms with the fact that he's a real motherfucking Dragon! What a mind snap.

I step back out slowly, making my way towards the Dragon when everything goes eerily quiet around me. The only noise is my bare feet padding along the soft grass and dirt beneath them.

Looking around me I'm surprised to find that all the people that were bustling about are now stock still and staring at me with wide-eyes and mouths open. Some of them are even sniffing at the air, it's really weird.

Reid laughs and speaks out, "Back to work, men, you're freaking out the female."

That's when I take note that they're all male, the whole village from what I can see. No women, no children, none of that. They're looking at me with awe simply because I'm a female and that makes me sad for them.

I turn to Reid, "Are there no girls here?"

"No, Summer, I told you, we don't have females and if there are any they're very few and far between. It's only the Valkyrie that we see and they don't like to be looked at or touched. We've learnt to see them as just Valkyrie and not females," Reid explains with a shrug. "Now these males have you and a couple of the others sleeping in their village, it's kind of blowing their minds, to be honest."

I look back at Salvatore and see him still staring at me, feeling a strong pull towards him. I know I need to go to him, so I continue my path, nothing else breaking my concentration. My heart is only interested in one thing.

Getting closer, I take in the Dragon shimmering like a mist and shrinking before my eyes, until there's only a very naked and super sexy Salvatore standing in front of me. His eyes search mine for judgement or fear, concern littering across his features. I smile at him with everything I have and run carelessly the rest of the way, my hair flinging back and forth through the breeze as I go.

Salvatore wraps his giant arms around me, holding me tight before grabbing my waist and lifting me off my feet, my eyes now level with his. I stroke his cheek and facial hair lovingly. "My beautiful beast." I kiss him hard and passionately on the lips, feeling my tongue gliding over his, claiming what's mine.

I love tasting this man. His lips are soft and full but his pressure is hard. His tongue is aggressive, his taste is oh so sweet. He nips at my bottom lip making me moan into his mouth and I strangle his waist with my strong thighs wanting to get closer to him.

Salvatore groans into my mouth, grabbing my ass hard and squeezing, earning a yelp from me before he slaps one cheek hard.

My kiss becomes even more aggressive, meeting his own fervour, his facial hair is probably going to leave my face red raw from our passion and I couldn't care less.

I grind my covered core against him as he lowers me over his rock solid cock. I moan deeply as I feel my pussy clench from the friction of it rubbing against him, my panties quickly growing wet from my building arousal.

"Far out, guys. You've got to stop or you're going to cause a mass jerk off session," Reid groans behind me.

I pull back from our frantic kiss, panting hard and

turn to see my Alpha rubbing his swollen cock through his clothes and a large band of men at the bottom of the hill smelling the air.

Embarrassment filling me I coyly mumble, "I can't help it." I say as I start to giggle from euphoria. An honest to goodness, girly giggle.

"Oh, shush up," Reid shakes his head with humour in his eyes. "We need to go somewhere private so we can fuck you. You're so sexy when you're wanton and you smell so good right now. There's nothing sweeter than the scent of your pussy drenching."

Damn his words are so hot, my core just got even wetter, squeezing tight from hearing those words coming from that delicious mouth. I bite my lip and look him up and down sensually while still wrapped around a very turned on Salvatore.

"Stop it," Reid moans, adjusting himself again. "Or we're going to take you right here on the hill in front of everyone," he warns, with hooded blue eyes.

I giggle and then unwrap my legs, regretfully. "Okay, okay. Where are the other girls? Are Bell and Shylo here?" Hope at seeing my friends distracting me.

Salvatore shakes his head. "No, Bell is, but Shylo's somewhere else. We have Bell, and two younger girls, they were in the same cottage as you and will probably wake up soon if they aren't already awake."

"Let's go then." Bummed about Shylo not being here but keen to see Bell, I grab Salvatore's hand and attempt to pull him down with me but he doesn't budge. "You need to move your legs for walking to work. I need to get some clothes on you before the other girls see you because that right there..." I point to his very large and still hard dick, "is mine."

Salvatore grins at me like I've never seen him do and it steals my breath. "Say that again." His voice is a deep, raspy tone. "Tell me I'm yours."

I lean up and kiss him on the mouth as he leans down to meet me halfway. "You're mine and I'm yours, now come with me, my sexy Kindred, so that I can clothe you. Otherwise, I'm going to have to rip out the other girl's eyes," I say super sweetly, batting my eyelashes. "I'll have no more of this standing on the hill business, you belong by my side. Let's go boys!"

Then I clasp both Salvatore's and Reid's hands and we head back to the village, Mr Big no longer fighting me... for once.

Chapter Thirty Five

Entering the cabin, Salvatore heads straight for the room that I came from, he must have clothes hidden in there. It was so weird watching him strut through town in all his naked glory and people were looking at me like *I* was the odd one. So strange.

I look around the cabin and see a beautiful, rustic, dark wooden kitchen and homely lounge made of more wood (surprise-surprise), filled with leather furnishings. Looking up, I notice the beautiful, inter-twined fine metal which looks like sculpted branches on the ceiling. Paying closer attention I realise they're lights, and in the corner is a lamp crafted the same way. I'm staring in amazement as that's some skill.

"Reid, how do you have electricity?" Wonder fills

my voice as I'm mesmerised by such craftsmanship.

He laughs at my question. "We're a land of magic, baby. Every home or building is run off an energized sphere, it's called a fission sphere. It powers everything with little effort."

Just then a door on the right creaks open and a mussed ash-blonde head of hair and big familiar blue eyes peep through. It's Janice.

"Janice! Hi, do you remember me? I'm Summer," I say eagerly in greeting of the familiar face.

She smiles at me instantly and replies with a friendly, "Howdy." Janice walks into the living room and looks around. "Where on Earth are we?" She asks, gazing out of the closest window.

I chuckle nervously. "Um, actually...about that..." I start and then just stare at her with no idea how to finish that sentence, my mouth opening and closing in search of words.

Reid clears his throat. "Sorry to interrupt that fascinating description, but why don't we wait until all of the girls are up before we go there?" I can't help but notice the humour in his voice at my discomfort.

"Yeah, great idea. I'm going to wake them up because I think it's time we all talked," I say, ignoring his jab at me.

"Okie dokie," says Janice, still smiling. She sits on the nearest couch while I go to the first door.

Opening it carefully, I peek inside. A big head of wild, curly black hair fans over the pillow, a small body attached and curled in on itself. Her hair's stunning!

I move over to her and gently tap her shoulder. "Rise and shine, sleepyhead," I coo as nicely as I can.

She mumbles and slowly turns her face to me. Eyes filled with thick dark lashes open and I can't help but stare in appreciation at the most captivating golden eyes I've ever seen.

"What? Who are you?" She asks in a quiet, husky voice. Looking around the room she sits up quickly and reaches for black-framed glasses that are on the bedside table. She puts them on her fear-filled eyes and adjusts them on her face, pushing wild hair out of the way as she whispers, "Where are we?"

This beautiful, young-looking girl looks so small and afraid hiding behind her thick glasses. I can't help but reach out for her, wanting to comfort her obvious distress.

Flinching away from my touch she backs against the wall. Somebody has hurt this small girl and I feel instantly angry and protective over her.

"You're okay, you're safe here. We're free now, no one will hurt you anymore," I say, wanting to reassure her. "What's your name, darling?" She looks so fragile.

Looking down at her hands she speaks in that low husky tone. "I'm Havana." Then she looks in my eyes. "I don't want to go home, there's nothing there for me." Her words break my heart.

"Havana, honey, we aren't back home. We're somewhere else, but you're safe and you'll be under my protection from now on." I hold my hand out. "Come with me, there's another girl in the lounge out here that would love the company. I have one more person to wake up and then we can all have a little talk."

Looking at my hand for a moment, she finally decides to trust me. Taking my hand, she lets me lead her to the lounge where she sits across from Janice, head down.

"I'll be right back." I let Janice do the introductions. She looks like a kid in a candy store having another person to talk to. What a huge comparison between the two young girls, they're both around twenty but clearly had very different upbringings.

The next door I open I see Bell laying with her mouth wide open, leg hanging off the bed and lightly snoring, and I can't help myself. With a cheeky smile, I run and jump on the bed yelling, "Wake up!"

"What the fuck? Holy meat-flaps you scared the fucking tits off me, bitch," Bell growls, throwing me off the bed.

I sprawl on the floor in hysterics and eventually, she joins in laughing with the odd, "Slut," comment thrown in here and there.

I climb back onto the side of the bed. "You shouldn't abuse pregnant women," I joke, giving her a mocking scowl.

Slam. The door to the room bangs open and Salvatore's by my side in a second, hands outstretched ready to pick me up.

"No." I slap his hands away. "It was just a joke, I'm fine. I only fell off the bed."

A deep growl rips from his chest before he says in a low voice, "You have to be careful, no more playing."

"Get fucked, Hulk. I'm gonna play with this wench whenever I damn well feel like it and I won't hurt your bloody baby." Bell rolls her eyes looking at me. "How do you put up with his he-man crap?"

I laugh out loud. "It's kinda sweet, though. Now get out of bed, tosser. There's a meeting in the lounge."

"Yeah speaking of that, why am I in a redneck lodge?" Bell's face becomes all scrunched up in disapproval.

I walk out the door saying, "Hey, I like it. Anyway, hurry up so you can find out."

After all the girls are seated and the guys are

standing guard at the door and window, I begin. I tell them everything that I've learned so far, it takes quite some time to get through, and some of it is almost too unreal to say out loud.

Crickets. That's all that can be heard in the silence that is the aftermath of reality setting in, dawning on us that this is our new life.

"So, when do I get a Valkyrie?" Bell breaks the tension.

We all turn as we hear a deep rumble of laughter boil out of Salvatore, I can't help but join in and so does everyone else, except Bell.

"What's so funny? I'm serious," she states, standing and folding her arms which makes everyone laugh even harder.

I wipe my eyes before chuckling out, "That's why it's so funny." I go over to her and put my arm around her shoulders. "I love you, bitch, don't ever change." Now she's smiling.

Salvatore claps his knees as he laughs. "I want to see her try to get one of those cold harpies," he cackles, shaking his head as he calms his laughter down, he points at Bell. "If anyone can handle a Valkyrie it's you." We all agree with that.

"Right." Clapping my hands together, I look at Reid. "I need food and I need to know what's happening next."

Reid straightens instantly. "I'm so sorry, baby. I forgot about food. Why don't you girls chat and get to know each other? Salvatore and I'll make sure all your needs are met."

"Also when will Blayze come back?" I need to know. "He's not in any danger is he?" My voice holds an edge of apprehension.

The guys both look at each other for a moment before Salvatore replies. "We don't know. He went straight to the Guardians with Leon and we haven't seen or heard from them since."

I feel sick. "How do we find out what's happening?" A slight quiver can be heard in my voice.

"We can't. We can only wait." Salvatore gives me a kiss on my head. "As soon as we know something, we'll tell you. I promise, Kindred."

I look up at him and know he's telling the truth. I have no choice but to wait.

As the men reach the door, Reid turns. "This village is Cheetah territory, also known as a coalition, and they're very respectful men. I'll have one of their top warriors stand guard at the door to ensure safety from any intruders, but we won't be far. Baxter is a quality male, if you need us, or anything else, please just ask him."

They walk out and a tall, and frankly picture perfect, guy steps in with a wide toothy smile and dimples for days. His long white-blond hair in a pony-tail, his face looks like it's been chiselled by the Gods, all perfect jaw, cleft chin, and straight masculine lines. Not to mention a strong, large, and yet defined physique.

"Good day, females, I'm Baxter," he says with twinkling eyes and a slight respectful bow to his head. "I'm at your complete service and will give you *anything* you require."

I try not to laugh at his obvious double meaning to *anything*. We have a cheeky one here.

"You can wait outside!" The booming angry voice of my Dragon Kindred calls from beyond the walls.

With a wink and a chuckle he exits and closes the door behind him.

"Good lordy that man's fine," I hear Janice drawl. I look back and see two very drooly-looking women. I can't help but laugh and so does Bell.

"Careful, beautiful, you might slip on that drool if you're not careful," Bell jokes.

We all settle down and chat some more to become what I'm sure will be lifelong friends in this crazy world that is now *ours*.

Chapter Thirty Six

Two long days of waiting with no word from Blayze or Baine pass, two days of refusing to move on to Reid's pack lands because I don't want to go without them, but now it's time to get going. I can't avoid it anymore, we have to move on to keep the girls safe.

"We'll stay until lunch and then we have to go, baby," Reid soothes playing with my hair. "They'll find us, I promise. They'll know where you are, we're drawn to you, my love. There's no way for us to be lost from you as our Kindred because you've accepted our claim, we're bonded to you forever in life and death. You would know if something happened to them."

I sigh and reluctantly agree to go. No matter how

much his words warm my heart though, I still can't stop worrying about my other Kindreds. "I know, I can feel it too. It's like my centre is being pulled and stretched, and I don't like it." I look over at the girls sitting by the town fire pit, talking to the local Cheetahs. "Okay, after lunch we leave." I have a responsibility to keep them safe.

"It's a shame that none of the girls have accepted any Cheetahs, they would've been fine males," I hear from behind me.

I turn and see a smiling Salem. "Hi, stranger," I greet, he really is a pussy after all. "I was kind of hoping the same, especially for you and Baxter. You're great guys but I guess they just think of you two as hunnys instead of potential Kindreds." I shrug.

A small growl comes from Reid. "Are you serious right now? I said *they*, not me." I roll my eyes at his ridiculous jealousy, these guys are super territorial.

Salem laughs. "It's fine, it doesn't work like that anyway. They should both feel pulled to each other. That's why no matter what you tried, you and your males kept getting pulled together. I can't wait to be in the position when I get to growl," he says, his voice jovial, a knowing smile on his face making me wonder if he already knows who his Kindred is.

All of a sudden I feel my stomach flip and tighten. I turn my body in the direction I feel a pull towards and spot what looks like a ball of fire zooming towards us.

I'm drawn to it and start walking in its direction, the closer I get the more I see that it isn't a ball at all but a humongous bird of flames.

My Phoenix, he's returned to me.

I hear gasps from all around. Cheetahs in human and feline form surround the women and form a barrier in front of me.

"Move," I demand. "He's mine." I shoulder through them towards my fire, my Blayze.

The majestic creature lands, it shrinks in size and transforms into a flaming man. The orange fire licks all over his bare skin. We walk closer to each other and his flames fizzle down until they disappear, leaving the most glorious, naked man. He really is perfect to look at and I feel very lucky to have him.

"You know, if I keep getting all my Kindreds greeting me naked like this I'm going to combust." I sweetly look up into his handsome face.

Beaming down at me, Blayze asks in his deep voice, "Did you miss me, little bird? Does this mean you're happy I'm your Kindred now?"

I waste no time climbing him like a tree and kissing him tenderly, his skin warm to the touch. "I was so worried about you. Are you ok?"

"Mmm... I am now," he says as he returns my soft

kisses. "I need you to come with me, so I can slake my need for your wet pussy around my cock."

I groan at his words and feel my core clenching. I haven't been touched by the other two because of not being in their territory, so this makes me very happy to hear.

"Fuck, yes!" I grind myself on him and lick him all the way up his salty neck.

I hear a rumble behind me and a throat clearing. I turn to see my other men staring at me with desire.

"I don't think so, baby. You know we want to but we need to go to our own territory first," Reid's voice apologetic.

Blayze squeezes my ass tight. "Stuff that, I want inside her now and I'm not asking your permission."

All three men tense up and I decide that's when I need to put my big girl panties on and suck it up for now.

I sigh deeply, and get down from him before admitting, "They're right." Damn it. "We're leaving straight after lunch. As soon as we get there and set those girls up, you three are going to fuck me senseless! That's an order, by the way. I'm so freaking horny and I want all of you in me ASAP."

Blayze grumbles his dismay but reluctantly agrees.

Walking away, I throw back, "The orgasms I get

better be endless after all the shit I've been through lately."

I leave them chuckling and realise too late that the guys in town are laughing also. I forgot about the town's good hearing, everyone's laughter was for me. Awesome!

Each of us girls has a leather satchel with spare clothes that the townsmen provided.

We're going to Reid's territory because it's vast with mountains, caves, and woods. Perfect for all my men's animal needs. Salvatore prefers to live in the mountains, and Blayze likes to have a home perched on the side of one, while Reid and Baine will need the woods to roam and run.

As soon as we get there we're going to find a nice mountainside to call our own, somewhere that'll make everyone happy.

"Let me be very clear here, Mr Big!" I say, my hands on my hips. "You want us to ride your freaking Dragon form? Up there? In the sky? On a Dragon?"

"For goodness sake, woman, do what you're told

for once," Salvatore grumbles, throwing his hands in the air. "You'll be fine, I won't drop you, unless you keep pissing me off."

I point my finger in his chest. "You wouldn't dare!"

"True, but if you don't play nice I'll strap you to my tail and you can flop around all the way there. Maybe that'll teach you who's in charge here!" His eyes narrow.

I scoff at him in defiance.

Blayze comes up to him holding a long rope. "Good idea. I'll gag her too, then she can't bitch so much."

They both start laughing and Blayze steps towards me with a cheeky smile.

"Reid!" I scream, running back towards the cabin. "Help!" I get out just before big arms lift me up. "Aarrgghh!" I scream out, kicking my feet in the air.

Reid comes running up the path. "What the fucks going on here?" He bellows, confused by seeing my other Kindreds manhandling me, while Bell stands at the side laughing so hard she's bent over in pain.

"They're trying to torture me," I squeal as Blayze throws me over his shoulder.

Umph. The air leaves me and I cry out as a joke, "My baby." Thinking it'll make him put me down, but all hell breaks loose instead.

Salvatore roars as Blayze rushes to put me on the ground. Reid runs over and tackles Blayze as soon as I'm down and Cheetahs come running over to surround my body with theirs protectively. One of them rubs his face on my belly, purring, and in the background, I hear Bell shouting, *"Fuck!"* Clearly shocked at the sudden chaos.

I lay down, squeeze my eyes closed, and scream at the top of my lungs. "Stoppp!!"

Everything goes quiet and I push the big cats off me while I sit back up. I get to my feet and dust myself off, scowling at the three stupid men that are laying on top of each other, paused mid-swing.

"For fucks sake, get up." I shake my head at them with my hands on my hips.

They unfold themselves and get back to their feet.

I turn and look at the girls. "Apparently we're going via Dragon. Get your stuff, we're leaving." Then I turn to the men of mine. "As for you lot, that's enough of that! I'm fine, but next time be more careful with my stomach."

Blayze steps forward, apology written all over his face.

I hold up my hand, "Not one word from any of you, let's go!" I turn around picking up my bag and address our hosts. "Thank you kindly for your hospitality, Cheetahs. I'll let the other ladies know about the quality males in this village." Waving a farewell to the men and big cats as we leave, many nod gratefully to me in response.

I turn and see a beautiful black Wolf sitting majestically next to my large red and black Dragon with a person-sized Phoenix perched on a rock nearby. It's hard to believe that these stunning creatures are mine. That they're the men that have brought me both heaven and hell, yet here they are, staring at me with longing.

We were told to stand in groups of two earlier and Salvatore would carry us in his large claws. We line up where we were told, all of us looking a bit green around the gills, except for my partner Bell who is grinning from ear to ear, her arms already raised and waiting, wiggling her fingers excitedly.

"Be gentle, Mr Big, or you'll hear about it," I say one last time as I lift my arms and wait.

Salvatore pushes into the air in one clean swoop and gently lowers himself, placing his claws around us and slowly lifts us.

I hold on to Bell for dear life and the weird woman squeals. "*Weeeee!*" Like it's the best ride ever. I clearly need new friends, I think to myself. Letting out a nervous laugh, I decide to just relax and enjoy this crazy ride.

Chapter Thirty Seven

The flight over to our new home was absolutely amazing after I got past my fear. This is such a beautiful land and there are so many little villages and animals surrounding them. There's plains, valleys, mountains, lakes, and lush forests, it's incredible to behold.

Coming up to a large forest next to lush mountains with a huge waterfall in the distance, we slow down and the girls and I are gently placed on the ground just before the treeline.

Luckily, during our flight Salvatore and Blayze went slow, keeping Reid always below us. He was so fast and strong as he ran and lept, his agility and speed took my breath away.

As Salvatore let me go, I ran over to where Reid is

running from and he leapt straight into my arms. A big, furry cuddle just for me, nudging me with his muzzle, and moving me towards the trees.

He runs ahead of me in the direction of the woods. It's then I see a line of large, ferocious Wolves growling and pacing at our presence. That is until they see Reid. The atmosphere changes immediately and they run and pounce at him with excited mewls. Then all as one they bow their heads to him and stay there in submission of their obvious leader.

Reid transforms back into his man-self and turns to me, ushering me over. I look at the other two guys and they nod. Moving forward, Reid takes me in his arms, showing his affection for me in front of his pack.

One by one they all change, but remain bowed down to us, heads looking up in awe at me.

"This is my Kindred, Summer. You'll accept her and protect her as your own. She's also chosen three other Kindreds, an Omega Wolf, a fire Dragon, and a Phoenix; they'll stay with us on our land and be a part of our pack. If you wish to challenge me on this, say so now." Reid delivers his speech loud and proud.

Not one man stands, they just bow their heads again in acknowledgement.

"Excellent, we also have with us three unmated females that we're to protect until told otherwise.

You *will* show respect and restraint, they'll choose their own male's, in their own time. It's the new way and we'll be proud to protect their honour." Reid waves his hands to the three girls still standing with Salvatore and Blayze, who have remained in animal form. Luckily for them, their junk is only for me to see, it's bad enough that Reid's exposed.

"There's one more piece of news that I wish to share with you. Summer is carrying a child, perhaps the first to be born in Rathe in a very long time. We as her Kindreds, and as her pack, are honoured by her," Reid shouts with joy filling his voice before turning back into his Wolf and howling into the wind. His pack shifts immediately, joining in with gusto.

The happiness squeezes my heart and threatens to bring me to tears. I go back to the girls. "We're literally saving their world just by loving them, I truly hope you ladies find someone that brings you the love and joy that these guys bring me," I wrap the girls up in a group hug and sigh my contentment.

Bell taps my shoulder. "Girl, you know I love you, but I'm not taking the D for anyone." Her face all scrunched up in disgust.

I laugh at her. "Who knows maybe they have IVF here and you just need to find a suitable donor and this sexy Valkerie you keep going on about."

She winks. "Now you're talking!"

"Speaking of the D, girls, you have to face over there and close your eyes because I don't want you seeing the guys naked. I'm going to pass them some clothes. I'll tell you when you can look." I cross my arms over my chest with one eyebrow up.

"Ew, you don't have to ask me twice," Bell grumbles, facing away with Havana who beat her to it. Janice follows soon after but less enthusiastically.

When all my guys are dressed, we all head into the woods until we come across the sweetest little village.

Reid had already told his pack that they needed to start construction on a new property for him, the guys, and myself. A bunch of them were already starting to take supplies towards where it's apparently being built, they work fast around here.

"So are you guys the only shifters in these woods?" I bring up while we have dinner in their big hall, it looks similar in design to what we had at Threshold but made of light wood, with Wolf carvings in the furniture and along the walls.

Reid shakes his head. "No, baby, we also have a Grizzly clan that uses the other side of the woods. We've always co-existed together in harmony and welcome them as neighbours, we even have get-togethers to encourage our standing as allies."

"Cool," I eat a big piece of meat, happy that it smells good to me and not bad for once, "I met a Grizzly once. I called him Chuckles, he's a regular comedian."

Blayze laughs next to me. "I remember that, the poor guy looked like he was going to shit himself when he brought you to my door. Keneth's a quality Bear but his humour isn't always activated at the best times."

"You're not wrong, when Derryn and I were fighting about him eating me, he was chuckling away in his bear form like a loon," I shake my head at the memory.

"Did you just say Derryn was going to eat you?" Salvatore all but growls out.

"I'll be having a talk with him when I see him next, Baine's brother or not, he'll not threaten to eat my Kindred!" Reid angrily adds.

Blayze just laughs harder than before.

"It's not a laughing matter, Blayze! Out here you don't outrank me, remember that," Reid snarls at him.

Chuckling, Blayze explains, "You're only freaking out because you didn't see the trouble she caused them, there was zero chance of that. I thought she was gonna poke one of their eyes out the way she was carrying on, it was hilarious."

Me being secretly proud of Blayze's ability to ignore Reid's ridiculous boasting, I put my arm around Blayze and kissed his cheek. "Thank you," I whisper in his ear with a smile.

"You're welcome, my little bird." He takes my mouth softly in a kiss.

I turn to see two sets of envious eyes. "If you learn to appreciate my ability to take care of myself instead of posturing then you'll also get a kiss." My voice a sweet promise.

On that note, I stand up and excuse myself from dinner.

"Where are you going?" Confusion written across Salvatore's handsome face.

I smile seductively over my shoulder. "Well, Mr Big, I'm going to bed. It's a shame no one's joining me, I guess I'll entertain myself." I walk out of the door, leaving behind hollering and hooting coming from the room of men, a knowing smile on my face.

I hear Bell yelling, "You better run, boys."

Next thing I know I'm hoisted up into Blayze's strong arms in a bridal hold and he runs me all the way back to the house we're staying in, me giggling and bouncing the whole way.

"Mine!" He kicks open the door and crashes his

lips to mine and fuck if that doesn't make me moist as hell.

I wiggle in his arms until my legs wrap around him. "About fucking time!" I deepen our kiss, his tongue caressing mine as passion takes over.

Someone pulls my shirt up and over my back and I realise we aren't alone, Reid's behind me stripping me.

Salvatore slams the door shut and approaches us, taking his own clothes off as he goes.

"Fuck!" I squirm at all this sexiness in one room. How did I get so lucky?

Blayze places me back on my feet running me down the front of his toned hard body. Reaching in between my breasts he releases my bra clasp and my heavy breasts pop free, rose nipples hardening instantly.

Blayze leans down and takes one into his mouth as Reid lowers my pants from my body.

I moan deep in my throat as I look over at Salvatore palming his heavy sac in his hand as he strokes his impressive length with the other one, eyes hooded and on me.

With my underwear still on, Blayze lays me on a soft rug in front of the fire, lowering himself until his face is right between my legs. Gazing up at me, he licks his lips and leans forward, nibbling on my wet cunt through my underwear. He nuzzles and nips, driving me crazy with need.

"Oh, please," I whine needing more.

Salvatore sits on his heels next to me. I reach over and grab his thick cock, stroking up and down, just the way he likes it, and he growls low, his head falling back.

Just when I think I can't handle anymore, Reid takes my hardened nipple into his mouth and laves at it lovingly, before biting down and making me squeal.

"More, please," I cry. Blayze pulls my panties to the side slipping one big finger in between my now soaking folds before sliding it inside my tight sheath, sucking on my clit at the same time and driving me over the edge. "Fuck!" I scream my release, cuming hard around his finger.

Blayze slips my knickers off and picks me up, laying back so I'm straddling him. I don't know when Reid and he got naked, they're so freaking hot.

I rub myself up and down his length, getting him all wet with my juices. Reid sits behind me, holding and moving my hips back and forth as I grind against Blayze, staring at my ass in worship. I lean forward and kiss Salvatore deeply as I stroke him and moan into his mouth, loving the sensation of Blayze's cock rubbing my clit.

Reid then lifts my ass up and I position Blayze at

my entrance, slowly lowering onto him, feeling my pussy stretch wide to make room for his massive size, it feels so good.

I make small up and down movements trying to lower myself fully, and Salvatore grabs my nipples, pinching hard, making me cry out and slip all the way down onto Blayze's impressive length. Pinching them again, my pussy clenches tight and I can feel myself getting even wetter.

"Holy shit, yes," I moan deeply.

I slowly and deeply ride Blayze, his hands holding so tight around my hips that I'll bruise, while Reid palms my bouncing ass cheeks.

"Lean forward and take me in your mouth," Salvatore demands and I comply happily, leaning right over Blayze. I open my mouth and lick the tip of Salvatores throbbing head. "You taste so salty and delicious," I say before I suck him deep into my mouth.

Grabbing my hair, Salvatore begins slowly thrusting his dick into the back of my throat, making me gag.

I feel Reid behind me, reaching around to strum at my aching clit and gathering my leaking pussy juices as Blayze continues bouncing me on his cock. He lathers my juices onto my asshole, making it pucker at his fingers. Reid slowly rubs in my cream relaxing my back passage and making me moan around Salvatores dick. He pushes one finger slowly into it and it feels really fucking good. I've always loved anal. My body trembles knowing what's coming, I want all of them inside me, filling me.

"I'm going to stick myself in your ass, baby, stay relaxed," Reid warns as he removes his finger and I feel his slick head sliding against my hole, staying still on Blayze in anticipation.

I groan again, gagging more on Salvatore as Reid slowly pushes himself into me, my hips arching slightly to accommodate both of their dicks.

Reid fills me up. I stay still for a moment longer trying to let my body adjust, but Salvatore has other ideas and grabs my hair tighter beginning to really fuck my mouth, hard and deep, making my eyes fill up with tears as I choke on his cock.

Reid and Blayze both start to fuck me in rhythm, slow at first and then just as hard as Salvatore. It feels so fucking amazing that within seconds my body starts to shake and I cum over and over again. They don't stop or slow, they just fuck me harder sending my eyes rolling in the back of my head.

I cum all over Blayze and feel my body turning to jelly, so they use their strength to hold me up when my body gives out. Fucking me harder still, Salvatore roars to the sky as his cum fills my throat and I swallow the thick saltiness down.

Blayze is next, tightening under me and losing his rhythm as he fills my cunt deeply. I cum again and Reid takes advantage, pulling me off Blayze, sliding his dick into my pussy and setting a hard tempo before he too fills me with cum. My ass is in the air and the front of my body simply rests on Blayze as I shiver and pulse from an orgasm that doesn't seem to end, just torments me and drives my mind into madness.

Finally, it finishes and I'm spent. I can't move, or speak and I fall asleep immediately in the same spot I came, wet, filled with cum and unable to think.

Chapter Thirty Eight

I wake up with a desperate need to pee, ah the joys of pregnancy. Then I remember what happened when I fell asleep and smile to myself, feeling very satisfied.

Opening my eyes, I look around and realise I'm laying on Blayze still, with Salvatore asleep on my left, with his hand on my ass, and Reid on my right, holding my hand while he sleeps.

A girl could get used to this, but how do I go pee without waking anyone?

I look back to Salvatore, his eyes are open and he's staring at me with tenderness, I smile in return and mouth, "I have to pee."

He tries not to laugh and then gets up, gently lifting me off Blayze so I don't wake him. Salvatore takes my hand and walks me down the hall to the bathroom.

"Thank you, Mr Big." I kiss him with a smile. "Sorry I woke you."

He brushes my hair behind my ear. "Summer, you wake me anytime, I'm always here for you. Do you want a bath? I'll run you one." His baritone voice sending delicious shivers down my spine.

For such a big tough guy, Salvatore's actually incredibly sweet and I appreciated both sides of him, it's what made him mine. "Will you join me?"

His face scrunched up a bit. "I don't normally do baths but yeah, I will. It's big, like a pool, so I'll fit, see you in there." With a kiss, he's gone.

I go to the toilet and walk into the bathroom to see this devastatingly handsome man up to his beard in bubbles and I feel my heart soar. All I need is my beautiful children back in my arms, Baine in our home, and I'll be complete.

Another week passes with no word, the girls have settled in well. Havana slowly comes out of her shell with the other girls, but is still very standoffish with all the men, Janice is having a blast and befriending every single person in the territory with her big smile and helpful attitude. Then there's Bell... She's managed to piss off 50% of the pack while the other half loves her crazy antics. Honestly, I can't take her anywhere, but I wouldn't want to be without her.

Salvatore and Blayze have settled in perfectly, they're just like one of the pack. My gorgeous men fill my week with love, laughter, and orgasms, and that makes me happy, but I ache for my babies and Baine. I'm starting to get depressed and fear that I'll never see any of them again.

I'm playing cards with the girls and a couple of their guards, when all of a sudden my stomach tightens when I hear, "Mum!" Called out into the wind.

Dropping my cards and standing instantly, my heart making its way out of my chest with how fast it's suddenly beating. I turn around and spot the most beautiful thing I've ever seen, two identical heads of flaming red hair, with big onyx teary eyes that start running towards me with their arms stretched wide.

"Oh my God!" I drop to my knees with my arms as wide as they can go and a sob caught in my throat. My sweet twin girls dive into my arms, crying their sweet souls out and I sob openly grasping at them with everything that I have. "My babies."

Looking past them I see my eight-year-old son Lawson holding hands with my nine-year-old daughter Meaghan, tears streaming down their faces. I hold one of my hands out to them to come to me, and they start to sob with us as they join in our family hug.

So many tears, so much time lost, so much relief, there are no words for the tightness in my chest as we heave sobs, holding on with our whole lives.

I have my children with me again, I have my home, I can't believe it.

I don't know how long we stay this way but nobody bothers us and time is irrelevant.

Eventually, I look down at my whole life sitting at my lap and I sigh, a sigh of complete contentment, now all I need is Baine.

I look up and see that everyone has gone except for my four wonderful men taking us in with tenderness, and an abundance of patience. I lock eyes with Baine and nod to him, showing him I see him and I'm grateful, he smiles in return, his cheeks wet with his own tears. My Baine, always filled with kindness and love.

"Guys, I hope you don't mind that you were brought here, if you'd rather stay with Dad then I'll understand but I hope that you'll give this place a chance because I missed you all so much and never want another day without you in it." I touch all of my kids, needing contact.

"Baine talked to us about everything on the way here and we want to stay with you, please don't make us go back, Mum," Meaghan says to me with a tremor in her small voice and damp eyes.

I kiss her on her head. "I'll never make you leave my side, I will keep you with me as long as you'll let me. Did Baine explain the animals here?"

Lawson perks up. "Yeah! Did you know that the people here can turn *into* animals?"

"We're in a magical land, Mummy," Llewellyn the twin to my left says excitedly.

"And they even have unicorns but we can't touch them because they're a bit grumpy," Cheyenne her sister, continues.

"Wow." My eyes animated for them. "I didn't know about the unicorns. Did Baine tell you that you need to stay safe by being close to us and not running off?"

"Yes, Mama," they chorus.

"Good."

"How come you have four husband's instead of one?" Cheyenne, always the honest one, asks.

I smile at them and then cock an eyebrow at Baine before answering. "Because, my darlings, I love them all very much and I don't want to be without any of them." I hear four loud gasps from my men, but I ignore them. "What do you think about that?"

Llewellyn jumps up. "It's great, now we get four great Daddy's instead of one that doesn't like us," she says, her tone becoming sad. My heart hurt for what their Father must have done or said to make them feel that way.

Lawson grabs my hand. "As long as you're happy, Mum, I don't mind."

I hear a giggle from Meaghan and when I look at her she says, "That's so romantic." Before she giggles some more.

"Well, in that case, would you like to meet them?" I point to where the men stand silently.

"Will they love us and be our Daddies?" Llewellyn whispers to me.

"We would very much like that if you'll have us?" I hear Blayze say with emotion in his voice.

"Yes, please," Meaghan says sweetly looking back at them.

I swear I just saw Baine try not to sob. I smile at them and stand.

"Right, well, let's be the best family ever. You guys already know Baine." I smile at Baine who nods with a grin that makes his dimples pop.

"This is, Reid," I motion for him to come over. "He's a Wolf too, in fact he's the boss Wolf and these are all his people in the village." Reid gives them a little wave before I move on.

"This is, Blayze." He steps up to us. "He's a Phoenix, which is a big, beautiful bird made from fire." The twins *Wow* in unison.

"And this is, Mr Big," I snicker at the use of his nickname and when he approaches, giving me the side-eye. "He can turn into a *humongous* Dragon." I hold my arms out really wide in animation.

Lawson's gasps, "Cool."

Baine comes over to join us and I introduce my babies while tapping each child on the head. "These are our children. Meaghan is nine, Lawson is eight, and these are the cheeky four-year-old twins, Llewellyn and Cheyenne. You'll notice that Cheyenne has a freckle on her neck but Llewellyn doesn't, it's the quickest way to tell the difference."

Reid smiles leaning down to them. "You can't fool us anyway, you smell completely different from each other."

"*Oh!*" They say in unison. They love trying to trick people, I guess those days are over.

While the kids and men get to know each other, already exchanging hugs and kisses, I sit at the table and watch with joy in my heart and my hand on my belly. I just know that this baby will change every-thing for the better. I feel so complete and happy that it seems like the fears and pain I've been through to get here are a million miles away. Who knew that from such a frightening beginning I'd find love, family, joy, friendship, and a place to truly belong.

Rathe is our home, now and forever, it's time for our people to be one. I look forward to what's coming next because I just know it's going to be epic...

Epilogue

Janice

The girls and I sit here flinching as we hear yet another scream coming from the Alpha lodges. It's been a long day and Summer's been a trooper trying to get out that baby. I can't wait to see what it is but it sucks that there's no epidural here.

There's a sudden silence followed by a resounding *Whoop!*

Reid comes running to the centre and calls out proudly to his pack. "We have a Dragon son! He's big and healthy, and Summer's amazing. A boy is born!"

Around us men change to animals and they howl and growl their victory into the world, and it once warms my heart to hear such joy, regardless of the species of child that's born. These people come together and rejoice in the birth of an innocent child, in a way that humans never do.

The appreciation of life regardless of gender or species is one of pure bliss and I feel so honoured to be a part of it.

One day this will be me and I'll gladly take it.

Today there are species other than the Wolves and the Alphas present. I see Tigers, Grizzly Bears, Eagles, and Owls. It's quite incredible.

"*Aaaaaahh!*" Another unexpected scream wrenches through the air and Reid goes white before racing back to his Kindred at warp speed.

More fierce screams follow and my stomach drops. What's happening? *No.* Fear fills me and I think of the worst.

Bell is up and racing towards the lodge in seconds, fear written all over her face and Havana and I look at each other with worry.

"She has to be ok," I try to lighten the mood. "She's too stubborn not to be."

Her kids walk over to us looking confused. "What's happening?" Summers' son, Lawson, asks nervously, gazing back towards the lodge.

I smile at him. "I'm not sure, sweety. Your mum is just finishing up. How exciting that you have a brother now, you must be glad since you have so many sisters?"

He nods but still stares off when another terrifying scream is let loose and then complete silence. "Mum?" He whispers with tears brimming his eyes.

Llewellyn comes and sits on my lap, her eyes wide and scared. "It's okay, darling, this is normal," I say reassuringly, stroking her hair softly but I look over to Havana's terrified face, my heart feels just as petrified as her expression.

Almighty roars come from the lodge before Baine comes barreling through the trees, tears pouring down his cheeks.

"A Phoenix rises again. A girl! We have a daughter and a son." The crowd goes wild, animals and men alike. A breath I didn't know I was holding blows out of my lungs in utter relief.

Baine comes over and picks up Cheyenne, giving her a kiss on the cheek. "Did you hear that, guys? Mama had more twins, a boy and a girl."

"What's their name, Papa? Is Mummy alright?" Meaghan asks, relief washing her tear-stained face.

Smiling at the kids like the proud Dad he is, Baine states, "Aye, your Mama did so well." Stroking Llewellyn's little face with love as she stands by him. "Demetrius and Mina are their names, and they're perfect. Come and see them, guys." Reaching his hand out for them and bouncing Cheyenne on his hip.

I know he includes us but I quietly decline because I want them to enjoy their special family time. I'm so happy for them, this is such a special day for everyone.

They all walk off happily, laughing with each other, and I silently slip away to the girl's lodge, where I stay.

Opening my door, I walk inside, it takes me a minute before I realise that the door took a longer time than usual to close and I turn around to see a large bald man with arms as thick as tree trunks leaning against my door, staring at me with dark sinister eyes. I know instantly that I'm in danger.

Before I can even scream something knocks me hard in the back of my head and everything goes black...

To be continued in Rathe Chronicles Book 2,
Janice's Entanglement

Acknowledgments

I want to thank, first and always, my husband. You read every word I write with enthusiasm, support and love. The unyielding support that you give to me throughout everything warms my heart and I will always be grateful to you. You tell me when I'm wrong, encourage me when I'm right and never let me give up, even when things feel impossible. Also a huge high five for being so cool about me writing about hot dudes and RH scenes, you're so awesome about it, it's ridiculous. Love you.

I want to thank my beautiful babies for dealing with me on days that are consumed with writing. They happily put up with having a vanishing mum on Sundays because they're excited about Mummy being famous and rich (like it's that easy haha). My sweet kids are such a blessing and their constant understanding and enthusiasm for me to keep going, makes me very proud to be their mum.

To all my loving family, for always backing me up and believing in me, thank you. From the bottom of my heart, thank you. It means the world to me. I love you Mum and Dad.

To the women who inspire me, Grandma, Branka, Winter and Eve, you have all inspired me in one way or another and I feel lucky to have such great women to look up to, with a level of awesome that I one day dream to reach.

Double thanks to Branka, I literally couldn't have done this without you!! Your support has meant the world to me. You have always pushed me to better myself and been there for me every step of the way, I feel truly blessed to call you and the girls my family. Miss you millions and love you loads.

Amanda, you awesome bitch, you have been the best alpha reader, not to mention my soul sister. It's such a shame the world couldn't handle us in the same place at the same time. Haha. Enjoy the ginger-nuts my friend. If I'm ever stuck in a hole (sometimes even literally) you help me out of it with conviction, ideas, hot guy pics, a shoulder to cry on, or dirty gifs that make me laugh so hard I choke.

Kalayna, you have saved my ass many times and I'm so very grateful to have found a friend in you.

Thank you for your time and energy helping me to bring this book to life and for teaching me what I'm capable of.

Rosie and Sam, you guys changed my life when I met you, you took me from a dream and into a reality. Having your 100% faith in my ability to change my life, no matter my hurdle, gave me the push I needed to become who I am today. You've helped me to become very proud of myself and to never give up.

I have been blessed to find great friends on this journey. Dahlia, your continual guidance and reminders that I can do it is so appreciated, I just know that in you I have found a great friend for life. Kira, you crazy girl, I get a great kick out of your many voice messages that have brought me an endless supply of smiles and laughter. Thanks girls!

To my amazing friends that have been there for me through laughter, tears, and all the inbetweens of life, Ashleigh, Jen, Julia, Rebecca, Steve and Amy. You guys have never let me down ... Thank you!

Lastly but certainly not least, I wouldn't be here without the hard work and talent of Tash from Dazed Designs, Hellhound Publishing, Moonlight Editing, and Kat Blak!

About the Author

Hi, I'm Alexandra, an Aussie/Kiwi mother of three, married to the best husband around.

My life is surrounded with lots of animals because I just can't say no to all their cuteness, I have a rare chronic illness that keeps me grateful for the beauty that life brings and my pen name is in honour of my amazing Grandparents who are everything to me.

My soul lives off coffee, family, reading, storms, good scotch and great wine, mountains, and is a real knowledge whore.

I'm a firm believer in being kind to others because it *does* matter, and it *does* make a difference. If I can make just one person happy with my stories or even to give them a reprieve they may desperately need to escape their harder reality, then I've done my job right.

My imagination is a constantly growing paradise

for me and I feel blessed that I get to share a little of it with you.

Thank you for coming on my journey with me; You *are* appreciated.

If you have enjoyed my story, please take the time to leave me a review on amazon. Reviews are the bread and butter of indie authors and everyone counts.

Here are some links to my social media accounts:

Amazon: https://www.amazon.com/Alexandra-K-Martin/e/B08NHK4JC4/ref=dp_byline_cont_pop_ebooks_1

Facebook Group: https://www.facebook.com/groups/261878653510451515

Facebook Page: https://www.facebook.com/Alexandra.K.Martin.Books

Website and Newsletter to come…

Also By Alexandra K. Martin

SERIES

Rathe Chronicles

-Summer's Confine, Book One

-Janice's Entanglement, Book Two (Coming 2021)

COLLABORATIONS & CO-WRITES

Sinners Fairytale Collaboration, Book Seven

-Lust: A Golden Bird Retelling (Coming Aug, 2021)

Coming on the 1st AUGUST 2021, A Sinners Fairytale Collaboration; LUST https:// books2read.com/Lustsins

Looking for new books to read? Try 'Embers of Phoenix' by AJ Blackburn

https://books2read.com/Eop

ncontent.com/pod-product-compliance
urce LLC
g PA
4120726
0001B/117

6 4 5 0 5 0 8 8 2 *